BULLETPROOF

MICKEY DUBROW

ISBN-13: 979-8-9865955-9-7
ISBN-10: 979-8-9897493-0-0

Published by Market Street Bridge Press.
Printed in the United States of America.

www.mickeydubrow.com

*"It is only one who is thoroughly acquainted with
the evils of war that can thoroughly understand
the profitable way of carrying it on."*

SUN TZU, *THE ART OF WAR*

CHAPTER ONE

N‍ELL CRADLED THE semi-automatic assault rifle like a baby, keeping it close to her body and giving it plenty of support with both arms. The rifle was fresh from the arms factory that birthed it. Dozens of the rifle's siblings hung on racks behind Nell at the Bulard Arms booth, one of the largest displays at the WAR (Weapons, Ammo, and Recreation) Industry Show.

"Harry," Nell asked. "Where can I get some ammo for this baby?"

Harry Pigott, the Bulard representative, scowled, causing his bushy mustache to puff out. His bald head was as shiny as Nell's rifle.

"Live rounds aren't allowed on the convention floor."

Nell pouted. The rifle was a Bulard Model 601, the company's version of the AR-15 semi-automatic rifle and their most popular product. Its nickname was the Beastmaster.

"But my baby is so hungry. She's starving for bullets."

"Explain to me again why you're here instead of Jolene?"

Nell nodded at the name tag attached to the lanyard hanging around her neck.

"I am Jolene. See? It says so right here."

"That reminds me," Harry said. "When I get a minute, we'll get your own name tag. I could get into all kinds of trouble for letting you wear Jolene's."

"Do I have to get a new one? I like being a Jolene." Nell sang the first line of Dolly Parton's iconic song.

"Don't argue with me. I'm in no mood for this shit today."

Kassie put herself between Nell and Harry. She was Nell's fellow booth babe. They wore matching skintight camo T-shirts, camo booty shorts, ball caps with the Bulard logo, and combat boots.

"Leave her alone," Kassie said. "I know you miss Jolene, but that's no reason to take it out on Nell. You should be nice to her. The agency was lucky to find a last-minute replacement."

"Did the agency say what was wrong with Jolene?" Harry asked.

"Stomach flu."

"That sucks. Maybe I should call her and see how she's feeling. You got her number?"

Kassie put her hands on her hips.

"Darn it, Harry. How many times do I have to tell you? Jolene has a boyfriend."

"Is it serious?"

"Extremely serious. Bordering on marriage."

Harry's mustache puffed out again. He stood behind the information desk and put on his best 'I'm-the-expert' expression. Nell followed Kassie to the other end of the booth and watched the crowd flow by. The Bulard Arms was in Central Hall of the Las Vegas Convention Center. The hall was like an indoor city with long rows of booths and hundreds of people checking out thousands of weapons and weapon related products. This was only the main hall. The North and South Hall were also filled with people and displays. Nell hadn't been surrounded by this many bodies since she went to the Riverbend music festival during her days at the University of Tennessee at Chattanooga.

Kassie looked over her shoulder at Harry before laying her assault rifle on a display case. Nell held onto her weapon.

"Aren't your arms tired?" Kassie asked.

"Not at all. I could carry it all day."

"You got kids?"

"No. You?"

"A boy."

"What's his name?"

"Logan."

"Why doesn't Harry like me?"

Kassie rolled her eyes.

"It's not you. He's hot for Jolene. You know how it is on these jobs. These company guys spend the day working with hot women like us and they get silly ideas in their heads."

Nell blushed. Her mother, Peggy, used to say she was cute, but never said she was attractive. Then again, by the time Nell was old enough to be attractive, Peggy was too busy to notice.

"How does Jolene feel about Harry?" Nell asked.

Kassie glanced back at Harry. He was talking to a potential customer.

"She can't stand him," Kassie said. "In fact, I wouldn't be surprised if she's not really sick. Jolene didn't want to do this show to begin with. She has no problem with shows for cars, golf, or video games. But when it comes to gun shows, she can't embrace the brand."

"Embrace the brand?"

Kassie glared at Nell.

"Duh. Embrace the brand. Our main objective as booth models. But Jolene hates guns. She said that those who live by the sword should die by the sword."

Nell scanned the crowd as they gawked at scopes, targets, pistols, revolvers, machine guns, shotguns, semi-assault rifles, gun oil, earmuffs, range glasses, sniper rifles, air guns, and more and more and more weapons and weapon accessories. There were so many American flags and NRA flags that they blended into the background.

"There's a difference between living by the sword and making a living by the sword," Nell said. "Everyone attending this convention makes their living by the sword. And a damn good living at that."

Kassie pulled a face at Nell.

"They're vendors selling a product that just happens to be guns. This is no different from cars, golf clubs, or video games."

"Guns are more like cigarettes and opioids," Nell said. "Except gun makers aren't held responsible for the deaths their products cause. Jolene should have said that those who profit from the sword should die by the sword."

"There you go. Refusing to embrace the brand."

Nell pretended to look hurt as she hugged her rifle.

"How can you say that when I'm clearly embracing it?"

Kassie giggled.

For the next two hours, Nell and Kassie smiled and posed with their Beastmasters. Kassie had told Nell that if a conventioneer quizzed her about her knowledge of Bulard's latest offerings, she was to refer any such questions to Harry. But it never happened. Mostly, the men wanted selfies with the girls. Many of them commented on how much they enjoyed the combination of Nell's blonde hair and Kassie's brunette mane.

"Has anybody tried to cop a feel during the selfies?" Kassie asked.

"No. Should I feel relieved or insulted?"

Nell felt someone staring at her. She turned and caught Harry watching her while talking on the phone. Their eyes met for a moment before he looked away.

The police arrived right before lunch. Nell ignored her aching feet and growling stomach and focused her full attention on the two men in tan uniforms and fully loaded duty belts. They were accompanied by a broad-shouldered man in a shiny blue sport coat. She made sure not to look too closely at their faces. If she thought too much about these men as people, she might lose her nerve. The three men spoke briefly to Harry before he led them to Nell.

"Ma'am," said the man in the blue sport coat. "My name is Keith Anderson. I'm head of security here."

"Pleased to meet you, Keith," Nell said.

"These two officers would like to have a word with you."

"Okay."

Keith stepped aside and the two policemen came forward. Nell read their nameplates: D. Palmer and M. Davis.

"Ma'am," Officer Palmer said. "Would you please come with us so we can talk in private?"

"Sure," Nell said.

"Leave the weapon here."

Nell laid her Beastmaster on a display case. Kassie placed herself between Nell and the officers.

"What the heck are you doing?" Kassie asked.

"Please stand aside, ma'am," Officer Davis said.

"Not until you tell me what's going on."

"That's what we're trying to find out. Please stand aside and allow us to do our job."

Kassie turned to Harry.

"You can't have her arrested for no reason. I'm calling the modeling agency."

"Knock yourself out," Harry said.

Officer Palmer turned to Keith.

"Is there someplace quiet we can go?"

"Yeah," Keith said. "There's an employee meeting room backstage."

Officer Davis turned to Harry.

"You need to come with us."

Harry's mustache huffed and puffed.

"I can't leave the booth unattended."

"We'll try to be as brief as possible," Officer Palmer said.

People were staring at them.

"I'll keep an eye on things," Kassie said.

Harry's shoulders slumped.

"I suppose I could step away for a few minutes."

CHAPTER TWO

As KEITH ANDERSON led the group though the convention hall, Officer Palmer kept a tight grip on Nell's arm. They left the main floor and entered the backstage world that surrounded the hall. Workers hurried down corridors with concrete walls, exposed overhead pipes, and harsh lighting. A few worker bees seemed surprised by the presence of policemen, but most hurried by with hardly a glance.

The employee meeting room was located along the backstage hallway that connected Central Hall and South Hall. Keith selected a key from his key ring and let them inside. The room had no windows. There were rows of chairs facing a table. The officers had Nell sit in the front row and stood before her.

Keith grabbed the radio clipped to his belt and pressed the speaker button.

"I'll be offline for a few. Sanders is in charge until I return."

"Sanders, here," said a crackling voice on the radio. "What's going on?"

"Potential security breach. It's under control. I'll fill you in later."

"Roger that."

Keith put his radio back on his belt. Officer Palmer looked down at Nell.

"Can you provide us with some kind of I.D.?"

"No, sir," Nell said.

"Can you call someone to come down here and vouch for you?" Officer Davis asked.

"No, sir, I cannot."

"No driver's license? No passport? Not even a utility bill with your name and address on it?"

"I don't have anything," Nell said. "Even the clothes I'm wearing aren't mine."

The policemen looked at each other.

"How the hell did you get past security?" Palmer asked.

Harry raised his hand.

"It's my fault. I was on my way to the convention center this morning when I got a call from the modeling agency that provides our booth babes. They said one of the two girls we hired called in sick. They promised to send a replacement girl as soon as possible."

"When did you discover that this young lady doesn't work for the modeling agency?"

"Just thirty minutes ago. I called the modeling agency to check up on Jolene; that's the girl who called in sick, and the agency apologized for not sending another girl. They said that all of their models were booked today, and they couldn't get me a replacement until tomorrow."

The men looked at Nell. She winked at them.

"How did this young lady trick you into believing she worked for the modeling agency?" Davis asked.

"I fooled myself," Harry said. "I saw this smoking hot babe standing at the front entrance looking lost. I asked her if she was the replacement. She stared at me with a blank look for a minute and then said she was the replacement. Models aren't known for their brains, so her confusion made sense."

"You think I'm smoking hot?" Nell asked.

Officer Davis faced Nell.

"Please, ma'am. Don't say anything until I tell you to." He turned back to Harry. "You didn't ask her for some kind of identification?"

"I'd overslept and was running late," Harry said. "I was relieved that the agency had found a new girl so fast. I figured she could wear Jolene's badge until there was time to take her down to security for her own badge."

"You should have taken her to security right away," Keith said.

"I see now that I made a terrible mistake. It will probably cost me my job, but at least this weirdo won't be wandering around the convention floor any longer."

"I'm not weird" Nell said. "You're weird."

"Please refrain from calling each other names," Officer Palmer said.

Nell pointed at Harry.

"He started it."

"Ma'am. What do you have to say for yourself?"

Nell crossed her legs.

"I would have found a way inside the convention eventually. But then Harry showed up. Next thing I knew, I was backstage with him and Kassie. They're telling me to put on this girl's costume and badge. Kassie was so sweet. She let me wear some of her make-up. Been so long since I wore make-up, it took me a moment to remember how."

"Why did you want into the convention?" Officer Davis asked.

"The way I see it, it was more than luck, more than a series of coincidences. It was meant to be. Harry was supposed to let me in, he was supposed to call Keith, and Keith was supposed to call the police so that I would be brought here to this room."

Harry snorted.

"She's either dumb as a rock or high as a kite."

"Why did you want inside the convention?" Davis asked again.

Nell looked at her nails.

"For the guns and ammo."

Officer Palmer exchanged glances with Officer Davis.

"Guns and ammo?" Palmer asked.

"What an idiot," Keith said. "Live ammo isn't allowed at the convention and even if she did get access to ammo, the firing pins have been removed from every weapon on the convention floor."

Officer Davis peered at Nell.

"Why do you want guns and ammo?"

"There are fully operational guns in this building with their firing pins intact. And plenty of ammo."

"I'm asking you again and this time I want an answer. Why did you want guns and ammo?"

"I checked the schedule. Tomorrow, the gun makers are going to give a demonstration of their latest products at a shooting range about ten miles from here. They also let potential buyers try out the weapons themselves. That means a lot of guns and a lot of bullets. My guess is that they won't haul all that gear out to range until tomorrow morning which means it has to be stored somewhere nearby. They wouldn't keep it in trucks. Too risky. They wouldn't keep it in their hotel rooms. Not enough room and also too risky."

Nell could feel the tension rising. It wouldn't be long now.

"Where do you think they're keeping the weapons?" Palmer asked.

Nell wiggled her fingers at the door.

"Somewhere backstage. Near the loading docks. Locked up in a secure area. I thought Harry could show me, but I'm beginning to think he doesn't know. I could walk around until I found armed security guards in front of a locked room. Or I could ask Keith. As head of security, he'd know exactly where they are."

She smiled at Keith.

"What do you want the guns and ammo for?" shouted Officer Davis.

Nell faced him. She noticed his blue eyes and wished she hadn't.

"What do you think I want them for?"

Davis's cheeks flushed. He put his hand on this holster.

"Ma'am. Get on the floor face down with your hands behind your back. You're under arrest for making terroristic threats."

Officer Palmer also put his hand on his holster.

"You have the right to remain silent. Anything you say can and will be used against you in a court of law. You have the right to an attorney. If you cannot afford an attorney, one will be provided for you. Do you understand the rights I have just read to you?"

Nell uncrossed her legs and gripped the edge of the chair.

"I just want to say one thing before we go any further. I respect the service and sacrifice of police officers. I admire how you risk your lives to protect society."

"Okay," Palmer said. "That does it. On the ground. Now!"

The policeman reached for his gun. Nell sprang out of the chair and was on him before he could get it out of his holster. She grabbed his wrist and wrenched his arm behind his back. A sickening snap announced that she had broken his arm. Palmer screamed in pain. Davis took out his gun, but she held Palmer in front of her. He couldn't shoot her without shooting his partner.

Nell steered Palmer about by holding onto his broken arm with one hand and gripping his belt with her other hand. Palmer tried to grab Nell with his free hand, but she managed to stay out of reach. Nell felt like she was dancing with a boy who wouldn't stop trying to grab her boob.

Keith pulled open his coat and took a gun from a shoulder holster. He tried to aim his weapon at Nell, but she dragged the policeman across the room so that her back was against the wall. Harry followed behind Keith.

"Shoot her!" Harry yelled. "Kill the bitch!"

"I'm trying," Keith said. "But I don't want to shoot the cop."

Still holding onto Palmer's broken arm, Nell let go of his belt and yanked his gun out of the holster. She fired three times into Davis's chest. His blood sprayed into Palmer's face. The sound boomed inside the limited space as Davis fell to the floor.

"Back up," Palmer said. "Need back up."

He fumbled for his radio with his free hand, but Nell snatched it away from him, dropped the radio on the ground, and stomped on it with her combat boot, smashing it into pieces. Out of the corner of her eye, Nell saw that Keith was still trying to get a clean shot at her. She pressed the barrel of Palmer's gun to the back of his head.

"I sincerely apologize to your loved ones for the pain and suffering I'm about to cause them."

"You don't have to do this," Palmer said.

"I'm afraid I do."

She blew his brains out. His body toppled to the floor.

The gunshot that killed Palmer was still echoing when Keith fired four shots into Nell's chest. She fell to the floor.

"I can't believe I just killed somebody," Keith said.

"You had no choice," Harry said. "She killed two cops. She was going to kill us next."

Keith gasped. He took a step back and bumped into Harry.

"This can't be real! She's not dead."

Keith and Harry watched wide-eyed as Nell climbed back to her feet. She wrinkled her nose as she inspected her hands.

"Damn it. You made me slip on Officer Davis's blood. Now I have it all over me."

"I shot you at point blank range," Keith said. "Why aren't you dead?"

"Look at her shirt," Harry said, pointing at Nell.

There were four bullet holes in her camo t-shirt. While Keith and Harry were staring at Nell's chest, she walked over to Keith. She snatched the gun out of his hand and yanked his radio off his belt.

"What does it look like?" Nell said. "I'm bulletproof, you stupid jerks. Sit down and don't move until I tell you to move."

CHAPTER THREE

Harry sat down. Keith hesitated before joining him. They stared at the two bodies on the floor. The sharp tang of blood hung in the air. Nell squeezed Keith's radio. It exploded into pieces. She placed the guns she took from Keith and the dead officers on the table, and then removed the officers' duty belts.

"Those gunshots were loud as hell," Keith said. "Someone's going to come busting in here any moment. There's still time to surrender before anybody else gets hurt."

"Nobody's coming," Nell said. "The sound of gunshots are all around us. It's the WAR Show, remember?" She held out her hand. "Harry. Give me your shirt."

Harry frowned but he took off his shirt. Like many bald men, his hair had migrated south to his torso. Nell used Harry's shirt to wipe blood off her face, hands, and legs. Her chest itched from the bullets bouncing off, but she didn't want to scratch her tits in front of these guys. Putting on Officer Davis's duty belt, she had to use the last punch hole. She stuck Keith's gun in the waistband of her booty shorts, and draped Officer Palmer's belt over her shoulder.

"Come here, Harry," Nell said, waving her hand. "Don't be shy."

Sweat beaded on Harry's bald head.

"What are you going to do to me?"

"Is Jolene prettier than me?"

"What?"

"I want to know."

Harry shrugged.

"No. But she's got big tits. You have decent medium sized tits, but I prefer a woman with more than a handful."

Nell glanced at her chest and nodded.

"Fair enough."

She had Harry lie face down on the floor away from the dead policemen. Taking two pairs of handcuffs from Officer Palmer's duty belt, she cuffed his wrists behind his back and then cuffed his ankles.

Keith bolted for the door. Nell tackled him before he could get his hand on the doorknob. They wrestled on the floor. Keith punched her in the face, but she didn't flinch. She got him on his back and straddled his chest so that her knees pinned his arms down.

"When I hit you, it was like hitting cement," Keith said.

"You sure know how to sweet talk a girl."

"You're not human. What the hell are you?"

"I'm the latest development in advanced weaponry. Order now for a special discount. Come on, Keith. Show me where they keep the good stuff."

"I'll die first."

"Okay."

Nell put her hands around his neck and squeezed. Keith's eyes bugged out. He kicked his legs and tried to buck her off, but she didn't budge. With her palm pressed against his carotid artery, she could feel his rapid heartbeat. Apparently, killing two policemen wasn't proof enough that Nell's cute girl act was just that, an act. She could see this from the fear in Keith's eyes as his face turned red.

"I was hoping I wouldn't have to kill you," Nell said. "Keep in mind. I'll still get the weapons. Nobody can stop me. It'll just take me a little longer without you."

"Wait," Keith said, barely getting the word out.

Nell eased her grip.

"Don't do it," Harry shouted.

"Shut up, Harry," Nell said. "Nobody asked for your opinion."

"I'll do it," Keith said.

She pulled her hands away. Keith wheezed as he drew air into his lungs.

Nell put a gag in Harry's mouth and took a last look at the two dead policemen. She and Keith left the meeting room and walked side by side with her arm around his waist. The hallways were almost completely deserted. Either Nell was lucky, or everyone was on their lunch break.

"Why didn't you kill Harry?" Keith asked.

"He certainly fits the category of people I want to kill, but I feel like I owe him for getting me into the convention."

Keith stared ahead.

"There it is."

Nell had guessed correctly. The secure area was near the loading docks. Two beefy men with long guns stood in front of a sliding metal door.

"Don't try running off while I'm killing the guards," Nell whispered.

"Wait," Keith said. "I can get us in."

"Okay. But don't do get cute. That's my job."

The guards glared at Keith and Nell. Keith held up his security badge.

"Security inspection."

"Who's she?" one of the guards asked.

"My assistant."

"Why is she carrying all those guns?" asked the other guard.

"It turns her on."

The guards grinned.

"Can't you find a better place to get a blowjob?" the first guard asked.

"Yeah," Keith said. "But none of them would be this much fun."

The guards chuckled and stepped aside. Keith used his master key to unlock the door. The wheels on the door squeaked as he slid it open. The storage room was filled with rows of bulky gun cases. The thick smell of gun oil hung in the air. Nell felt a flutter in her stomach as she searched the cases until she found ones with a Bulard Arms logo.

"The cases are locked," Keith said. "I don't have the key to any of them."

Nell gripped the case and pulled it open, breaking the clamps.

"I'm sorry. What were you saying about locks and keys?"

The case was filled with handguns. Disappointed, Nell tossed it aside and opened the next case. It contained pump action shotguns, which Nell tossed aside as well. While she searched, Keith inched toward the door.

"If you run, I'll have to kill those two guys who think I'm blowing you right now," Nell said. "Do you really want their deaths on your conscience?"

Keith moved away from the door.

Nell opened the next case. Her eyes lit up at the sight of four Beastmasters nestled in foam padding. She ran her fingers over the cold metal before taking two rifles out of the case and putting them aside. She forced open four more cases before finding thirty round-loaded magazines for the semi-automatic rifles. With two Beastmasters, two standard issue police pistols, and Keith's big ass handgun, Nell had enough firepower to make her point today.

"I need something to carry the extra ammo in," Nell said as she inserted a magazine into each Beastmaster. "Do you see any magazine pouches?"

"I don't see shit," Keith said.

He leaned against the wall with his arms crossed. His clothes were scuffed from when they wrestled on the floor.

"Give me your jacket," Nell said. "And your shoulder holster."

Keith took them off without an argument. The hem of his coat came down to Nell's knees, and she had to roll up the sleeves. She managed to fit three magazines into each side pocket. Slinging a rifle over her shoulder and cradling another in her arms, she put the other duty belt on above the one she was already wearing.

"How do I look?"

"Like you're batshit crazy," Keith said.

Nell rolled her eyes.

"Why did I even bother asking you?"

"Now that you have what you want, what do you plan to do?"

"Those who profit from the sword should die by the sword."

"What the hell does that mean?"

Nell didn't respond. Keith would get the answer soon enough. She rushed out of the storage room past the two beefy guards.

"Stop her!" Keith yelled.

Despite her heavy arsenal, Nell outran them. Turning a corner, she slammed into a janitor. She got a quick glimpse of his surprised face before he tumbled to the ground.

"Sorry, but I'm in a hurry."

As she ran through the backstage hallways, the equipment in the duty belts jostled and rattled. Her footsteps echoed off the concrete walls and sweat poured down her face, causing her makeup to streak. She wondered if victims of gun violence would understand why she was doing this. Would anybody understand? Or would everyone just assume that mental illness ran in her family?

Nell slowed to a stop. She wasn't sure how to get back to the Central Hall. Closing her eyes, she heard combat sound effects and patriotic music on the other side of the wall. She burst through a double door and found herself in the middle of the convention floor. A few men stopped to admire the cute girl holding big guns, but mostly the endless river of humanity kept flowing because a girl loaded with weapons didn't look out of place.

"You can't be the Beastmaster forever!" Nell shouted. "But I'm the Beastmaster today!"

Nell switched from Safe to Fire on the Beastmaster, picked a man at random, and pulled the trigger three times, shooting him in the chest. He died with a look of surprise on his face.

A security guard saw her kill the man. He barked into his radio for assistance as he ran toward her. Nell swung the rifle around and squeezed the trigger four times. Bullets tore into him, and he immediately fell to the ground.

Panic spread faster than gossip at a slumber party. People screamed and ran in all directions. They created log jams at the exits. Nell opened fire on them. The thirty round magazine was empty in less than a minute, leaving many dead or dying. She pulled the magazine out and replaced it with a fresh round of ammo.

Walking briskly, Nell swung the rifle back and forth, shooting into the crowd. Many people cringed as if she were merely tossing water on them, and they could somehow sidestep the death about to spill on them. A few heroic souls rushed toward her, but she shot them before they reached her. Blood soaked the carpet and squished under Nell's combat boots. Leaving a trail of spent cartridges, she pulled the trigger so rapidly that the rifle's barrel overheated. She dropped the rifle, switching to the second Beastmaster.

Security guards took position behind booths and fired at her. Nell braced her legs so that the force of the bullets wouldn't knock her over. She ran to the booths and mowed down the guards shooting her.

There was too much noise in the hall to hear sirens approaching, but Nell knew the police would arrive soon. That didn't leave her much time. Nell checked her pockets. She still had two magazines plus however many bullets left in the magazine she was presently using. More than sixty bullets. At least sixty more weapon profiteers would die if she hurried. She hadn't touched the handguns, hoping to save them for when she made her escape.

Working her way through the center of the convention hall, Nell continued her killing spree. Inserting the next to last magazine, Nell scanned the area for more targets. She found a woman crouching behind a table and aimed the rifle at her.

"Please don't shoot me," Kassie cried as she held hands over her head.

Nell lowered her rifle. She was standing next to the Bulard booth.

"Damn it, Kassie! I almost shot you."

"What the hell are you doing?"

"I'm making sure people who profit from the sword die by the sword."

"You're using a gun to kill people who sell guns. Isn't that hypocritical?"

"No. It's ironic. There's a difference."

"Tell that to the dead people."

"Just get the hell out of here. I don't want Logan to grow up without his mommy."

Kassie ran for the exit. The dead and wounded were strewn about the convention floor. Combat sound effects and patriotic music still played on the loudspeakers. The WAR Show really did look like a war movie.

Gunfire echoed off the walls as multiple bullets tore up the carpet and ripped into the booths around Nell. The police had arrived. SWAT teams in heavy armor and artillery advanced towards her. Following them were emergency medical teams, ducking low as they scurried toward the victims.

It was time for Nell to leave.

Along with guns, rifles, bows and arrows, tactical gear, and camouflage lingerie, the WAR Show had large, armored vehicles. Not for sale, for display only. Nell dashed to them. She considered the bulky SWAT truck just to stick it to the guys shooting at her but decided on the tank parked next to it. She climbed inside and locked the hatch. She'd never been in a tank, but she only had to touch the controls to know everything about the machine. It was like learning all a lover's secrets just by laying her hand on his chest. The machine gun was neutered, the ammunition rack was empty, but it had a full tank of gas.

Nell turned the ignition, and the motor woke with a grumpy roar. Checking the periscope, she saw the SWAT team closing in. She assumed they wouldn't waste ammunition shooting at a tank, but she assumed incorrectly. Bullets pinged off the metal hull. Nell drove away from the bullet litterbugs, turned left, and headed towards Central Hall's front entrance.

"Stop the tank now and surrender."

The hairs on Nell's arm stood up. The tank had a ghost. Then it dawned on her that the police had managed to tune into the tank's radio communications. She flipped on the transmitter.

"Sorry. Can't stop now. I'm late for a very important date."

"Give yourself up. Don't make this any worse than it already is."

"But making things worse is what I do best."

Nell drove over booths, snapping wood and metal tables, scattering brochures, pulling down drapes, knocking over loudspeakers, and crushing weapons under the tank's caterpillar tracks. She also drove over the bodies of the people she'd killed, crushing skulls, ribs, spines, arms, and legs. The tank busted through a double door, rumbled across the lobby, and shattered a glass wall on its way out of the convention center.

Outside, SWAT trucks and ambulances were parked on the front curb. The area was cordoned off with patrol cars. News trucks with satellite dishes on the roof and bold logos on the side waited behind the police barrier for the latest developments. Helicopters hovered above like giant gnats.

Avoiding the ambulances, Nell drove toward the other vehicles. There was a moment of hesitation in which everyone must have thought that surely she wouldn't drive over them, but then police and reporters dove out of the way as the tank crushed patrol cars and news vans.

Tires screeched when drivers on the road saw the tank coming their way. Nell did her best not to run any of them over, but she couldn't avoid sideswiping a few vehicles that failed to get out of her way. Traffic got even worse when she turned onto South Las Vegas Boulevard. She considered taking the sidewalk, but she only wanted to kill those who profit from the sword, not those who gamble away their life's savings.

Cars honked and swerved out of the way. Police sirens wailed. The voice on the tank's radio demanded that she stop stop stop. Nell did stop. She braked in the middle of the intersection of South Las Vegas Boulevard and East Flamingo Road. The tank was surrounded by the heavy traffic on the Las Vegas Strip.

Nell swung the turret around three times before opening the hatch. As she climbed out, police officers and tourists shouted and pointed at her. A policeman climbed onto the tank. Nell whacked him on the side of his head with the nightstick from Officer Palmer's duty belt. The policeman tumbled to the street. She scrambled down the side of the tank and dashed into the crowd. A civic-minded tourist tripped Nell. Getting to her feet, she thought about shooting him, but there wasn't time. His action encouraged more tourists to rush her. She squirted pepper spray into their faces and pushed them out of her way. Glancing over her shoulder, Nell saw officers chasing her.

Nell zigzagged through casinos and hotels, malls and fast-food restaurants, parking lots and alleys. She gave no thought to where she was going, and after two hours of constant motion, she was drenched in sweat and her muscles ached. Her legs felt like lead, but she kept moving through the maze of Las Vegas like a starving rat.

When Nell finally slowed to a shuffle, she found herself in a dim basement hallway. Leaning against a wall of peeling paint, her lungs burned as she waited for her heart rate to return to normal. Her forefinger ached from pulling the trigger so many times. After five minutes, she decided that the police had lost her trail.

She was far from home free. There was still the matter of getting out of Las Vegas. Limping along the hallway, Nell found a room with stacks of linens and towels. Next to it was a room with lockers and benches. Dark gray maid uniforms of various sizes hung on a rack. This was the second time today that Nell felt that something more than luck was helping her.

She chose a uniform two sizes two big. Before putting it on, she located the maids' bathroom. First, she peed, something she had been needing to do for hours. There was no shower, but there was soap and towels by a row of sinks. She stripped off her bullet-ridden camo outfit and stuffed it into a trashcan. Her bra and panties were nasty sweaty, but she kept them on as she washed off blood and grime. She scrubbed her face and rinsed her hair. When she was done drying herself with a towel, she felt rejuvenated.

The maid's uniform was pressed and clean. The elastic waistband of the pants hung loosely on her hips. She wore the duty belt over the pants to keep them from slipping down. The oversized tunic hid the belt and made her look heavier.

At some point, she'd lost the Bulard logo ball cap and Keith's gun. She had Officer Palmer and Officer Davis's handguns. At this point, she only needed one. She stuffed the extra gun in the trashcan with her ruined clothes, took the extra clips of ammo out of the second duty belt, and put them in the pockets of her maid's uniform before throwing the belt away. Whoever emptied that trashcan was in for a big surprise.

Nell studied her reflection in a mirror mounted on the wall. She looked like a fresh-faced maid who was a little on the chunky side. Then she noticed her dirty combat boots. Taking another towel, she rubbed them until they shone.

A service elevator took her to the first floor. It wasn't until she got out of the service area and into to the lobby that she realized she was in the Cosmopolitan of Las Vegas Hotel and Casino. She wondered how much it cost to stay here, knowing all too well that it was too rich for her blood. Then again, any place was too expensive for her. Nell crossed the lobby and walked out. The sun was going down. The glowing pinks and oranges in the sky competed with the Strip's bright lights.

As Nell sauntered among the crowd, she breathed in cooling desert air and almost relaxed, but then she saw two policemen standing at the intersection. Her heart raced as she approached them. They had to be looking for her. Hell, the whole world had to be looking for her. She could have turned around and walked in the opposite direction, but that might make them notice her. Instead, she stood next to them and waited for the light to change. They looked at her and then looked away. Nell glanced down at her uniform and grinned. Nobody paid attention to maids. They were practically invisible. When the walk sign came on, Nell crossed the street and walked toward the night.

CHAPTER FOUR

FORENSIC SCIENTISTS IN white papery Tyvek coveralls placed yellow markers next to every bullet casing they found. They looked like ghostly gardeners planting a field of daffodils, moving carefully and respectfully past the dead covered with blood-stained sheets. Las Vegas Convention Center's cavernous Central Hall was quiet except for camera clicks and the whirring of the building's industrial air conditioning units. The air was cool, but not cold enough to slow down the growing stench from decomposing bodies.

Special Agent John Easter watched the investigators from the ragged hole in the wall where the main doors used to be before a tank rolled through them. His hands were buried in the pockets of his FBI jacket. As a Marine, Easter had done three tours in Afghanistan. As a special agent with the Bureau, he'd been involved in twenty active shooter incident investigations. The aftermath of an active shooter incident was almost identical to the aftermath of a battlefield.

Easter's partner, Special Agent Mara Zavala, joined him. "Hey, Bunny."

Zavala was the only person to call him Bunny, as in Easter Bunny. He didn't mind, especially coming from her, though he was surprised that no one else had made the connection.

"The total so far is sixty-two fatalities and four hundred twenty-six injured," Easter said.

He made sure to add the words "so far," because of the vast number of bullets that had been pumped at a rapid rate into human bodies. There was a good chance that some of the victims were going to move from the injured column to the fatality column.

"That music festival was just down the road from here," Zavala said. "How many did Paddock shoot?"

"Fifty-eight dead and five hundred forty-six wounded."

"I don't care if this is Sin City. Nobody deserves this much killing."

Their shoes crunched on the broken glass in the lobby. Outside, they walked around the crushed police cars and ducked under the yellow police tape. They nodded at the officers standing guard.

"What do the police know at this time?" Easter asked.

"Single shooter," Zavala said. "Female. Still at large."

"Mass shooters are almost always male."

"Yeah. They can't believe a girl did this. Fucking misogynists."

Easter and Zavala walked past the line of law enforcement trucks to the FBI Mobile Command Center. The long truck was blue and white with the FBI shield on the side. Beyond the law enforcement trucks was the herd of television news remote trucks. Easter knew that as soon as the reporters spotted his FBI jacket, they would try to get an official statement or an off-the-record tidbit of information. Easter was authorized to speak to the press and under normal situations, he would be inclined to talk to them, but not now. Or at least, not yet.

It was a typical summer day in Las Vegas, with stifling heat and blinding sun. Easter took out a handkerchief and mopped his brow.

"Two eyewitnesses, Harry Pigott and Keith Anderson, were present when Slagle murdered the two LVMPD officers," Zavala said. "Pigott believes the shooter wore high tech body armor. Anderson claims the shooter is bulletproof."

Easter shook his head.

"It was a tense situation. It's easy to get confused."

"Anderson's the chief of security. He shot Nell four times in the chest. Apparently, she didn't like it and tried to strangle him to death."

"If he becomes a problem, we'll deal with him."

Easter was about to knock on the door of the FBI Mobile Command Center, but Zavala held up her hand.

"Wait."

"What?"

"Tell me again why we agreed to work this case?"

"We didn't. We don't choose what to work on. We're given assignments."

"Did we not voice strong opposition to the conditions of this case?"

"We did. We told the Bureau we didn't think the classified information on this case should be classified. The public deserved to know what the killer was capable of."

"And how did they respond to our concerns?"

"The Bureau promised that if we did this case as instructed, we wouldn't have to do any more active shooter incidents."

"And if we refused?"

"They would assign it to someone else, we would still be under strict orders not to reveal what we know about Nell Slagle, and we'd still have to do active shooter incidents."

Zavala stared at the sky.

"That's right. It's all coming back to me now."

Easter first met Zavala in 2007 as members of the FBI team investigating the Virginia Tech Shooting. A senior, Seung-Hui Cho, killed thirty-two people and wounded twenty-three before killing himself. At the time it was the deadliest mass shooting committed by a lone gunman in United States history.

Easter and Zavala were both new to the Bureau. They worked more diligently than any of the other agents on the case because that was the kind of people they were. Their hard work impressed their superiors. They were assigned to another active shooter incident, and another, and eventually they were considered experts. The Bureau made them official partners who only worked active shooter incidents. Easter should have known better. If you do a dirty job too well, you get stuck doing it all the time.

The problem with investigating active shooter incidents was that there were so many of them, one after the other. The incidents got uglier after semi-assault rifles like the Bulard 601 became the weapon of choice among mass shooters. Rifles like the Beastmaster caused the same kind of pulverizing body damage as military assault rifles. Every case they worked reminded them that U.S. citizens were at war with each other. Easter and Zavala each had a belly full of this revelation and longed to be assigned to an organized crime case or a public corruption case; crimes motivated by greed, crimes that made sense.

"Can we go inside now?" Easter said. "The heat's killing me."

"Don't let me stop you," Zavala said.

Easter knocked on the door of the FBI Mobile Command Center. An agent opened the door, acknowledged Easter and Zavala, and held the door open for them. It was cool inside and smelled like burnt coffee mixed with stale deodorant. They climbed into the truck and squeezed past a line of agents seated in front of computers. At the end of the row, a young man with red hair and freckles sat hunched over a keyboard.

"Hey, Archie," Zavala said.

Agent Wayne Driscoll glanced up at Zavala and Easter before looking back at his computer screen.

"My name's not Archie."

"I know," Zavala said. "But admit it, you look like Archie Andrews."

"Well, you look like Dora the Explorer."

"I love Dora."

"Enough," Easter said. "Agent Driscoll, what do you have so far?"

"Later today, the LVMPD will officially identify the shooter as Nell Slagle," Driscoll said. "They will remind reporters with short memories that nine years ago her brother, Carson Slagle, killed twenty-five people, most of them children, at Red Clay Middle School in Cleveland, Tennessee. You and Special Agent Zavala were team leaders on that case."

Easter rubbed his forehead.

"When reporters ask us what we remember about Nell Slagle, we'll say we only had minimum contact with her."

"Which, by the way," Zavala said, "is completely true."

Driscoll brought up the FBI report on the Red Clay incident on his computer screen.

"Soon the press will track this down and see that before

Carson drove his mother's car to Red Clay, he killed his mother, Peggy Slagle, and wounded Nell. The injury left her paralyzed from the waist down."

"They'll ask if we have any information on when she regained the ability to walk," Zavala said.

"What will we tell them?" Driscoll asked.

"We're investigating and will get back to them later," Easter said. "But right now, our main objective is locating and arresting Slagle."

Driscoll nodded.

"Got it."

Easter glanced at his watch. "Zavala and I have to go."

The two special agents left the truck and went to their rental car parked on the street in front of the convention center. Zavala popped open the trunk and they exchanged their blue FBI windbreakers for black suit jackets. They drove north on Paradise Road past liquor stores and fast-food restaurants. They turned left onto Elvis Presley Boulevard, where the street ran between an unfinished resort on one side and a parking lot on the other. A sad tribute to the king.

"Are you worried too many agents know who is responsible for Slagle?" Zavala asked.

"I'm more worried about the civilians who don't know."

They parked in the Circus Circus Casino parking garage and took the elevator to the roof. A soldier stood guard at the entrance to the helipad. Easter and Zavala showed their badges and he let them pass. A military helicopter waited for them. They climbed in, buckled up, and put on their headsets. Facing them was Lieutenant General Buck Carter. He wore a camouflage combat uniform and mirrored sunglasses.

"You're right on time."

He gave the pilot a thumbs up. The helicopter's blades rotated slowly at first and then quickly gained speed. Soon, they were airborne and traveling over the tall glittering buildings on the Las Vegas strip.

"The press doesn't like it when we create more questions than answers," Zavala said.

There were many things Easter admired about Zavala. Her no bullshit approach was near the top of the list.

Carter shrugged.

"It's better if they're kept in the dark."

"The lack of evidence is just going to make them look harder. They won't stop until they find something."

"Taken care of."

"How?"

"Don't worry about it."

"We're on the same team. Remember? You agreed not to keep any secrets from us."

Carter scowled at Zavala.

"We have created a series of diversions."

"Such as?" Easter asked.

"The bullet next to Slagle's spine shifted, and once she was able to walk again, she decided to follow in her brother's footsteps."

"Why?"

"Mental illness runs in her family."

Easter nodded.

"That might actually work."

"We've also planted a conspiracy theory on various websites that she was recruited by either Russia, China, or North Korea and trained to be an American hating assassin."

Zavala laughed and then glared at Carter.

"Wait. You're serious."

"If we find her soon enough, it won't matter what people believe."

Zavala started to respond, but Easter put his hand on her arm. She glanced at him and then looked out the window. As much as Easter admired Zavala's no bullshit approach, sometimes she pushed too hard. Like it or not, they needed Carter as much as he needed them.

The helicopter headed north. They left the city behind and flew over the desert, a reminder that Las Vegas was built in the middle of nowhere. The helicopter followed the two-lane highway that meandered over the desert. The mountainous terrain looked like the broken crust of a sourdough bread loaf with smatterings of white flour. Power lines hugged the sides of the road, and occasionally they passed a gas station or a house sitting by its lonesome on a flat plain.

"At our team's briefing, we were told Nell Slagle had enhanced abilities that included abnormal strength and invulnerable skin," Easter said.

"Despite what happened at the convention center, we find this hard to believe," Zavala said.

"Nell Slagle is the latest development in advanced weaponry," Carter said. "She was bought and paid for by the United States Armed Forces. If we don't catch her, or if the public finds out about her, then we've lost fifteen years of hard work, amazing scientific discoveries, and a truckload of taxpayers' money."

Easter and Zavala glanced at each other.

"What on earth possessed you to create this weapon?" Easter asked.

"Sixteen years ago, I attended a private dinner with Pentagon officials and defense contractor chief executives," Carter said. "I had the best Porterhouse steak I'd ever eaten. After the meal, I had a Courvoisier Napoleon Cognac. I don't normally order such expensive cognac, but Boeing was picking up the tab."

"Nobody ever buys us dinner," Zavala said.

Carter grinned at her before going on.

"I was feeling relaxed. There was no specific agenda. It was a friendly get together. We shared stories about where we grew up. I happen to mention that I loved comic books as a kid. Turned out so did most of the men. We talked about our favorite superheroes and how it was too bad that our soldiers didn't have the same powers. Wouldn't be great if they had bulletproof bodysuits as lightweight and skintight as the Black Panther's? Or even better, what if their bodies were bulletproof like Luke Cage, Hero for Hire? They wouldn't need helmets or heavy body armor. They'd be able to move around more freely."

"Are you telling me this all started because of a comic book?" Easter asked.

Carter shrugged.

"Comic books have inspired all kinds of technology. How different is an Apple Watch from Dick Tracy's 2-Way Wrist Radio?"

"Yeah, but that's a device that you put on and take off. You're talking about extreme genetic modification."

"When I went home that night, I considered our talk about bulletproof soldiers as nothing more than alcohol-infused wishful thinking and that would be the end of it. But defense contractors are fiercely competitive, and they smelled a possible lucrative military contract. By the end of the week, I had received proposals from three different companies to create bulletproof skin."

"Why didn't you tell them to stop reading comic books and grow the fuck up?" Zavala asked.

The helicopter veered away from the two-lane highway and shadowed a paved road that led up into the mountains. They passed over a gated entrance with barbed wire fencing stretching out in either direction.

"Two of the companies gave us give-us-money-and-we'll-figure-it-out proposals," Carter said. "But Honeydew's R&D departments came up with ideas that looked promising enough to show the top brass. They gave me the green light to proceed."

The whole thing started to make sense to Easter. The Pentagon was always paying obscene amounts of money for the development of outlandish war toys like unmanned combat vehicles, laser cannons, cyborg bugs, amphibious rifles, and hypersonic missiles. The more badass the weapon, the more the Pentagon got a hard-on to have it made, and what was more badass than superpowered soldiers?

"And Honeydew delivered the goods?" Easter asked.

"Better than we ever expected," Carter said.

The paved road below ended at the Honeydew Industries Research Facility. The helicopter hovered over the network of buildings. Only one of the structures was untouched. The rest had been reduced to rubble. A battle had been waged here and Honeydew lost.

CHAPTER FIVE

Skeeter woke to the ammonia smell of urine and a feeling of dampness in his groin. It didn't take a genius to figure out that he'd pissed his pants during the night, something he hadn't done since he'd stopped drinking ten years earlier. He groaned. The cushions would have to be pulled out of the sleeper cab, hosed off, and sun-dried to burn out the smell. And he needed to change his jeans.

But he couldn't do any of those things until he got his hands and feet untied.

Skeeter wasn't too proud to call for help and would have if it weren't for the duct tape over his mouth. Now that he was awake, he continued trying to loosen the power cords that held him prisoner in his own truck, but all he'd managed to do so far was rub the skin raw around his wrists. The sunlight filtering through the heavy curtain separating the sleeper from the cabin and the increasing heat of the cramped space told Skeeter that a new day had begun, the second day of his captivity.

The first day had begun with a painful need to urinate and a terrible thirst. For hours he dangled between the desperate cravings to intake liquid and to expel it. During his darkest moments, he whimpered like a whipped dog. At the end of the day, Skeeter passed out from exhaustion and dreamed that he was drowning in a bottle of Fireball Cinnamon Whiskey and the cinnamon was burning his skin off. While the scorching pain was unbearable, he figured it was safe to piss because nobody would notice the difference between his urine and the amber whiskey.

And now the second day was here. He'd lost the battle to control his bladder, he was still tied up like a Christmas turkey, and his nose itched.

Staring at the dirty laundry scattered on the floor of his sleeper cab, Skeeter thought of people who had wronged him. That included his ex-wife Edie, who had subjected him to eight years of cruel and unusual punishment before their divorce, the dispatcher at Friou Trucking Service who had always given him the worst routes until Skeeter couldn't take it anymore and quit, and the evil girl who had tied him up and left him to die.

She had said her name was Nell. Nell, straight from hell.

The blonde-haired blue-eyed demoness appeared Monday night in the Morton Travel Plaza truck lot where Skeeter had parked his rig. He was sitting in the driver's seat watching his *Tombstone* DVD when he noticed her walking past his truck. He assumed she was a lot lizard, a truck stop prostitute. Since his next assignment wasn't until Wednesday, he welcomed the distraction she would provide from the lonely wait. He had turned off the DVD and flipped on his interior lights to let her know that her services were required. When she didn't respond, he'd opened his door.

"Hey, there, little lady. Are you offering commercial company?"

The girl had peered up at Skeeter in the cab of his semi-truck.

"You talking to me?"

"Yeah. I'll do a forty. What do you say?"

"A what?"

"A forty. Don't tell me the prices have gone up."

"Do you have any water? I'm about to die of thirst."

Skeeter realized he should have suspected something was amiss when she didn't recognize the common terms used by lot lizards, not even the well-known 40-60-80: $40 for oral sex, $60 for sex, and $80 for both. Instead, he'd assumed she was new to the world's oldest profession, which made her all the more enticing. Maybe he was her first customer, the one against whom she would measure all future customers.

"I got water," Skeeter had said. "Come on in."

He'd leaned over and opened the passenger side door. She'd climbed in, bringing a dust cloud with her. Skeeter took a close look at her. She wasn't dressed in fishnet stockings, high heels, a tight dress that barely covered her butt, and slutty make-up like the stereotypical hooker. Then again, most lot lizards didn't dress like that. Too obvious and unreasonable attire for climbing in and out of trucks. Most wore jeans, T-shirts, and tennis shoes. This girl had on a light blue coverall and black combat boots. The number forty-eight was stenciled on the coverall's right chest pocket. He'd figured the rips and burn holes were some kind of new fashion trend, like ripped jeans.

All hookers had a tendency to be a bit dirty, which was understandable considering their work environment, but this girl was downright filthy. Her coverall was mud splattered and there were streaks of grease on her face and hands. Her hair was a tangled mess. Skeeter had seriously considered insisting that she shower before they do the deed, something he'd never asked a hooker to do before.

"How about that water?" she'd asked.

Skeeter had taken a gallon jug of water out of his mini-fridge and handed it to her. She twisted off the cap and tilted it up. Her throat bobbed as she guzzled the cold liquid. Some of it ran down her throat and into her clothes. She lowered the jug after drinking half of its contents and wiped her mouth with the back of her hand.

"Oh, man. I needed that."

She'd handed the jug to Skeeter. He'd wiped the spout with a paper towel before returning it to the fridge.

"You got a name?" Skeeter had asked.

"Sorry. Where are my manners? My name's Nell."

"Skeeter."

"Is that the name your mama gave you?"

"My real name's Terry. But I've always been called Skeeter."

Despite the layer of grime, Skeeter could tell that Nell was good looking. Give her a hard scrubbing and she would be girl-next-door cute. Through the slashes in her clothes, he could see she was muscular. Not like a musclebound weightlifter, but lean and ripped like an American Ninja Warrior.

"As I was walking into town, I saw a billboard out on the highway for something called the WAR Show," Nell said. "Do you know anything about it?"

"You mean the billboard southbound on I-15?"

"Yeah, that's the one."

"You couldn't have been walking because there ain't nothing but snakes and lizards out there."

Nell had shrugged.

"Okay. I didn't walk miles through the desert. Do you know what the WAR Show is?"

There was something not right about this girl. Skeeter should have kicked her cute butt out of his rig right there and then, but the little head was thinking for the big head. He'd figured that if she was this freaky during a casual conversation, then imagine how freaky she'd be once she was naked in his bed. He might even be willing to go for an eighty.

"The WAR Show is an annual tradeshow for the weapons, ammo, and recreation industry. It's the biggest event of its kind in the world," Skeeter had said.

He knew about the show because his Wednesday assignment was for one of the gun makers at the convention center, but he had no intention of sharing this information with the dirty super freak in his cab.

"Can anybody attend?" Nell had asked him.

"It's not open to the public. Only buyers and sellers in the business are allowed."

"Then why the hell do they have a billboard for it?"

"It's a big deal. The sign is an advertisement for the convention center."

Nell had leaned back in the seat and stared at the sky.

"As I was walking here, I wondered what I was going to do with my life, but then I saw that billboard, and I knew exactly what I had to do. It's the only way things are going to change in this country."

"They won't let you in," Skeeter had said.

"I'll figure something out."

Skeeter enjoyed conversing with anybody about anything, but his tolerance for crazy talk was limited and he'd reached it with Nell. It was time for her to do her job. He took out his wallet and pulled out two twenties.

"Here you go."

Nell had taken the money and put it in her pocket.

"Thank you. I really appreciate it. I hate to be rude, but could you give me some more?" She counted on her fingers as she listed the things she needed. "I need to buy a shower at the truck stop here because as you can see, I'm a hot mess. I'll need clothes. I obviously can't go around in this. I saw there's a Citi Trends just down the street. I'll need bus fare. And something to eat. I'm so hungry I could eat my leg."

"Forty is all you're getting," Skeeter had said. "I was going to do an eighty but changed my mind. I only want a blowjob."

Nell had laughed.

"Oh my God! You think I'm a prostitute. Well, of course you do. I get it now. How embarrassing."

Irritation had gnawed at Skeeter.

"Are you trying to make a fool of me?"

"Even when I was at the lowest, most desperate times of my life, I never had sex for money. I knew women and men who did, and I understood why. They did what they had to do to get by. The truth is that back then, nobody wanted to have sex with me."

"I don't want your damn sob story. I want the sex I paid for. Either get to work or give me my money back."

Nell had crossed her arms.

"I'm not having sex with you and I'm not giving you your money back."

Skeeter's anger boiled over. He'd slid his hand down beside his seat to the holster he had strapped there and grabbed his concealed weapon. He pulled it out and aimed the snub-nosed pistol at Nell.

"You think you can just climb into my truck and rob me?" he'd said. "Give me my money and then get your ass out of here."

Nell had pointed at his weapon.

"That's a taser, isn't it?"

"It'll still fuck you up," Skeeter said. "Hand over my money."

"I'm sorry. I can't. I guess I am robbing you."

Skeeter had seen that reason wasn't going to work with this lunatic. He pulled the trigger. Twin probes shot out of the muzzle and buried into Nell's coverall. Electric current traveled through the wires connected to the probes. The charge should have shocked her into a writhing ball of pain. Instead, it was Skeeter who had been shocked as he watched blue tendrils of electricity crackle around her as she sat calmly in her seat. When the electric charge ended, Nell had grabbed the wires and yanked the probes out of her clothes.

"You're lucky. I would have killed you if you had used a gun."

Skeeter's eyes had widened.

"What the hell? You're not human."

Nell rubbed her forehead.

"Damn it. I can't have you telling anyone about me until I'm ready for people to know."

She had disconnected the microphone and the coaxial cable from Skeeter's CB radio. Skeeter's mouth had gone dry as he realized that this was no ordinary lot lizard. His life was in danger. Escape was essential. He would worry about his truck later. He threw his door open. The air was cool. He could smell diesel fuel and fried chicken. He glanced back at the monster he'd foolishly invited into his truck. She had moved so quickly that he didn't realize her fist was coming at him until it connected with his head.

Pain had shot through his body like a taser. He struggled to stay conscious as he slumped in his seat. Nell pulled Skeeter back into the truck, closed the door, and tossed him onto the bed of the sleeper cab.

"I'm really sorry about this," Nell had said. "Very rude of me especially since we just met."

She'd moved his arms and legs like a rag doll as she wound the cables around his wrists and ankles. Digging through his personal space, she located a roll of duct tape and tore off a strip.

"Why you doing this to me?" Skeeter had asked, slurring his words.

"It's not personal."

She'd placed the duct tape over his mouth. He felt her take his wallet out of his back pocket. She waved two twenties in his face. The girl got her eighty after all.

"This should cover everything I need," Nell had said. "Keep in mind, I could have taken all your money."

She pulled across the curtain between the sleeper cab and the cabin, plunging him into darkness. He'd tried to scream at her, but his voice was muffled by the tape.

Here it was two days later and Skeeter about to die from dehydration. He would miss Edie most of all, because despite all the venom they'd pumped into each other's systems, he still loved that woman. Hopefully, somebody would find his body before it bloated and blistered so he would look good at his funeral.

A loud rapping on his door snapped him out of his pitiful thoughts. He tried to call out to whoever it was, but he was weak and had a damn piece of tape over his mouth. The rapping happened again. Skeeter prayed that Nell hadn't locked the doors to the cab. Though his body ached, he rocked back and forth. More rapping. The door opened. Praise Jesus, it wasn't locked.

"Hey," a woman's voice said. "You only paid to park here until this morning. You have to pay more if you're planning on staying longer."

Mustering all his strength, Skeeter rolled off the bed. His momentum carried him under the curtain. The woman shrieked when she saw him and ran away. Minutes later, a man wearing a green Subway T-shirt and a dirty apron entered the cabin with the woman.

"Damn, Marcia. You weren't lying," he said. "There really is a dude tied up in here."

"Hey, man," Marcia said. "Why you tied up like this?"

Skeeter shook his head. Tears rolled down his face. Subway Man tore the tape off Skeeter's mouth. It stung like hell but was a tremendous relief.

"I was robbed," Skeeter croaked. "She left me to die."

"A female did this to you?" Subway Man asked.

"A woman can rob somebody just as well as a man can," Marcia said.

"No doubt. Hey, man. You want us to call the police?"

"Untie me," Skeeter said. "I want to get out of the truck."

Subway Man tried to untie the cables, but the knots were too tight. He had to use a cable cutter to free Skeeter. Once Skeeter got feeling back into his arms and legs, he drank the rest of the water in his jug. He did not want to call the police. He didn't want to spend hours talking to them.

After a shower and a change of clothes, he bought a Subway sandwich and a bag of chips. Normally, Skeeter avoided Subway because their food was lousy, but since one of their employees helped save his life, he felt the least he could do was buy a meal from them.

As he ate his ham sandwich, Skeeter hated how much he wanted a drink. A shot of whiskey would have steadied his shaking hands. But he didn't dare. One was one too many.

Instead, Skeeter took comfort sitting in the truck stop's dining area, even if it did smell like cleaning fluid and burnt cheese. He was no longer a prisoner in his own truck. Though there was a baseball game playing on the TV mounted on the wall, he watched the bumper-to-bumper traffic on the highway. Skeeter checked his watch. The morning rush hour should have been over by now. Panic seized him. He was supposed to have been at the Las Vegas Convention Center three hours earlier to pick up cargo for Bulard Arms and take it a shooting range a few miles away. Bulard was his best steady client. He couldn't afford to lose them.

He took out his phone expecting to see a voicemail or a text. To his surprise, there were no messages. That might be a good thing or a bad thing. There was only one way to find out for certain. He called Harry Pigott, his contact at Bulard.

"Who is this?" Harry said when he answered the phone. "What do you want?"

"Harry. It's Skeeter."

"Skeeter? Oh, hey, Skeeter. Forgot all about you."

"I can't tell you how sorry I am that I wasn't at the

convention center this morning. I won't waste your time with excuses. I can be there in an hour."

Harry chuckled.

"Unless you're a block away, I seriously doubt you can get to the convention center or anywhere in this city in an hour. There are roadblocks everywhere. And even if you did get to the convention center, it's sealed off."

"Sealed off? What for?"

"Have you been living under a rock for the last couple of days? There's no pickup today. Or any time soon. That cargo you were supposed to haul is now part of an active police investigation."

"What happened?"

Harry sighed.

"The police just cut me loose so I'm in no mood to go over it again. Turn on a TV, a radio, or a computer. You'll find out all about it."

Skeeter got a lump in his throat as he considered the possibilities of what had gone down at the convention center.

"Should I check with the dispatcher about another haul?"

"Don't waste your time," Harry said. "He's going to tell you to see if your other clients have a job for you. Bulard is shut down until this shit gets sorted out."

Harry hung up.

Skeeter had Subway Man change the TV from the baseball game to a news channel. Grim-faced reporters discussed the mass shooting that had taken place at the WAR Show. Sixty-two dead, four hundred twenty-six injured, and the shooter was still at large. The FBI and the National Guard were assisting the local police with the manhunt.

A photo appeared on the TV of the suspected killer. Skeeter gasped.

"Oh my God!"

"You didn't hear about this?" Subway Man said. "Oh right. You wouldn't have because you were all tied up and shit. Turns out robbery isn't the only thing a woman can do as well as a man."

Skeeter pointed at the TV.

"That's who attacked me."

Subway Man leaned over the counter and shouted at the manager's office.

"Hey Marcia! The guy we cut loose was attacked by the convention killer."

Marcia hurried into the dining area.

"Really? It was her?"

Skeeter was still staring at the TV.

"She said her name was Nell. Straight from hell!"

"She told you she was from hell?"

"No. I added that part because she's a blonde-haired blue-eye demoness."

Icy fear ran through Skeeter. He thought about the other thing Nell had told him. It was right after he'd shot her with his taser. She said she would have killed him if he had used a gun.

Skeeter wanted a drink worse than ever.

CHAPTER SIX

Lt. General Buck Carter led John Easter and Mara Zavala around the chunks of concrete, strands of rebar, and clouds of dust that had once been Honeydew Industries Advanced Research and Development Southwest Facility. A military helicopter that resembled a giant dung-colored metallic insect was nose down in a pile of rubble, as if it had been swatted dead. Men in hazmat suits dug through the ruins while armed guards watched over them. The scent of sagebrush and scorched metal hung in the air.

Easter nodded toward the diggers.

"What are they looking for?"

"Anything they can salvage," Carter said. "Project Bulletproof wasn't the only thing they worked on at this facility. Honeydew lost a ton of valuable data."

"There are no backups at other facilities?"

"The only backups were kept here. Honeydew was in constant fear that a competitor might get access to their research, so they kept it contained in one location."

"Honeydew Industries Advanced Research and

Development Southwest Facility," Zavala said. "That's quite a mouthful."

"They use an acronym," Carter said. "HARD-SOW."

Easter glanced over at Zavala expecting her to say something snarky. She shrugged.

"I got nothing."

On the barren plain to the north of the facility, the flat roof of a bunker rose out of the ground like a rectangular boil on the skin of the desert. Beyond the bunker was a wooden shed with white bullseye targets painted on the walls.

Easter marveled at the mass destruction Slagle had left behind, both here and at the Las Vegas Convention Center. She was a one-woman army razing everything in her path. The only building still standing contained the living quarters and cafeteria. With its corporate architecture of sharp-angled boxes, metal panels, and mirrored windows, the three-story structure could have just as easily been an insurance company headquarters.

Two armed guards stood at the entrance. Even though they were private security contractors, they saluted Carter. They were probably ex-military conditioned to salute a superior officer.

"They're with me," Carter said, gesturing at Easter and Zavala.

The guards nodded and the three entered a lobby with dark wood polished floors and modern chairs and sofas set up around glass coffee tables. Sunlight streamed through the windows. The walls were bare except for a Honeydew logo etched into a shiny plate bolted to the wall between two wide-door elevators.

One of the elevators dinged and the doors slid open. A man came out to greet them. Everything about him looked expensive, from his tailored suit, silk tie and shiny shoes, to his designer frame eyeglasses and stylish haircut. Even the sling on his left arm looked expensive. He flashed them a smile with bright white teeth.

"Buck," Wilson said. "Punctual as always." He turned to the FBI special agents. "You must be John Easter and Mara Zavala. I'm Rex Wilson, CEO of Honeydew Industries."

He reached out his right hand and gave Easter and Zavala a firm handshake.

"I'm glad to see that the air conditioning is still working," Easter said as he mopped his forehead with his handkerchief.

"This building didn't suffer any damage," Wilson said, "Almost as if Number Forty-Eight had saved it on purpose."

Easter noticed a few hairline cracks in the windows, so the building wasn't completely damage free.

"Did Nell have a reason for sparring this building?" Zavala asked.

Wilson winced at the use of Slagle's first name.

"Number Forty-Eight lived here with the other test subjects. I suppose she didn't want to hurt her friends. The rest of the world be damned."

"The test subjects live here?" Zavala looked around the lobby. "I'm impressed."

"Most of the staff, including researchers, administrators, and maintenance crew, live here as well."

"What about you?"

Wilson narrowed his eyes at Zavala.

"I have a house in the city."

"I'm curious why you have guards for this place," Easter said. "Seems like you're closing the barn door after the horse is gone."

Wilson looked past them at the front door.

"The massacre at the Las Vegas Convention Center is proof that Number Forty-Eight is insane. My employees feel safer knowing the guards are there in case she decides to come back and finish what she started."

"Speaking of what she started," Zavala said. "I understand you have a video to show us."

"About that," Wilson said. "Before I show you, I'll need you both to sign a confidentiality agreement not to disclose anything you see here today."

"I don't think that's necessary," Carter said.

"It's my duty to protect the interests of Honeydew."

Zavala put her hands on her hips.

"Tell you what. We'll promise not to tell the world that Honeydew created an unstoppable killing machine that slaughtered dozens of people and in exchange, you cram your confidentiality agreement up your ass."

Wilson's face turned red. Carter jumped in front of Zavala.

"Damn it, Special Agent Zavala! That was uncalled for. Apologize to Mr. Wilson."

"I don't work for you," Zavala said. "Or him."

"Then maybe I should call the director and have you removed from this assignment."

"Go ahead. You'd be doing me a favor."

Easter put his forefinger and thumb in his mouth and blew a loud, shrill whistle that bounced off the barren walls. Carter, Zavala, and Wilson turned their attention to him.

"Everybody calm down," Easter said. "Mr. Wilson. Understand that Special Agent Zavala and I were chosen for this assignment because of our field experience."

"So, I've been told," Wilson said. "However…"

"I wasn't finished. We didn't volunteer for this. But if we're going to capture Nell Slagle, we're going to have to trust each other."

The group took half a minute for their tempers to cool and to regain their composure.

"Very well," Wilson said. "You don't have to sign anything. Follow me. We've set up a video monitor in the cafeteria."

Wilson headed for a corridor to the left of the elevators. Carter, Easter, and Zavala followed close behind him, their footsteps clacking on the wood floor. On the walls hung photos of HARD-SOW. Easter would have considered the photos entirely too self-referential, but they let him see what the facility had looked like before Nell obliterated it. Besides the residence building, there had been four other buildings. They had all been taller and wider than the residence building. And unlike the residence building, they'd had few windows. They were more like rectangular fortresses than office buildings. Considering how solid they looked, it made Easter even more curious to see how Nell brought them down.

"Mr. Wilson, you said most of the staff lives here," Zavala said.

"That's right."

"Do they live here year-round or just during the week?"

"Year-round. I see what you're getting at. You're wondering where is everybody?"

"Exactly."

"When I received your request to question the research team, I instructed them to wait in their rooms so that they'll be easier to locate."

"That's a good plan. Thanks."

Wilson looked over his shoulder at Zavala.

"I'm so glad you approve."

The inviting aroma of baked bread greeted them when they entered the cafeteria, but the serving lines were shut down and the whole place was scrubbed clean. The only evidence of food was a refrigerated display case filled with packaged sandwiches and juice bottles. On a side table was a coffee machine with coffee cups. On another side table was a soft ice cream machine. Zavala tugged Easter's sleeve and pointed.

"Go ahead," Easter said. "I'm sure they won't mind."

Zavala frowned.

"Maybe later."

At the back of the dining area, a large high-definition monitor hung from the ceiling. A dining table with four chairs had been set up with the chairs facing the monitor. On the table was a laptop computer. Wilson took the chair that gave him access to the computer. Carter, Easter, and Zavala took the remaining chairs.

"When Honeydew rolls out a new product," Wilson said, "we do a live demonstration for our client. At the same time, we videotape the demonstration for advertising purposes."

"Initially, the Pentagon wasn't going to allow Honeydew to make this video," Carter said. "Since we directly financed the product, it's exclusive for our soldiers. We eventually agreed so that there would be a video record of the event."

Wilson typed on the keyboard. The overhead lights dimmed. On the monitor, Rex Wilson appeared. He wore a dark blue suit, held a microphone, and stood on a platform surrounded by desert. Parked ten yards behind Wilson was the military helicopter that was now crashed in the rubble.

"Today, a long difficult journey comes to an end," Wilson said. "Honeydew Industries is proud to present the latest development in advanced weaponry. Project Bulletproof!"

Wilson thrust out his arm and Nell joined him on the platform. She wore a light blue coverall with the number forty-eight stenciled on the right chest pocket, a light blue ball cap with the Honeydew logo on it, and black combat boots. Nell stood next to Wilson and faced the camera. She showed no emotion. Wilson was at least four inches taller than she was. It took Easter a moment to recognize that this young woman dressed as a car mechanic was the same woman in heavy make-up wearing the skintight camo T-shirt and camo booty shorts that he'd seen in photos from the WAR Show.

"Using test subject Number Forty-Eight," Wilson said, "Honeydew will demonstrate the next generation of body armor. And how will we do that?"

He reached inside his suit jacket, took out a handgun, and held the weapon inches from Nell's head. She didn't look at Wilson but kept her gaze straight ahead. Wilson pulled the trigger. The gunshot rang out across the desert.

Easter and Zavala gasped in unison. Easter noticed that Wilson and Carter seemed almost bored, as if a woman getting shot in the head was something that they'd seen every day.

In the video, Nell staggered but didn't fall.

"That's how," Wilson said. "But this is just the beginning of the demonstration. Before we continue, gentlemen, I will join you in the bunker. Number Forty-Eight may be bulletproof, but I'm not."

He left the platform. Nell wiggled her forefinger in her ear on the side of her head where Wilson had shot her and then stood with her back straight and her hands by her side. After a minute, Wilson spoke from off-camera.

"Honeydew's latest invention will dramatically change modern warfare. History will look back on this day as the moment between before bulletproof soldiers and after. The advantages are legion."

A man in full military tactical gear joined Nell on the platform from stage left. He fired a shotgun into her stomach. She grimaced, but the only damage was a hole in her coveralls. The man fired three more times. The third shot finally knocked Nell off her feet, but she quickly scrambled back to a standing position. The man gave a short bow to the camera and then walked away.

"There will be no need for a soldier to wear a bulky vest or a helmet. Soldiers will move more freely, carry less heavy gear, and will be more fearless as they protect our country from its enemies."

Another man in tactical gear entered from stage right. He fired a machine gun at Nell. A flurry of bullets bounced off her. One of the bullets hit the man shooting her. He dropped the machine gun and grabbed his arm. Men rushed out and led him off the platform.

Wilson's voiceover continued.

"As Honeydew's advanced research division toiled away on Project Bulletproof, we realized that it wasn't enough to make the soldier's skin bullet proof. What good was having bullets bounce off if the impact broke bones or damaged internal organs? How would we treat injured soldiers if the Army surgeon was unable to penetrate their skin? We had to make every part of the body invulnerable."

While he spoke, men attacked Nell with a variety of weapons, including a Gatling gun, a grenade launcher, and a flamethrower. Easter felt like he was watching a living cartoon character, like Wile E. Coyote, that kept going despite getting hammered by one deadly calamity after another.

"Honeydew's research team successfully fused human DNA with foreign elements to create bulletproof skin, shatterproof bones, and damage-proof internal organs. But then something truly amazing and unexpected happened. We discovered that Number Forty-Eight's improved body picks up internal vibrations from machines even when the machine is dormant. As a result, she can operate anything mechanical just by touching it. No longer will the military have to waste months training soldiers to operate advanced weapons systems. The soldiers will only have to lay their hands on the weapon once and will instantly have the knowledge necessary to use it."

Even though Nell's body was unscathed, her coverall was torn and dirty, her hair stuck out in all directions, and there were dirt smudges on her face.

"Number Forty-Eight will demonstrate this bonus feature of Project Bulletproof by flying the advanced multi-role helicopter you see behind her," Wilson said. "It has laser-guided precision hellfire missiles, 70mm rockets, a 30mm cannon, advanced target acquisition designation. Intensive testing and training are required to operate the helicopter. I swear to you on my mother's grave that Number Forty-Eight has never been in a helicopter of any kind much less flown one."

Nell turned and headed off across the field toward the helicopter. Midway to her destination, an explosion threw her ten feet into the air and blew her boots off her feet. She sat on her rump and shook her head as smoke drifted off her.

"We added that little surprise," Wilson said, "to demonstrate why future soldiers will never have to worry about IEDs again."

Walking in her socks, Nell located her boots, and put them back on. She brushed some of the dirt off her coveralls as she continued to the helicopter. She paused next to the imposing military aircraft before placing her hands on the metallic shell.

"Come on, Number Forty-Eight. Climb in and show us what you can do."

With her hands still on the shell, Nell looked toward the bunker. She said something but since there was no microphone on her, Wilson and Zavala couldn't hear her words. She got into the helicopter. The engine started and the blades rotated.

"For this part of the demonstration, Number Forty-Eight will hover in the air and fire a missile at the hut," Wilson narrated.

The aircraft lifted off the ground, floated in place, and turned towards the hut. But it didn't fire. Instead, it spun back in the direction of the bunker, stirring up a cloud of dust, and shot a missile at the bunker. For a brief moment, the camera captured the projectile growing rapidly as it got closer. There was a deafening explosion. The scene shook, stuttered, and died. Shouting and explosions could be heard for thirty seconds before the video ended.

Zavala turned to Easter. Her eyes were wide with fear.

"We are so screwed."

"You just have to find her," Carter said. "We'll bring her in."

Carter made it sound so simple, but Easter knew better. He and Zavala would have to find a way to keep Nell in one place long enough for the military to arrive.

"We've seen the structural damage she caused," Easter said. "What was the number of casualties?"

"Twelve dead," Carter said, "and seven wounded. All of them were Honeydew employees. The bunker withstood the missile and no one inside was harmed."

Easter turned to Wilson.

"You were inside the bunker, but I see you were wounded."

Wilson looked down at the sling and frowned.

"It's just a sprain. I tripped and stuck out my arm to break the fall."

It was tempting to laugh, if only to relieve the tension after watching the video, but Easter didn't and neither did Zavala. Wilson only made weapons of mass destruction. He probably had never been in a combat situation, which meant he'd never had any real-world experience with the products Honeydew made. This had to have been the first time one of their weapons had fired back at them.

"We'd like to get started interviewing the Project Bullet-proof research team," Easter said."

"You can do the interviews in here," Wilson said. "I'll send them in one at time."

"Yes, that'll work."

"I'll stay with you," Carter said.

"I'd rather you didn't," Easter said.

"I promise I won't say a thing. I'll be a fly on the wall."

"An enormous distracting fly. There are CCTV cameras all over this building. You can watch the interviews from the monitoring station."

Carter got to his feet.

"Hey, before you go," Zavala said.

"What?" Carter said.

"Actually, my question is for Mr. Wilson."

Wilson looked down his nose at her.

"Yes?"

"Nell, I mean Number Forty-Eight, said something before she got into the helicopter. Do you know what it was?"

Wilson stared at the blank monitor.

"We sent the video to Honeydew's main offices so that the technical crew could do advanced video forensics. They were able to isolate her mouth movements and then had a lip reader decipher her words."

"And?"

"We had hoped she had something that might help us understand her motivations or her next move. Anything that would assist the effort to get her back. But what she said was meaningless and not worth repeating."

"Let us be the judge of that. What did she say?"

Wilson glared at Zavala as he answered her question.

"Number Forty-Eight said, 'See you later, fornicator.'"

CHAPTER SEVEN

A MAN WITH salt and pepper hair and thick rimmed glasses balanced on his beak nose entered the cafeteria.

"I'm Dr. Ethan Troutman, head of the research department and lead developer on Project Bulletproof."

After giving Easter and Zavala a soft handshake, Dr. Troutman settled into a chair at a table. Easter and Zavala took seats on the opposite side. Before Easter could begin, Troutman asked a question.

"How soon can you return Number Forty-Eight?"

Easter decided right then and there that he didn't like Troutman.

"That depends on the information you provide us."

"I don't know what I could possibly tell you about her that you don't already know."

"Once we know why she attacked HARD-SOW and the WAR Show, we'll have a better idea of where she might strike next."

"You think she'll attack again?"

"What do you think?"

From the surprised look on his face, Easter guessed that Troutman hadn't realized the obvious. As long as Slagle was free, people were in danger.

"Number Forty-Eight represents an historic opportunity," Troutman said. "Invulnerability will change how America engages in combat and provide an incredible benefit for our nation's soldiers. But it won't happen unless she's returned to us. When Number Forty-Eight destroyed the facility here, she obliterated the entirety of our research. That's years of trial and error that can't be replicated."

"If I'm hearing you correctly," Easter said, "you're saying that Nell's body holds the secret to invulnerability."

"Exactly."

"Nell is test subject number forty-eight," Zavala said. "That means there are at least forty-seven other test subjects. Why can't you examine them?"

Troutman looked up at the security camera. He adjusted his glasses before turning his attention back to the FBI agents.

"Unfortunately, test subjects with significant markers died during experimentation."

Easter felt a chill as Troutman's words sank in.

"Nell is the only one out of forty-eight test subjects who's still alive?"

"Her number has nothing to do with how many test subjects were involved with the project," Troutman said. "There are plenty of living test subjects, but none from her group. Without Number Forty-Eight we would have to start from scratch, and there's no guarantee that we'd find the formula again."

"Did any test subjects have contact with Nell?"

"Certainly. The test subjects' quarters are two floors below this one. They have their own cafeteria and common areas."

"After we're done talking to members of your staff, I want to talk to them."

Troutman frowned.

"Whatever for?"

"Nell might have told a test subject something that will help lead us to her."

Troutman glanced at the security camera again.

"They're not here. All the test subjects were moved to another location. For safety reasons."

"Safety reasons?"

"Their floor was damaged by the attack."

Zavala rolled her eyes. Rex Wilson had just told the special agents that the building hadn't suffered any damage.

"Why don't you examine the dead test subjects that led to your success with Nell?" Zavala asked.

Troutman took a handkerchief from his jacket pocket and cleaned his glasses. He put his glasses back on and stuffed the handkerchief into his pocket.

"After the test subjects died, we performed autopsies and archived samples of bone, skin, and blood. They were stored in one of the buildings destroyed by Number Forty-Eight's assault."

"We saw people in hazmat suits searching the rubble," Zavala said. "Are you hoping some of the samples survived the attack?"

"It's probably a lost cause, but we're looking anyway."

As Easter took a sip of his coffee, he had a thought.

"Couldn't you exhume the dead test subjects' bodies?"

Troutman shook his head.

"Their remains were cremated."

"Is that standard procedure?" Zavala asked.

Troutman glanced at the security camera for the third time. Easter groaned.

"You can tell us," Easter said. "We're on the same team, remember?"

Troutman sighed.

"Rex was worried that a competitor might find out what we were doing here and steal one of the corpses."

"It wasn't because the test subjects died?"

Troutman scowled at Easter.

"There are risks in any kind of human subject research, whether it's for a new treatment for heartburn or for invulnerability. They volunteered and signed consent forms."

"Is Nell completely invulnerable?" Zavala asked.

"That's a good question," Troutman said. "Despite her enhanced body, Number Forty-Eight is still a human being. She needs fluids to avoid dehydration, food to avoid starvation, and sleep to avoid exhaustion."

"But can anything hurt her? Can she be killed?"

"Yes, but obviously not easily. Her skin can be pierced with a laser. A bunker buster bomb or ballistic missile would blow her to pieces. She wouldn't survive being hit by a speeding train. And drowning. She could die from drowning. Beyond that, I'm not sure. We had planned to do more testing before delivering the final product to the Pentagon."

"But you can't do that now, can you?"

"For the time being, no. But hopefully, you will return her quickly so that we can."

"We'll do our best. Thank you for your time, doctor."

Troutman left the cafeteria. Easter and Zavala made two more cups of coffee.

"He was a bundle of laughs," Zavala said. "We should party with him."

"I almost feel sorry for Dr. Troutman," Easter said. "He spent a decade and a half creating a magnificent weapon and not only did the weapon run away, she blew up the instruction manual on how to build her."

Zavala sipped her coffee, grimaced, and added more sugar.

"There's still a chance that someone will come forward who knows her. Considering the media coverage, I'm surprised an ex-boyfriend, a neighbor, or a friend from school hasn't used their connection to her as an excuse to get on TV."

"She was one of those people who everyone wants to forget. That's why Honeydew used her. People like her are as disposable as lab rats."

Easter and Zavala proceeded to interview six members of the Project Bulletproof research team. They interviewed them individually, and though the agents poked and prodded with the skills they gained from years of questioning suspects and witnesses, the six research team members failed to provide any more information than what they had gotten from Dr. Troutman.

The seventh and final research team member they interviewed was Dr. Gina Li, a Korean American. She shook the agents' hands vigorously before taking her seat.

"Before we start," Zavala said as she pointed at the soft ice cream machine, "do you mind? It's been calling my name all freakin' day."

"I don't mind at all," Li said. "It only has chocolate and vanilla, but you can get the two swirled together."

"I love chocolate and vanilla swirl."

"Me too. Do you mind if I join you?"

"No. In fact, you'd be doing me a favor. This way I don't

look like a complete pig eating ice cream by myself. What about you, Bunny?"

"I'll stick with coffee for now," Easter said.

While Zavala and Li filled their bowls from the soft ice cream machine, Easter made another cup of coffee. It had been a long day, and they still hardly knew anything about Nell.

Once they were back at the table, Zavala ate a spoonful of ice cream and smiled.

"I needed that."

"There are pints of gelato in the freezer, but there's something wonderfully decadent about soft ice cream," Li said, gesturing at her bowl with her spoon.

"Reminds me of drive-through burger joints. Damn it. Now I'm craving a hamburger."

"When Nell first came here, ice cream was all she ate."

Zavala and Easter glanced at each other.

"You're the first member of the research staff not to call her Number Forty-Eight," Easter said.

Li ate a spoonful of ice cream before answering.

"In our reports, we identified the test subjects by their assigned numbers. When we spoke directly to them, we used their names. Top management like Rex Wilson will only refer to the test subjects by their number."

"Getting back to the ice cream," Easter said. "Did Nell give a reason why it was the only thing she would eat?"

Li looked at Easter as if he were a buffoon.

"She didn't have to. Nell was a heroin addict. Most of the test subjects were addicted to something when they arrived. The heroin addicts spent the first months here lined up at the ice cream machine. It was the only thing they could keep down, and they craved sugar."

Easter was taken aback. Nell's file included an arrest for misdemeanor drug possession. He had assumed she had been busted for marijuana.

"You experimented on heroin addicts?" Zavala asked.

"*Former* heroin addicts. We put the test subjects through rehab, fed them healthy meals, and had them go through a rigorous exercise program."

"That's a lot of time and trouble."

"Our goal was to transform their bodies into something new and amazing. The test subjects needed to be in peak physical condition to endure a process which was often painful and dangerous."

"What was your impression of Nell?" Easter asked.

Dr. Li ate more ice cream before answering.

"Nell was our sweetest, most agreeable test subject. Polite. Adorable Southern accent. Never complained."

"I'm surprised that Honeydew uses women in their experiments," Zavala said.

Li's forehead knitted.

"Why? As test subjects, they're just as good as men. In fact, women deal with pain better than men."

"I was thinking of the optics," Zavala said. "When I watched the video of Rex Wilson presenting Project Bulletproof to the Pentagon, I got the feeling that he would have preferred that Nell had been a big burly dude."

"What gave you that impression?"

"His body language gave it away. Here was his great new weapon and he could barely bring himself to look at Nell."

Li laughed.

"You're right. Rex was furious that adorable Nell was our breakthrough test subject."

"Nell had been shot in right leg just below the buttock," Easter said.

"That's right. She had a bullet lodged in her T10 spinal column that paralyzed her from the waist down."

"How did you get her to walk again?"

Li ate the last of her ice cream and let her spoon clang in the metal bowl.

"This is Honeydew Industries. We have surgical equipment that is decades ahead of civilian hospitals. Our surgeons were able to safely remove the bullet, and then we put her on an advanced physical therapy program that had her walking again in less than a year."

"I don't get it," Zavala said. "Why go to all that trouble for just one test subject?"

"We did this for every test subject. There was no way of knowing which one would respond best to the procedure."

"Did Nell ever talk about how she was shot?"

"No."

"She never mentioned that it was her brother who shot her?"

"Her brother?"

"You never asked?"

"It's not like Nell was the only test subject who was homeless with a gunshot wound and a heroin addiction."

Easter stared at Li.

"Nell was homeless?"

Li placed her palms on the table.

"I can't believe this is news to you."

"The last time we saw Nell, she was recuperating from her gunshot wound in a hospital in Cleveland, Tennessee," Zavala said. "The FBI file on her ends there as well."

"She was from Tennessee? That explains her accent."

"Nell wasn't recruited in Cleveland?"

Li shook her head.

"Honeydew never went to Tennessee to find test subjects."

Easter glared at the security camera. Every scrap of information Honeydew had on Nell Slagle should have been gathered and delivered to Easter and Zavala the minute she'd escaped, instead of forcing the special agents to waste hours questioning their staff.

"Do you have any idea where Nell was recruited?" Easter asked.

"Philadelphia," Li said.

"What makes you so certain?"

"There was a list of where the test subjects were recruited. It was in the building Nell destroyed, so the list no longer exists. But I recall that test subjects forty to sixty-five came from Philadelphia. Nell was number forty-eight."

"That's twenty-five people."

"Which is why I remember their assigned numbers. Largest group from a single city."

Zavala put her hand on Easter's arm.

"I think we're done here."

Easter nodded.

"Dr. Li. Is there anything you'd like to add before we conclude the interview?"

Li held up her forefinger.

"One more thing. Probably not important."

"Tell us anyway," Zavala said.

"After we removed the bullet from her spine, we offered to eliminate the wound scar on her leg. It wasn't a bad scar, but young women are so concerned about having perfect bodies. Nell refused. She said she wanted it as a reminder of her past life."

CHAPTER EIGHT

Nell napped on the city bus for hours. Her invulnerability didn't include an endless supply of energy. Shooting bullets into people's bodies and having bullets bouncing off her own body combined with running in and out of hotels and casinos had plumb worn her out. She slept on the bus's hard plastic seat with her head rolled back and her mouth open. Nobody paid Nell any mind. In her maid's uniform, she blended in with the exhausted domestic workers taking long bus rides home.

She would have been fine sleeping on the bus for days, but every time a rider signaled for the bus to drop them off, the ringing bell woke her up, and she worried that someone would eventually recognize her despite her disguise. She needed a quiet hiding place to rest and decide what to do next.

It was late afternoon when she got off the bus and walked toward the My Place hotel. She chose the hotel because it sat all by its lonesome off a six-lane road in a barren-looking part of North Las Vegas in a neighborhood that was nowhere near the Strip. The hotel looked like a row of alternating light cream, burnt orange, and soft blue Legos.

Walking around the building, Nell was stymied. Going through the lobby was too risky. The maid's uniform worked against her. The front desk clerk would probably know the cleaning crew well enough to realize that she didn't work there. There was a side door, but it required a card key for entry. Breaking it open might set off an alarm. She was about to try sneaking through the lobby when a man wearing chinos and a dress shirt came out the side door and held it open for her.

"Room one twenty-four," he said.

Nell was confused. Was he was propositioning her?

"Excuse me?"

"One twenty-four. I called the front desk over an hour ago for more towels and I'm still waiting."

She glanced down at her maid's uniform. This was the best disguise ever.

"Yes, sir. I'll get right on it."

The hotel's interior was quiet and clean. The walls and floor featured varying shades of beige. She took the stairs to the top floor and stood outside the room closest to the stairwell. She chose this room because it was in a far corner of the hotel and next to an exit in case she needed to leave in a hurry.

Pressing her ear against the door, she heard nothing. That didn't mean the room was empty. There might be a sleeping guest inside, but the promise of a soft bed was too strong. Looking both ways to ensure that the hallway was empty, Nell leaned against the door until the lock broke. The break sounded like a gunshot. Nell looked around again before slipping inside and closing the door behind her. Peering back into the hallway through the peephole, she waited for someone to come investigate.

A minute passed, and Nell decided that she was safe for the

time being. The setting sun streamed through the window and dust motes meandered in the orange light. Gazing at the bed, Nell was tempted to dive under the covers, but while she'd been waiting to make sure no one responded to her breaking in, she thought she had smelled a dead animal. She scanned the room but saw no evidence of a decomposing corpse. An exploratory sniff of her underarm brought tears to her eyes.

"Oh, my Lord," Nell said. "I stink something awful."

The bathing she'd done in the maids' bathroom had been what her grandmother would have called "a lick and a promise." What she needed was a full body scrubbing.

Nell took the extra ammunition magazines out of her pockets and put them on the dresser before removing the tunic that had done an excellent job of hiding the police duty belt around her waist. Running her finger on the nubby black leather, Nell wondered if this was Officer Palmer's or Officer Davis's belt. She'd worn it for so long today that she had gotten used to the heavy weight of the Glock 17 service pistol and assorted police accessories. Taking it off made her feel light enough to float away. She put the belt on the dresser next to the magazines.

Sitting on the edge of the bed, Nell unlaced her combat boots, peeled off her socks, and wiggled her toes. Other than her invulnerability, the boots were the only thing she had that belonged to Honeydew. Once she was fully undressed, Nell examined herself in the mirror. The bruises on her torso from where she'd been struck by bullets had receded to faint shadows. Except for the air conditioner's steady hum blending with the ocean wave-like sound of the traffic outside, the room was blissfully quiet. After four years sharing a room with five other female test subjects, she savored the solitude.

Nell hadn't known what to expect when she'd agreed to be

a Honeydew test subject. She hadn't bothered to read the fine print of the contract she signed. She had barely listened to the man who came to her homeless camp and gave a speech about how volunteers would not only get three square meals a day and a comfy bed to sleep on at night, they would also be saving the lives of the brave men and women who protected America's freedom. Nell wasn't trying to escape being a homeless drug addict with dead legs, and though she did respect and honor the troops, she didn't buy the man's patriotic sales pitch.

She had her own reasons for signing up.

Honeydew recruited homeless people because they didn't expect most of them to survive the experiment. Despite all the poison she'd injected into her bloodstream, Nell had been careful not to overdose, and though she had access to guns, she'd never put the barrel of one in her mouth and pulled the trigger. Truth be told, Nell never had the nerve to kill herself. Maybe these guys would do it for her.

Nell got into the shower. The luxury of a long steaming hot shower more than compensated for the hotel's tiny bar of soap. Shampooing *and* conditioning her hair was another luxury. Standing under the hot water, she examined her skin. It looked normal. It felt normal. But it wasn't. Her skin was a reminder that some monsters look like everyone else.

Stepping out of the shower into the steam-filled bathroom, Nell twisted a towel into a turban for her hair and wrapped another towel around her body. She washed her underwear and socks in the bathroom sink. Somebody's blood had somehow managed to get on her bra. She hung her underwear and socks on the shower curtain rod to dry.

Nell considered putting on the maid's uniform, so that she wouldn't be caught naked if someone came into the room, but she really wanted to feel clean, crisp sheets against her bare skin. Besides, she'd come a long way from wearing the same clothes for weeks at a time. That girl had stained her panties and jeans with piss and menstrual blood. She would have shit her pants too if the heroin hadn't made her constipated.

She laid the uniform on foot of the bed, slipped the Glock under the pillow, closed the drapes, and got under the covers. The pillow was divinely soft. Her stomach grumbled, but she was way more exhausted than hungry. Other than getting up once to pee, she slept through the night and all the next day.

CHAPTER NINE

THE NIGHT BEFORE Carson Slagle killed twenty-five people and wounded three, Nell went on a date. Her date's name was Scott. He was hot. He made her laugh. They had pizza and beer for dinner. Nell was prepared to pay her half, but Scott insisted on paying for everything. After dinner, they went to a bar to see a local band play because Scott knew the bass player. They ended the evening making out in Nell's dorm room.

The date almost didn't happen.

A half hour before Scott picked her up, Nell was in her dorm room deciding which shoes to wear when the phone rang. Nell guessed it was Peggy before she checked the number. She always called at the worst times.

"I need you to do something for me," Peggy said.

"When?" Nell asked.

"Tonight."

"I can't. I have a date."

"This is important."

"What does Carson want this time?"

"This has nothing to do with what Carson *wants*. This is about what Carson *needs*."

Nell wished Peggy could see her roll her eyes.

"Whatever it is Carson *needs*, why can't you do it? You don't work."

"I can't leave the house. I'm in the middle of doing Carson's laundry. He ran out of underwear."

Nell wrinkled her nose.

"You want me to buy him more underwear?"

"Of course not. He has plenty, but you know how he feels it gets dirty after a few hours."

"Then you end up doing laundry every other day. Buying him more underwear might not be a bad idea."

Peggy sighed.

"I got behind and now all his underwear is in the washer. That's why I can't leave the house. Your brother is in his room right now wearing no underwear."

"Thank you for that disgusting image of Carson sitting bare-assed in his room."

Nell checked the time on her computer. Scott would be arriving soon, and she wasn't ready. She rubbed her forehead. To think, she used to admire Peggy and wanted to grow up to be like her. That was before Peggy became Carson's slave.

Nell heard Peggy's phone ding.

"Hold on," Peggy said. "It's Carson."

Even though they were in the same house, Carson only communicated with Peggy by texting.

"What does the little prince want this time?" Nell asked.

"He wants to know when his underwear is going to be ready," Peggy said. "He's feeling very uncomfortable."

"Going commando isn't that bad."

"I need you to pick up his medication. I wouldn't ask if it wasn't important."

Nell's blood boiled and she almost threw her phone against the wall.

"Important?" Nell said. "Like that time you ran out of mayonnaise and you couldn't go to the store because you had to look after Carson even though he never leaves his bedroom. Just sits in there all day playing shooter games. So instead, you had me rush to the store because the only thing Carson will eat is mayonnaise sandwiches. The reason he's so skinny is because all he eats is mayonnaise on white bread. And not just any fucking mayonnaise. Had to be the jar with the red lid not the blue lid. I went to three different grocery stores before I found a jar with a red lid."

Peggy's phone dinged.

"Hold on," Peggy said. "It's Carson again."

Nell took advantage of the pause in their conversation to check the time. Scott was due in ten minutes.

"Carson's getting more upset about his underwear," Peggy said. "I lied and said they were in the dryer."

"I'm not getting his medication," Nell said. "Downtown Chattanooga to Cleveland this time of day? You'll be done with the laundry before I get there so there's no reason why you can't pick it up."

Peggy sounded more exhausted than usual.

"I've already called the pharmacy and told them you were going to pick it up."

"What's the point? He's going to flush it down the toilet like he did last time."

"He said the pills made him dizzy. I talked to Dr. Spiel, and he prescribed a new medication. A better medication."

Nell rubbed her forehead.

"Peggy. Mom. I've said it before and I'm going to say it again. Carson needs more than medication. He needs professional medical help. This is more than you can handle. You need to tell Dr. Spiel it's time to send Carson to Moccasin Bend."

"Okay," Peggy said.

She spoke so softly Nell wasn't sure she heard her correctly.

"Really?" Nell asked. "You're really going to do it?"

"Yes," Peggy said. "I'll talk to Dr. Spiel…about Moccasin Bend."

The phone dinged.

"Carson's really wound up about that underwear," Nell said.

"That wasn't my phone," Peggy said.

Nell checked her text messages.

"Oh shit," she said. "My date's here. He's in the lobby."

Nell texted Scott that she would be there soon.

"What about Carson's medication?" Peggy asked.

"I'll skip class tomorrow and pick up his prescription first thing in the morning. It'll be easier to get there because traffic will be going the opposite way. Then let's call Dr. Spiel and set up a meeting. Maybe he'll even be able to see us that day."

Nell tapped her foot impatiently as she waited for Peggy to respond.

"I'd rather you picked up his medication tonight," Peggy said.

"I can't," Nell said. "I have a date."

"I'd rather you did it tonight."

"I can't do it. Not this time."

Peggy paused. Nell worried Scott would get tired of waiting for her and leave.

"Okay," Peggy said. "I'll see you tomorrow."

"And I'll tell you all about my date," Nell said. "Well maybe not everything."

"You're a good daughter."

They said their goodbyes. Nell quickly chose which shoes to wear then rushed downstairs to the lobby. Scott hadn't left. He smiled when he saw her.

The next morning, Nell arrived at Peggy's house with Carson's new medication in her purse. She felt optimistic for the first time in a long while. Peggy was going to get Carson the help he needed. Nell was going to make sure Peggy got Carson the help he needed. She wasn't going to let Peggy wiggle out of it this time.

Then Peggy would get her life back.

So would Nell. She could concentrate on being a college student. She could go on dates without worrying about Peggy calling her at the last minute. Speaking of dates, Nell couldn't wait to tell Peggy about her evening with Scott.

Nell would have pulled into the garage next to Peggy's car, but the doors to Peggy's car were open blocking her access. Leaving her car in the driveway, Nell entered the garage and peered inside Peggy's car. Boxes of ammo sat on the passenger seat. Confused but not overly concerned, Nell went into the house.

"Hey, Peggy," Nell called. "You planning on going to the range today?"

No answer.

"Peggy? Where you at?"

Nell left her purse on the kitchen counter before checking the dining room and living room. No sign of life.

"Peggy. I picked up Carson's pills."

Nell checked the laundry room and the den. Nobody there. Could Peggy have gone for a walk? She used to jog but not lately. Peggy's bedroom was at the end of a hallway. Nell had to pass by Carson's bedroom to get there.

A plastic laundry basket filled with underwear sat next to Carson's bedroom door. A sign on the door read KEEP OUT! DO NOT DISTURB! ENTER AT OWN RISK! The door was never open, so the fact that it was open now seemed wrong. Inside it was dark as a cave. Nell flipped on the light, went into the room, and reared back. The stench of body odor and rotten food was so strong she had to hold her nose.

Peggy had begged Carson to let her clean his room, but he had refused. The floor was covered with wadded up paper towels. There were plates with half-eaten mayonnaise sandwiches on the unmade bed. Juice boxes filled a garbage can.

A gaming set up and gaming chair dominated the room. On the video monitor, silent footage from a first-person shooter game showed a phantom player roaming from room to room shooting opponents. Nell thought about Carson spending endless hours playing these games. She had gone through a gaming phase but nothing this obsessive.

The hairs on the back of her neck rose. Where was Carson? Where was Peggy? What the hell was going on?

Nell headed toward Peggy's bedroom.

"Peggy? Peggy? Mom?"

The door was ajar. Nell pushed it open and stepped inside the dark room. She flipped on the light switch and screamed. Peggy was in bed with the covers up to her chest. Half her head was missing. Brains and blood splattered the pillow, the sheets, and the wall next to the bed. Nell stared as if her mother was a car accident. Horrible but unable to turn away.

Nell stumbled out of the bedroom, struggling to catch her breath. Her face was wet with tears.

"I need to call…I need to call somebody," she stammered.

Moving on autopilot, she went to the kitchen and fumbled in her purse for her phone. Her hands shook and she dropped the phone on the floor. As she bent to pick it up, she looked through the kitchen door into the dining room and gasped. A homeless person sat at the table. Then Nell realized it was Carson. He hadn't been in the dining room earlier when Nell searched the house.

She hadn't seen him for months. His skin was as pale as a boiled potato. His hair was shaggy and oily. He was emaciated from only eating mayonnaise on white bread. He was eating a mayonnaise sandwich now. A Glock 20, a Smith and Wesson nine-millimeter, and Carson's Beastmaster were spread out on the table in front of him. The S&W 9mm was Peggy's favorite gun.

An absurd thought popped into Nell's head. She was surprised Carson was able to make his own sandwich.

She joined him in the dining room.

"Mom's dead," Nell said.

Carson giggled. "I know," he said.

Nell gawked at her little brother.

"Did you shoot her?"

Carson nodded vigorously then continued eating his sandwich.

"Why?" Nell asked.

Carson glared at Nell. There were dark circles under his eyes.

"I don't have to explain myself to you," he said.

Nell glanced in the direction of Peggy's bedroom.

"What you did was wrong, Carson. I have to call the police."

Carson pushed his plate away from him.

"Don't," he said.

"I have to," Nell said. "Mom's dead."

Carson stood and picked up the S&W 9mm.

"I said, don't."

A chill ran through Nell. She had been too stunned by Peggy's death to recognize the danger she was in until this moment. And for what seemed like an endless moment, she was unable to move.

The animal instinct for survival kicked in and Nell was outside before she knew she'd made the decision to run. As she bolted across the front lawn, she didn't dare waste a second to look behind her to see if Carson was after her.

She heard the crack of the handgun and felt a sharp sting near her butt. The ground seemed to come up and hit her in the face. Pain spiraled through her. Spitting out dirt, Nell tried to stand but not only wouldn't her legs move, she couldn't feel them. Sobbing, Nell dragged herself with her arms across the grass. She knew she couldn't get away, but desperation kept her going.

"Help!" Nell screamed. "Somebody help me!"

Carson stepped in front of her. She peered up at his smirking face.

"Admit it," Carson said. "That was a good shot considering you were a moving target." He kneeled and nudged her cheek with the gun's muzzle. "This close would be much easier."

"Don't do it," Nell said. "For fuck's sake, I'm your sister."

"From the way you're bleeding all over the yard, I must have hit an artery. Not worth the bullet if you're going to bleed out anyway."

He walked away. A minute later, Nell heard car doors slam and an engine start. She watched Carson drive by in Peggy's car. He didn't bother looking at her.

With Carson gone, the immediate threat of death had passed leaving Nell exhausted and too tired to move. She laid her cheek against the cool grass. An effort was made to stay awake, she was sure of it, but she lost the battle quickly. She closed her eyes and passed out.

For days, Nell drifted in and out of consciousness. Every time she woke, she got a snippet of information.

She was alive.

Peggy was dead but she already knew that.

She was alive because Peggy's next-door neighbor, Mrs. Nina Holtzclaw, came home from the grocery store shortly after Carson left, saw Nell unconscious in the yard, and called an ambulance.

She was paralyzed from the waist down and would never walk again.

Carson had gone to Red Clay Middle School and killed a bunch of people, most of them children. The last person Carson killed was himself.

Because she was a mass shooter's sister, she was given a private room and a police guard outside her door.

There were two FBI agents who wanted to speak to her when she felt up to it.

"I don't feel up to anything," Nell said. "But I'll talk to them any time they'd like."

The agents came to Nell's room later that day. The man was tall and handsome with short brown hair. The woman was Hispanic and slim.

"I'm Special Agent Mara Zavala," the woman said. "This is my partner, Special Agent John Easter."

"Are you going to arrest me?" Nell asked.

"Why would we arrest you?"

"Peggy asked me to get Carson's pills the night before… everything happened, but I wouldn't do it."

"Why didn't you pick up his medication?" Easter asked.

Nell picked at her blanket. "I had a date."

Easter and Zavala glanced at each other.

"We just want to ask you a few questions," Easter said.

"Do you mind if we sit?" Zavala asked.

"Where are my manners?" Nell said. "Please. Have a seat."

The special agents pulled two chairs close to the bed. Zavala put her purse on the floor next to her.

"We're not here to arrest you," Easter said.

"You should," Nell said.

"Why should we arrest you?"

"I told Peggy that Carson needed serious medical help," Nell said. "But I didn't try hard enough to make her do something about it."

"You did try."

This caught Nell off guard. She didn't expect the FBI to be so nice.

"Yes. I did try."

Zavala pointed at the TV mounted on the wall. It was tuned to a shopping network.

"Do you mind if I turn this off?" she asked.

"Go ahead," Nell said. "I wasn't really watching it."

"Then why is it on?"

Nell shrugged.

"Company, I guess. I tried watching other channels, but

they all seemed to be either old westerns, cop shows, or news. This was the only one that didn't have guns or somebody talking about Carson."

Zavala searched for the remote, found it, and turned off the TV.

"I'm afraid we are going to have to talk about what happened at Red Clay," Easter said.

"Did you know I went to there as a kid?" Nell said.

"Did Carson also go there?" Zavala asked.

"No. We moved, and he ended up going to a different school."

"Do you know why he targeted Red Clay Middle School?"

Nell furrowed her brow and tried to think of a reason. One thing she was certain of was that Carson didn't choose Red Clay because she'd gone there. That fact that he wouldn't waste a bullet to her brain to make sure she was dead made it clear she didn't matter to Carson.

"I'm sorry," Nell said. "My head's fuzzy from the pain meds. I can't think of anything."

"That's okay," Easter said. "Answer the best you can."

"Your parents are divorced," Zavala said.

It wasn't a question but Nell answered anyway.

"Yeah," Nell said. "Three years ago. Dad remarried a year later."

"Was your brother a factor in their divorce?"

"Definitely. Dad wanted to send Carson to Moccasin Bend, that's the mental hospital in Chattanooga, but Peggy refused. She said she could take care of him herself."

"When was the last time you spoke to your father?"

"Yesterday. Or maybe it was the day before. Time's been slippery lately."

"Are you close to him?"

"I'm closer to Peggy." Nell got a catch in her throat. "Or rather, I was."

Nell tried to hold back the tears and failed. Uncontrolled sobbing had been happening a lot lately. Easter picked up a box of tissues from the table next to Nell's bed and held it for her. She pulled out some tissues, wiped her eyes, and blew her nose.

"Thank you," Nell said.

Easter and Zavala stood.

"We should let you rest," Easter said.

"Yeah," Nell said. "I wear out pretty fast."

"Do you want us to turn the TV back on?"

"Not really. The next time the nurse comes by I'll ask her for a magazine."

Zavala pointed at a New Testament sitting on the table.

"You could read the good book," she said.

Nell narrowed her eyes at the bible.

"I suppose I should, but I'm just not ready."

"Did the hospital give it to you?" Easter asked.

"No, Mavis did."

"Is she one of the nurses?"

"I thought she was, but it turns out she's a volunteer. She's sweet as can be."

Easter nodded at Zavala. She nodded back.

"Do you like romance novels?" Zavala asked.

Nell grinned. "I admit they're a guilty pleasure."

"They are for me too," Zavala said.

The special agent took a paperback out of her purse and handed it to Nell. The cover was a typical historical romance novel illustration of an attractive couple in period clothing embracing except that instead of being shirtless, the man was dressed in heavy furs and breathing an icy cloud into the woman's face. The title was *Frigid Heir*.

Nell's eyes grew wide.

"Really? I can borrow it?"

"I just finished it so you can keep it," Zavala said.

"Thank you."

The FBI agents left as Nell opened the paperback to the first page and began to read.

CHAPTER TEN

NELL OPENED HER eyes. The My Place hotel room was dark. The clock on the bedside table read 7:35 p.m. Reaching under the pillow, her fingers touched the butt of the Glock. Remembering how she got the gun caused a pang of guilt.

Later, Nell would watch the news to find out how many people she'd killed. They caused her no anguish. They had as much blood on their hands as she did. They sold the lie that guns were protection from evil. Her mother Peggy had kept an arsenal in her house and none of them prevented a demon from slipping inside and eating her soul.

Officer Palmer and Officer Davis were different. They had been trained to use their guns only to serve and protect. Maybe they were racist cops who abused unarmed people of color and got what they deserved, but then again, maybe they weren't. Maybe she had killed two good men.

Nell's pity party was interrupted by voices in the hallway. A man and woman were having a heated argument. Nell felt an urge to leap out of bed, throw on the maid's uniform, and dash out of the room, but another urge, the one that wanted to stay in bed and get a few more hours of sleep, was stronger. Besides, there were a lot of rooms on this floor. What were the chances that they were headed toward her room? She closed her eyes and tried to ignore them, but they were too damn loud.

"Give me a break, Martha," the man said. "There's nothing wrong with this hotel."

"It's a dump, Louis," Martha said.

So, now she had names for the loud couple. Louis and Martha.

"I've stayed in dumps," Louis said. "This is no dump."

"It's not the Bellagio," Martha said.

Louis groaned like a wounded bear.

"We can't get into the Bellagio. The Strip is on lockdown. How was I supposed to know that there was going to be a mass shooting the same day we arrived?"

"It's bad enough that I'm forced to stay in this dump. I know you, Louis. Next, you'll try to take me to one of North Las Vegas's crappy casinos."

"Why not? It would just be a couple of days. I'm sure the Strip will be open by then."

"What if we blow all our money before the Strip re-opens?"

"I brought enough cash so that even you can't lose it all before then."

"I'm not the lousy gambler in this family. You are."

"I'm a lousy gambler? Need I remind you how much I've won this year?"

"Look. The door's busted. I told you this place was a dump."

Nell cringed. There wasn't time to get dressed. She decided to keep her eyes closed and pretend that she was asleep. Maybe the couple would assume they were mistakenly given a room that was already booked. That would certainly justify Martha's negative opinion of the hotel.

Nell heard a creak and then a gasp.

"What am I looking at?" Louis asked.

"Isn't it obvious?" Martha said. "The maid got drunk, took off her clothes, and passed out in the bed."

"You're right, Martha. This place is a dump."

"That's it! We're going downstairs right now and telling the manager that there's a drunk maid in our room."

Nell grabbed the handgun under her pillow and pointed it at the couple.

"Don't move."

"We don't want any trouble." Louis raised his hands over his head.

"I know this is none of our business," Martha said. "But the first step toward recovery is admitting that you have a problem."

"I'm not drunk. I was sleeping." Nell scooted out of bed, holding the bedsheet up to her chest with one hand and holding the gun with the other. "Sit on the bed."

Louis and Martha did as they were told. It was hard to maneuver with one hand, but Nell didn't dare put the gun down. She awkwardly wrapped the bedsheet around her naked body, shut the door, turned on the TV, and raised the volume. She snatched Martha's purse out of her hands and then studied the couple. They looked to be in their forties. Louis had a goatee and wore a white polo shirt, khaki cargo shorts, and boat shoes with no socks. Martha wore a floppy straw hat over her platinum blonde hair, a low-cut cheetah romper that showcased fake breasts the size and shape of cantaloupes, chunky gold bracelets, and flip flops embellished with rhinestones.

"Why are you staring at me?" Martha asked.

"You're bigger on top than me," Nell said. "Otherwise, we're about the same size."

Nell got two pairs of handcuffs from the police duty belt and put the gun down before cuffing Louis and Martha's wrists behind their backs. Tearing a towel into strips, Nell used the strips to tie the couple's ankles. Once they were securely bound, she went through their suitcases.

The first one was filled with men's clothing. Nell pushed it aside and opened the second suitcase. It was much bigger and filled with Martha's clothes. She rifled through them and picked out a pair of ripped jeans and an American flag tank top.

Nell went into the bathroom for her bra and panties. They were dry but there was a brown stain on the bra. She put it on anyway. After she was finished dressing, Nell carried Martha's purse to the dresser. She was about to search its contents when she noticed that it was a Louis Vuitton monogram handbag.

"Is this real or a knock off?" Nell asked.

"What?" Martha said.

Nell held up the purse and spoke louder so that Martha could hear her over the TV.

"Real or a knock off?"

Martha sighed.

"It's a knock off."

"It's still a nice purse."

"It's my favorite."

If Martha thought that would keep Nell from taking the purse, she was wrong. Nell emptied the purse's contents onto the top of the dresser. She pushed aside things like the phone (traceable), house keys, and a battered Danielle Steel paperback. She kept the make-up, sunglasses, and granola bars.

Once these items were stuffed back in, Nell removed the baton, taser, and flashlight from the police duty belt and put them into the purse. She checked the two magazines from the belt and the two extra she took from the other belt. The magazines had room for seventeen bullets, and they were fully loaded. She put them and the Glock into the purse. The police belt would stay in the room since it was too bulky to wear with her new outfit.

Going through the wallet, Nell checked out Martha's driver's license. She was forty-four. She looked good for her age. Nell tossed aside the license, the credit cards (also traceable) and receipts. She kept the bills and loose change, which totaled sixty-three dollars and eighty-eight cents.

As Nell tried to calculate how far she would get with sixty-three dollars and eighty-eight cents, she was distracted by sobbing that was even louder than the TV. Nell investigated and found Martha was crying so hard that she was hyperventilating.

"Come on," Nell said. "It's not that bad. The insurance company will cover your losses."

But Martha wasn't watching Nell pilfer her belongings, and neither was Louis, whose face had paled. They were staring at the TV. Nell didn't have to look at the screen to see why they were freaking out. She could hear the news reporter.

"Las Vegas Convention Center shooter, Nell Slagle, is still at large and considered to be armed and very dangerous. The LVMPD is urging the public not to approach her. Instead, call 9-1-1 immediately if you see her."

Nell took the remote and turned off the TV. She went into the bathroom, pulled a handful of tissues out of the tissue box, and soaked a bath towel in warm water. When she came back into the room, Martha was leaning against Louis' shoulder and still sobbing heavily. Nell knelt in front of her.

"You got snot running out of your nose," Nell said. "Here. Blow into this."

Nell put the tissue against Martha's nose, and she honked into the tissue. Nell wiped Martha's nose and threw the soiled tissue into a trash can.

"You're not a maid, are you?" Martha said.

"That's right. I'm not a maid."

"You're her, aren't you? You're Nell Slagle."

"Yes. That's me."

Nell knew what it was like to face a monster, so she knew that Martha's fear was a terrible thing that filled a body to the brim.

"I have four thousand dollars cash in my pocket," Louis said. "Take it. It's yours. Take the keys to our rental car. It's a sweet cherry red Jaguar convertible. Just don't hurt my wife."

Nell kept her attention on Martha.

"All that crying has ruined your make-up. Can I clean you up?"

Martha nodded. Nell wiped Martha's streaking eyeliner off her face with the warm bath towel. Most women Martha's age looked older without their war paint, but she looked younger.

"Are you going to kill us?" Martha asked.

"No," Nell said. "But I am going to take your husband's offer of money and a car. Now I'm going to reach into his pockets. It's nothing personal. I'm not trying to feel him up."

That broke the tension. Martha and Louis laughed. Nell carefully searched Louis's pockets. She found the rental car key and a fat roll of fifties and twenties. She couldn't believe he walked around with this much money on him. Somebody might rob him.

"I'm only going to take half," Nell said. "That should do me for a while."

"You can have it all," Louis said. "Just don't hurt us."

"I only need half and I'm not going to hurt you."

Nell counted out two thousand, and stuffed the money into the purse along with the rental car key. She left the rest of Louis's money on the dresser next to the police duty belt and items belonging to Martha that she couldn't use. Nell looked at herself in the full-length mirror next to the dresser. Something was missing. She turned to Martha and Louis.

"You've been so generous that I hate to do this, but I feel I must." Nell lifted Martha's floppy straw hat off her head and put it on, along with Martha's sunglasses. "How do I look?"

"You look great," Louis said.

"You're such a flirt. Be honest. How do I really look?"

"Like a tourist," Martha said. "Shit. That means I look like a tourist."

Nell smiled. That was exactly what she wanted to hear.

CHAPTER ELEVEN

Harry Pigott and Keith Anderson were at the Palomino Club drinking at the bar when a stripper tried to entice Harry into buying a lap dance. The two men had had their butts glued to their barstools for over an hour. During that time, three strippers had approached Harry, but not once had Keith been propositioned. This annoyed the holy heck out of Harry because it indicated that they believed that Keith was so damn handsome that he didn't need to pay a beautiful woman to rub her naked body on him, but the only way Harry would ever experience that kind of proximity to prime female flesh was if he paid for it.

"No thank you," Harry said to the petite brunette wearing what could only be described as red satin dental floss that barely covered her private parts.

"You sure?"

"I said no. Besides, I've had better. For free!"

"Sure you have."

She giggled and as she walked away, Harry saw that she had the word "Nice" tattooed on her left butt cheek and "Ass" on her right butt cheek. Though the words were certainly true at this point in her young life, she did nothing for him. Harry was a breast man, the bigger the better.

"Next round is on me," Keith said.

"Are you offering out of pity or camaraderie?" Harry asked.

"Don't you remember? You paid for the last round."

Harry rubbed his bushy mustache.

"In that case, I accept your offer."

Keith waved the bartender over and ordered another round, a gin and tonic for Harry and a Corona for himself. The bartender took away their empties and wiped down their area of the bar before going to get their drinks. The air smelled of stale beer, stale perfume, and stale testosterone. Like most strip clubs, the interior was dark as a cave with subdued blue, red, and purple lighting, making it impossible to tell if it was day or night.

A cave was exactly where they wanted to be, after surviving both the convention shooting and endless questions from law enforcement on how they had managed to survive. They needed time alone to process their experience.

"I can't drown my shame," Harry said. "But I'm going to try anyway."

"Shame?" Keith said. "Shame for what?"

"It was my fuck-up that led to the deaths of two of Las Vegas Metropolitan Police Department's finest officers."

"You didn't fuck up."

"How can you say that?"

"You're not dead."

Harry groaned.

The way some people turned to the Bible for guidance, Harry turned to *The Art of War* by Sun Tzu. He prided himself on always thinking like a warrior. But he'd allowed his senses to be dulled by his many years of working for Bulard Arms. The high salary and excellent benefits had softened him. He'd forgotten Tzu's lesson that all warfare was based on deception. He should have sensed that the cute blonde booth babe with an ass so firm that it deserved its own tattoo was a psychopath in disguise.

If that sin wasn't egregious enough, when Harry came face to face with Nell Slagle, instead of attacking her, he had meekly allowed her to cuff his wrists and ankles like he was her personal bitch.

The bartender arrived with their drinks, and Keith handed him cash. Harry took a sip and hardly noticed the alcohol burn in his throat. Their afternoon of self-medication had numbed him to physical pain. Only existential pain remained as a constant thrum in his brain. He looked around the strip club. The place was half full, but probably half empty in the eyes of management. The customers were mostly overweight tourists in Hawaiian shirts and khakis who acted bored by the beautiful naked women, their skin glowing from the stage spotlights. Yet another dancer asked Harry if he wanted a lap dance and even though she had large breasts, he turned her down.

"How long did the cops question you?" Keith asked.

Harry shrugged.

"Not sure. I kept thinking they were going to arrest me for aiding and abetting. The charge wouldn't have held up in court, but I figured they wanted to arrest somebody for something."

"They had me repeat what happened fifty times."

"Really? Fifty times?"

Keith took a swig of his beer.

"It felt like fifty." He leaned close enough for Harry to

smell his beer breath. "There was something I never told the cops."

The promise of a hidden secret perked up Harry from what had otherwise been a dismal day.

"Really?"

Keith looked around the club as if expecting to spot an undercover cop.

"You know Nell and I were alone in the supply room before she went out and killed all those people."

"Yeah," Harry said.

"The guards stayed outside the supply room because they thought Nell was in there giving me a blow job."

"Is that what you didn't tell the cops?"

Keith shook his head.

"No. What I didn't tell them was that Nell wouldn't use just any gun. She kept opening cases until she found a specific rifle."

Harry knew that Nell had used two Bulard Model 601 semi-automatic rifles in the mass shooting. He had thought it was just a coincidence that earlier that day she'd been prancing around with a demonstration model of the exact same weapon at the Bulard Arms booth.

"She kept looking until she found a Beastmaster?"

"That's the one," Keith said. "Weird, huh?"

"Why didn't you tell the cops?"

"Honestly, I forgot. I was about to shit my pants the whole time the cops had me in the interrogation room. I didn't remember about the rifle until this morning."

Harry ran his hand over his bald head.

"Makes sense."

"You think I should tell the cops?"

"Only if you want them to make you repeat that part fifty times."

Harry stood and weaved his way to the bathroom. After emptying his bladder, he washed his hands, and then glared at his reflection in the mirror.

"Come on! You just took a piss and that was a dick in your hand. Don't let that little bitch turn you into a pussy. Man up!"

He went back to the bar. Keith was starting to wobble on his barstool.

"That little bitch is going to pay for what she did to us," Harry said.

"Yeah. The police are going to find her and put her in jail for the rest of her life."

"Forget the police."

"Who then? You?"

Harry straightened his spine.

"Not many people know this about me, because I prefer to keep a low profile, but I'm the leader of the Real American Freedom Force."

"Is that part of your job at Bulard Arms?"

Harry scoffed.

"Selling guns is how I pay the bills. Leading true patriots is my real job."

"What exactly does Real American Freedom Fries do?"

"Real American Freedom *Force*. We're a small but well-trained militia dedicated to defending the Constitution and keeping our borders safe. With our lives if necessary."

"Slagle's not trying to sneak into the country to pick strawberries. She's already here."

"The Real American Freedom Force is going find Nell. And

when we find her, if she doesn't surrender peacefully, we'll have no choice but to use deadly force."

"Is that legal?"

"Depends on which state you're in but that's beside the point. Sometimes the only way to stop a bad girl with a gun is a good guy with a gun."

"Those gin and tonics are going to your head."

"I'm not shitting around. Why don't you come with me? I know you're not afraid to use a gun."

"You're offering me a job?"

"I'm offering you a chance for revenge."

Keith sipped his beer.

"Thanks, but no thanks. I've got a wife and two kids to support. I need steady employment with benefits."

Harry was disappointed. He thought they shared the connection of soldiers who'd experienced battle together, but now he could see that Keith was pussy-whipped.

A dancer with enormous breasts sauntered by.

"Hey," Harry said.

The dancer stopped, gave Harry a onceover, and grinned.

"You talking to me?"

"I am. You available for a lap dance?"

She put her hand on her hip.

"As a matter of fact, I am."

He followed the busty dancer to the V.I.P. rooms without saying goodbye to Keith. As far as Harry was concerned, he no longer existed.

CHAPTER TWELVE

By the time Lt. General Buck Carter's military helicopter headed back to the Circus Circus helipad, night had fallen. Easter and Zavala were treated to the dazzling multi-colored lights of the Las Vegas strip. The sight left a sourness in Easter's stomach because he was too angry to enjoy it.

"What the hell were you thinking?" Easter asked.

Carter tore his attention away from the window.

"About what?"

"Experimenting on the homeless."

"Drug companies do it all the time. Why not defense contractors?"

"And the Pentagon?"

"Yes. The Pentagon approved Honeydew's plan to recruit them."

"Did the Pentagon know test subjects died from the experiments?"

Carter raised his eyebrows in mock surprise.

"I'm in the business of winning wars. In every war there is collateral damage. In this battle, it was homeless people."

"A high percentage of homeless people have mental health issues," Zavala said.

"What's your point?"

"The test of a civilization is the way it cares for its most helpless members."

"Didn't Gandhi say that?" Easter asked.

"No. Pearl Buck."

"I thought it was Hubert Humphrey," Carter said.

"He said something like it," Zavala said. "Once again, a man takes credit for something a woman did."

Easter nodded at Zavala.

"Going back to what she just said about mental health issues, didn't the Pentagon or Honeydew consider that before they started scooping up people off the streets and injecting them with strange chemicals?"

Easter could see the Circus Circus helipad. They would be landing soon.

"Of course, we were aware that they had personal problems," Carter said. "That's why they were homeless."

"But don't you see?" Easter said. "It's like the movie 'Frankenstein.' Dr. Frankenstein puts a criminal brain in the body of a superhuman monster. As a result, the monster becomes an unstoppable killing machine. At least Dr. Frankenstein tries to destroy the monster. The Pentagon and Honeydew are trying to capture it so that they can mass produce monsters."

Carter smiled.

"And what if Dr. Frankenstein had used a normal brain, or better yet a soldier's brain, into that superhuman body? It would have been a much different story."

Easter looked at Zavala. She shrugged.

"I hate to admit it, but he's right. A soldier is trained to follow orders. He or she will only kill who they're ordered to kill."

Easter wanted to continue arguing, but the helicopter had landed. Carter unbuckled his seat belt and grabbed his laptop.

"Thanks for an interesting conversation," Carter said, "but I really must go now. You have my direct line. Contact me the moment you hear anything about the girl's location."

"And then what?" Zavala asked.

"We'll take it from there."

Carter slid the door open. He got out of the helicopter and dashed to the edge of the heliport where his limo was waiting for him. Easter and Zavala got out just in time to watch the limo drive away.

"Really?" Zavala asked. "Frankenstein?"

They went to their rental car and drove to the Convention Center. A police guard checked their I.D.s before allowing them through the barricade. Easter parked on the street corner, and they walked to the FBI Mobile Command Center. Inside, they found Agent Wayne Driscoll at his computer monitor.

"Hey, Archie," Zavala said. "Isn't it time for you to go back to Riverdale?"

"Stop teasing him," Easter said.

Driscoll grinned.

"Hey, Dora. I see you're back from your latest quest."

Zavala chuckled.

"See? He likes it."

Easter checked his watch.

"All kidding aside, isn't your shift over?"

"Almost," Driscoll said. "Night shift should be here soon."

Easter sat in the chair next to Driscoll. Zavala leaned against the console.

"When night shift gets here, I'll brief the entire team on what Zavala and I learned from Honeydew," Easter said. "While we wait, give me an update."

"All of the bodies have been transported to local morgues," Driscoll said.

"What's the latest on the search for Slagle?"

"Even though she's in the facial recognition database, they still haven't located her."

"Why not?" Zavala asked.

"False positives. Las Vegas is full of young women with blonde hair and blue eyes with almost identical facial features."

Easter wasn't surprised. Facial recognition technology was a tremendous tool for law enforcement, but it had its flaws, especially when it came to minorities, women, and children. The software had trouble telling them apart, just like in real life. Nell was a stereotypical all-American girl.

"What about the police tip line?" Easter asked.

"As you would expect, the police have gotten hundreds of calls. A cop told me that it feels like everybody in Vegas has seen Nell but them. The LVMPD is investigating as many as they can."

"Can I see the list of calls they've gotten so far?"

Driscoll tapped on his keyboard and brought up the Las Vegas police department's internal website. He pulled up the list of calls to the tip line. Easter and Zavala looked over his shoulder. Easter noticed that all the sightings happened near the Strip except for one that took place in North Las Vegas.

"Let me see that one," Easter said, pointing at the North Las Vegas call.

Driscoll clicked over to the full police report. Easter read through it.

"A truck driver sitting in his truck at the Morton Travel Plaza's parking lot was assaulted by a woman. She bound his wrists and ankles and then robbed him. The assault happened the night before the shooting, but he remained tied up in his truck until the day after the shooting when the manager of the truck stop found him."

"He identified Slagle as the attacker?" Zavala asked.

"Yes and no. The driver didn't report the assault. The manager who rescued him made the call and claims that the driver told her that his attacker was Slagle."

"All we have is the manager's word?"

"That's correct."

"We can forget that one."

Normally, Easter would have agreed with Zavala, but the time and location told him to look into it.

"Morton Travel Plaza in North Las Vegas," Easter said. "Show me that on a city map."

Driscoll typed on the keyboard. The LVMPD site was soon replaced with a map of Las Vegas with a red flag indicating Morton Travel Plaza. Zavala peered at the map.

"What exactly are you looking for, Bunny?"

"The incident happened the night before the shooting. The truck stop is next to I-15 in North Las Vegas."

Zavala nodded.

"Yeah, I get it. If Nell had started walking from HARD-SOW in the early afternoon and followed the highway, then she would have arrived at the truck stop after the sun went down."

"She'd only have the clothes on her back. Badly damaged clothes. She'd need money for a new wardrobe."

"A truck driver in a parking lot would be an easy target."

"What's HARD-SOW?" Driscoll asked.

"The place we just came from," Easter said. "I'll explain when I do the team briefing."

"We should go out to the truck stop and talk to the driver," Zavala said.

"I'll go," Driscoll said.

"That's okay. We'll take care of it."

"Come on. I've been cooped up in here all day."

Easter looked at Zavala. She nodded.

"You got it," Easter said. "If you find out anything significant, call me right away. Otherwise, give your report tomorrow."

The night shift arrived. Easter gathered the entire team and briefed them on what he and Zavala learned at HARD-SOW. This prompted several questions which Easter did his best to answer.

"She really is bulletproof?"

"We saw it for ourselves."

"How exactly does her learn-how-to-operate-any-weapon-by-touch work?"

"No clue."

"When are we going to warn the public?"

Easter crossed his arms.

"If it were up to me, they would have been warned the second she escaped. Until we hear otherwise, her abilities and where she got them are still classified information."

CHAPTER THIRTEEN

THE TEXAS ROADHOUSE waitress didn't bat an eye when Nell ordered cheese fries, a bowl of Texas red chili, a salad with Ranch dressing, a ten-ounce ribeye cooked medium rare, grilled shrimp, buttered corn, a baked potato, strawberry cheesecake, a brownie with a scoop of vanilla ice cream, and sweet iced tea. Nell assumed the waitress had seen Las Vegas tourists do just about everything under the sun.

When the waitress brought the cheese fries and chili, Nell almost cried with joy as she breathed in the intoxicating combination of oil-fried potatoes, gooey cheese, overcooked beef, and chili powder. She had to force herself not to stuff her face in a white-hot frenzy.

Before she finished one course, the waitress showed up with the next round. Nell was so absorbed with eating that she only nodded whenever the waitress asked, "How's everything tasting?" "Can I take some of these empty plates?" "More tea? You ordered the sweet tea, right?" Along the way, Nell licked cheese off her fingers, scrapped the bottom of the chili bowl with her spoon for every last morsel, gnawed the bone of her ribeye steak, and buried her baked potato in whipped butter and sour cream before digging in.

Nell was halfway through a big ass slice of cheesecake smothered in strawberry sauce when she felt someone watching her. She kicked herself for letting her guard down. Without making it obvious, Nell scanned the room. Two women in a booth four tables away kept stealing glances of her. One of them was drop dead gorgeous, with wavy honey blonde hair, high cheekbones, and smooth skin. Despite her baggy sweatshirt, Nell could tell that she had huge breasts. The other woman was Kassie, her former booth babe at the Bulard Arms display at the WAR Show. A boy around nine years old sat next to her. Kassie and Nell's eyes met. Kassie quickly looked away.

Her appetite gone; Nell pushed the cheesecake aside. She took four fifty-dollar bills out of her purse, which she figured would be enough for dinner and a tip, and put the money on the table. As Nell sauntered toward Kassie's table, the two women stared at their plates. The boy's attention was focused entirely on his cheeseburger. Nell stopped at their table, put her palm on her cheek in mock surprise, and spoke loudly enough for everyone at the nearby tables to hear her.

"Kassie?" Nell said. "Oh my, goodness! What a pleasant surprise. What's that, Kassie? Why I'd love to join you."

Nell slid in next to the attractive blonde. The blonde tried to put as many inches as she could between her and Nell by scooting against the opposite side of their seat. Kassie looked sick. Her auburn hair was tied back into a neat ponytail. The boy glanced at Nell and then turned his attention to dipping his fries one at a time into a pool of catsup on his plate before popping them into his mouth.

"Please don't hurt us," Kassie said.

"I only wanted to say hello," Nell said. She leaned forward and lowered her voice. "And to make sure you haven't called the cops."

Kassie looked at the boy next to her.

"I swear. We didn't call anybody."

The boy looked familiar. Of course he did. He looked like his mother.

"Is that Logan?" Nell asked.

Kassie put her arm around the boy's slim shoulders and leaned her head against his. He wiggled away and turned his attention back to his food. Nell didn't understand why mothers treated their boys like little princes. There was nothing special about them.

Nell's little brother had been special, but not in a good way. Carson had untreated mental problems and there had been a time when Nell even felt sorry for him. But their mother, Peggy, had allowed Carson to behave in ways that Nell never would have gotten away with. It got to the point where Peggy had spent all her time and energy on him.

"If you do anything to hurt Logan, I'll kill you," Kassie said.

"I have no intention of hurting your precious little boy," Nell said.

"You'd better not," the blonde said. "Or else I'll call the police."

Nell turned to the blonde, who tried to squeeze even tighter into her side of the seat.

"Where are my manners?" Nell said. "We haven't been properly introduced. I'm Nell Slagle. Who the hell are you?"

Nell held out her hand and the blonde flinched. Seeing that the blonde wasn't going to shake her hand, Nell pulled back.

"This is Jolene," Kassie said.

Nell slapped the table, causing Kassie and Jolene to jump.

"*The* Jolene?" Nell said. "The one whose name tag I wore at the WAR Show?"

"If I had known that you were going to sneak in and use my name tag, I never would have called in sick," Jolene said.

"No wonder Harry Pigott has a crush on you. You're hot stuff."

Jolene glared at Nell.

"That guy is a creep."

"Tell me about it. I probably should have killed him when I had the chance."

Sweat beaded on Jolene's upper lip.

"What are you talking about?"

Nell shrugged.

"You kill some, you lose some. I really love your name. I wish I was named Jolene."

Jolene shrank further into her corner.

"What are you doing here?" Kassie asked.

"What most folks do at a restaurant," Nell said. "Eating."

Kassie leaned forward and whispered loudly.

"How can you be out in the public like you don't have a care in the world? The police are looking for you."

"I figured the best place to hide was in plain sight," Nell said. "But since you recognized me despite my clever disguise, I'm not so sure."

Logan burped loudly.

"Logan!" said all three women in unison.

"I thought I was a good judge of people," Kassie said. "But you fooled me. I honestly believed that you were a decent human being."

Before Nell fired her first shot into the crowd at the WAR Show, she knew that folks like Kassie would see her as another crazy killer. She accepted that, but it still hurt to hear Kassie say it out loud, especially after Nell went out of her way to make sure Kassie survived the shooting.

"I'm sorry I disappointed you," Nell said.

"There's still time to make things right," Kassie said.

Nell wrinkled her nose.

"I don't see how that's possible."

"Turn yourself in."

"If I did that, then you would see me on display at next year's WAR Show as the latest development in advanced weaponry."

Kassie's lower lip quivered.

"If you won't turn yourself in for your own sake, then do it for the fifty-eight people you murdered. Do it to help bring peace to their loved ones."

"They were bad people," Nell said. "They deserved to die."

"How can you say that? You didn't know them."

"They bought and sold weapons at the WAR Show. They were literally merchants of death."

"Not all of them sold weapons."

"Okay. Some of them were merchants of death accessories."

The waitress came by the table to see if they needed anything, and to ask Nell if she needed change from the cash she'd left on her table. Logan asked for more soda and Nell said she didn't need change. Nell had no idea what her meal cost, but based on the waitress's huge grin, she must have left a generous tip.

"You can't escape," Kassie said. "I saw on the news that there are roadblocks everywhere. The police are watching the airports and the bus stations. Unless you can sprout wings and fly, there's no way you can get out of the city."

Nell looked directly into Kassie's eyes.

"Even if they find me, they can't catch me."

"If you're so sure, then why are you running?"

"I don't want to kill any more policemen."

Kassie and Jolene gasped. Logan yawned.

"I'm tired, Mom," Logan said as he leaned against Kassie. "I want to go home."

"Soon," Kassie said. "We're going soon."

"How soon?"

"That's up to Nell."

"Oh my," Nell said, glancing at her bare wrist. "Will you look at the time? I really must be going. It was great seeing you, Kassie. Pleasure to meet you, Jolene. And it was an honor to meet you, Logan."

"Thank you," Logan said.

Nell smiled.

"Your mamma raised you right."

"Goodbye, Nell," Kassie said.

Nell grabbed Kassie's hand.

"Behave yourself, now," Nell said. "You don't want me coming back in here for any reason."

Kassie paled. Nell decided that she was sufficiently scared shitless and hurried out of the restaurant. The Texas Roadhouse was located next to the My Place Hotel. Nell jogged to Louis and Martha's rental car. She glanced up at the top floor of the hotel and hoped that the couple was still securely tied up. She also hoped they were okay.

When Louis had told Nell that he had rented a cherry red Jaguar convertible, Nell hadn't paid much attention to the type of car. She had never been impressed by flashy sports cars and she simply saw the vehicle as much-needed transportation. But as she slid behind the driver's wheel, pressed the starter, and felt the motor roar to life, Nell was pleased with Louis's choice. This kind of car was built for speed, something she would sorely need if the police spotted her.

Rather than pull onto the highway, Nell drove into the adjacent neighborhood. She followed winding roads past identical ranch houses. In the distance, she heard the police sirens she had been dreading. Nell cursed. She wondered if it was Kassie or Jolene who had gotten up the nerve to call the police.

Taking back roads until she found an entrance ramp to the freeway, Nell also found police cars blocking it. Turning left at the next intersection, Nell headed in the opposite direction. Taking a right onto Rancho Drive, she drove the speed limit and wondered what to do next. The North Las Vegas Airport was on her left, with more police cars with flashing lights blocking the entrance.

She turned right onto West Cheyenne and continued to study the airport. This wasn't the main airport that brought tourists and conventioneers to Las Vegas so that they could lose their hard-earned money. A chain link fence topped with barbed wire surrounded the airfield, the buildings were industrial flat and plain. Single and twin-engine airplanes sat in neat rows. Nearby, a line of helicopters looked eager to be airborne. Nell found an airport viewing area, a circular parking lot with a tiny grassy oasis with two picnic tables. She parked the car and walked to the fence. A crescent moon hung in the night sky, while landing lights blinked like fallen stars on the tarmac. Nell hugged herself against a cool wind blowing in from the desert.

The wind carried the scent of sagebrush, stirring memories

of jogging with her fellow test subjects. The physical trainers at HARD-SOW had them run before daybreak to avoid the relentless heat of the desert sun. They ran next to an electric fence. Nell had done the pre-morning jogging ritual for two months before she realized that the buzzing she heard was from the fence and not in her head.

Most of the other test subjects had bitched and moaned about jogging. But not Nell. First, she had savored the pain as punishment she deserved, then she had exulted in regaining the use of her legs, and finally, the jogging had filled the hole in her that she used to fill with heroin. Long distance jogging became her new addiction. Though this definitely wasn't the time for it, she was tempted to jog around the airport. That was an itch she would have to scratch later. Right now, she had to find a way out of Las Vegas.

A few yards on the other side of the fence, two couples walked toward a helicopter. Nell wasn't surprised to see a tour group this late in the evening. A late-night ride over the Strip had to be a big tourist attraction.

What was it that Kassie had said back at the restaurant? That unless Nell could sprout wings and fly, there was no way she could get out of Las Vegas. Maybe she could sprout wings after all.

The barbed wire above the chain link fence would have seriously injured a person without Nell's invulnerable skin. She grabbed the wire with both hands and climbed over the fence. As she ran toward the helicopter, she kept one hand on top of the floppy straw hat so that it wouldn't fly off.

When she got to the helicopter, everyone but a large man had boarded. Nell grabbed the man's shoulder and yanked him backwards. He landed on his butt and make a sound like a moose snorting. Nell reached inside her fake Louis Vuitton handbag and took out the Glock.

"Sorry, folks, but tonight's flight has been cancelled."

At first, the tourists and pilot stared at her in confusion, but then they saw Nell's gun, which quickly cleared away their bewilderment. One of the women screamed. The pilot climbed out with his hands up.

"I'll take you anywhere you want to go. Just don't hurt these people."

"I only want the helicopter," Nell said.

"You know how to operate this machine?"

"How hard can it be?"

The tourists stumbled out. They helped the man Nell had thrown to the ground get back to his feet and then they ran.

"The police keep their helicopters here," the pilot said. "You won't get far before they come after you."

"I figured I would be cutting it close," Nell said.

She placed her free hand on the helicopter. After absorbing the internal mechanics for operating Honeydew's advanced military helicopter, this one seemed like a child's toy. She climbed into the cockpit and started the motor. The blades began to rotate. The pilot ran toward one of the flat buildings. The aircraft lifted and the ground got smaller. Spread out below her were the lights of the city. Nell took a moment to admire them before she headed east.

CHAPTER FOURTEEN

Easter and Zavala drove their rental car south toward the Hampton Inn near McCarran International Airport. Away from the casinos, the streets were lined with identical shopping centers filled with peach and yellow buildings. Zavala pointed at a strip mall ahead.

"Stop at the Walmart. I need my fix."

"You said you were hungry. We can go after dinner."

"Come on. I know you need it too."

Easter pulled into the Walmart parking lot. Inside the store, they went past the alcoholic beverages, the condoms, the pharmacy, and the candy aisle. They stopped at the books and magazines. Zavala peered at the glossy paperbacks and her face lit up. Snatching a book, she held it up for Easter to see. On the cover, a cowboy with his shirt unbuttoned to reveal his muscular torso embraced a buxom woman with long flowing hair wearing jeans and a white shirt. Horses pranced in a corral behind them.

"Look!" Zavala said. "It's Katie Kemp's latest."

Easter leaned in for a closer look. The title of the book

was *Spurs of Love*. He congratulated her on her find. Cowboy romance was Zavala's favorite. Easter preferred sports romance. He picked a baseball romance titled, *Take Me at The Ballgame*. On the cover, a baseball player with his jersey unbuttoned to reveal his muscular torso embraced a buxom woman with long flowing hair wearing Daisy Dukes and a skintight T-shirt. People filled a baseball stadium behind them.

Zavala was responsible for Easter's interest in romance novels. She had needed a way to deal with the stress of investigating mass shootings and had seen how fellow agents self-medicated with booze, drugs, sex, and food only to have the cure end up causing as much damage as the stress. Zavala had a cousin, a trauma nurse, who loved Harlequin Romance novels. After a day of dealing with the horror of broken bodies and broken lives, the books provided a reliable escape. The plots were predictable, the sex scenes were fun, and the couples always found true love by the end of the story.

The cousin gave Zavala a romance novel. Zavala read it, loved it, and couldn't stop talking to Easter about it. He read one so that he could tease Zavala about reading girly trash, but ended up also loving the book. Here was the safe stress reliever they both needed. That didn't keep Easter from being embarrassed by this guilty pleasure. He and Zavala had worked out a deal where she bought his books when she bought hers, and he paid her back by buying dinner.

Zavala purchased the books. On the ride back to the hotel, Zavala kept her nose in her paperback. Just as Easter parked the car, her phone rang.

"It's mobile command." She answered the phone. "Special Agent Zavala."

As she listened, she jerked her thumb back in the direction

they'd just come from. Easter started the car and was back on the street when she hung up.

"Did they find Slagle?" Easter asked.

"A woman stole a helicopter from the North Las Vegas Airport. Climbed in and flew away like she'd been flying helicopters her whole life. LVMPD called us to ask if we thought it might be her."

"It's her."

"Agent Teal, the night shift supervisor, agrees. She wanted to touch base before relaying an answer to the police."

"When did Slagle take the helicopter?"

"She's been in the air for thirty minutes. The police are tracking the aircraft. So are we."

"Call Carter."

"Almost forgot about him. I'll put him on speaker phone."

She called Lt. General Buck Carter's private number.

"Special Agent Zavala," Carter said. "I hope you have good news for me."

"It's news. Not sure how good it is. I have you on speaker phone with me and Special Agent Easter."

"Hello, Easter."

"Good evening, sir. Slagle stole a helicopter from North Las Vegas Airport. She's airborne and heading east."

"Do you know who she stole it from?" Carter said.

"Deluxe Helicopter Tours," Zavala said.

"That's enough intel for us to find the aircraft data. My men will be waiting for her when she lands."

He ended the call.

"So, I guess we did have good news for him," Zavala said.

Easter and Zavala had to show their badges again to get through the barricade at the Las Vegas Convention Center.

Once inside the FBI Mobile Command Center, they made their way to the back of the truck. Agent Jenni Teal looked up briefly from her computer to acknowledge their arrival. On her monitor was a radar screen with a moving white bullseye.

"That's the helicopter," Teal said pointing at the bullseye. "It crossed the border into Arizona heading southeast."

Easter and Zavala peered at the screen.

"Do we know how much fuel she has?" Zavala asked.

"Deluxe Helicopters confirmed that the tank was full when the helicopter left the airport," Teal said. "According to the model she's flying, she can almost make it to Mexico before she runs dry."

Easter pointed at the screen.

"Nell doesn't appear to be headed for the border."

"The Arizona state police have been informed and are also following her flight data," Teal said. "Wherever she lands, they'll be waiting for her."

"The military is on its way too."

"Lucky girl. Everybody wants to dance with her."

The bullseye flickered and then disappeared. Agents watching on other monitors shouted and cursed.

"Where'd she go?" Zavala asked.

"I don't know," Teal said.

Easter called the LVMPD and spoke to them briefly.

"Near as they can tell," Easter said, "the helicopter's GPS stopped functioning."

"We lost her?" Zavala asked.

"Afraid so."

"The GPS didn't malfunction," Zavala said. "Slagle disabled it."

"Is this an example of her touching and learning a machine?" Teal asked.

"And she did it while she was operating the aircraft."

"How the hell are supposed to catch her if she does shit like this?"

"I was just asking myself that same question."

Easter and Zavala left the mobile command truck and stepped into the cool night air. They walked towards the convention center. Yellow police tape stretched across the broken entrance. If Easter and Zavala had been smokers, now would have been an ideal time to light up.

"You have to admit," Zavala said. "The girl's smart as a whip. She knew how to throw us off her trail."

"I agree that Nell is intelligent, but she's making it up as she goes along. She was in the air for an hour before it dawned on her to turn off the helicopter's GPS."

"What about the convention center shooting? That wasn't a spur of the moment decision."

"Not entirely. I think she left HARD-SOW without a long-term plan, and somewhere between there and Vegas she decided to attack the WAR Show."

Zavala leaned against the mobile command center vehicle. "Then how do we catch her?"

Easter leaned against the vehicle next to her. He stared at the half moon above them.

"We figure out Nell's next move before she does."

CHAPTER FIFTEEN

SKEETER EXPECTED THE police roadblock in Las Vegas.

He waited patiently as officers searched his rig, even though he had assured them that there were no fugitives hiding inside. His patience was an act. Inside, his brain squirmed like a worm on a fisherman's hook. Skeeter wanted to get the hell out of there. If he never saw Las Vegas again it would be too soon. The police eventually finished poking around and told him to have a nice day. Skeeter told them the same and he meant it. He knew they were just doing their job. As if anyone would choose to bake in the hot morning sun while dealing with irate commuters.

Skeeter was surprised by the roadblock in Flagstaff.

He was five miles outside city limits when I-40 East became a parking lot. He slowed down to a grinding stop. As he inched toward the Arizona State Troopers standing in front of their cruisers, police helicopters flew overhead. Cops set up roadblocks where they thought their target was headed. So, unless there was another murder suspect at large, the police believed that the Las Vegas Convention Center shooter might be coming this way. That meant that the blonde-haired blue-eyed demoness who had tied Skeeter up and left him to die had managed to slip past the Las Vegas checkpoints and was now somewhere in Arizona.

Nell straight from hell. Just thinking her name sent a shiver down Skeeter's spine. She tried to kill him and would have succeeded if that truck stop manager hadn't found him when she did. If the manager had come a day or two later, then she surely would have found Skeeter's stinking corpse.

Skeeter should have been happy to be alive. The sobering truth was that no one would have given a rat's ass if he had died. He was a divorced recovering alcoholic. And he was a truck driver, the world's loneliest job. Maybe it would have been better if the truck stop manager hadn't found him. A car horn blasted behind Skeeter. He gave the driver behind him a middle finger salute and inched closer to the roadblock.

Skeeter finally got his turn to have his rig searched for the second time that day. This time he was too deep into a blue funk to hide his impatience. If the mass shooting hadn't happened, Skeeter would have been carrying a load of firearms from Vegas to the Bulard Arms headquarters in Connecticut. And Harry Pigott had been right. Skeeter had called the Bulard truck dispatcher. He told Skeeter that there wouldn't be any gun shipments until further notice. Until further notice could mean a week or months.

Calls to his other clients didn't pan out either. Skeeter had no choice but to go home and wait. But that didn't mean he wanted to spend all his free time dealing with roadblocks.

Once he was through, Skeeter got on his CB radio. Many young truckers had abandoned citizens band radio, but old-timers like Skeeter still relied on it. He went straight to

Sesame Street, trucker slang for CB channel 19, to warn other truckers about the roadblock and to find out if there were any more to deal with further along the highway.

"Heads up if you're traveling east on I-40," Skeeter said into the microphone. "Arizona state bears are having a picnic just outside Flagstaff city limits."

A man's voice crackled through the speaker.

"Flagstaff? I knew Vegas was sealed up tighter than a nun's asshole. But Flagstaff?"

"That's right," Skeeter said. "I just crawled through."

More truckers joined the conversation, and through them Skeeter learned that there were roadblocks all around Flagstaff, Phoenix, and Tucson. And that was just Arizona. The police search extended to New Mexico with roadblocks around Albuquerque, Santa Fe, and into El Paso, Texas.

"Son of a bitch," Skeeter said. "I'm trying to get to Georgia. At this rate, I won't arrive until Christmas."

"You think you're screwed?" one of the truckers said. "My deadline's all shot to hell."

A chorus of truckers joined in to gripe about their late shipments. Skeeter would have felt sorry for them, but he could only handle feeling sorry for himself today. He signed off and rode in silence, ignoring the satellite radio and the CD player in favor of listening to the forlorn rumble of his engine.

There was no roadblock in Winslow, Arizona.

Skeeter pulled into the Flying J Travel Plaza, filled his tank, and parked in the truck lot. If he was going to be sitting through a series of roadblocks, then he should eat now while he had the chance, and a hot lunch might lift his spirits.

The store was busy with truckers and tourists filling tanks and emptying bladders. Skeeter idled by the DVD stand before going to the Denny's connected to the plaza. He sat at a table by the window and studied the menu. The smell of vintage cooking grease hung around like a deadbeat relative that refuses to take the hint that it's time to move out. The waitress came over with flatware, a glass of water, and the day's specials. Skeeter ordered the pot roast, mashed potatoes, and biscuits.

"Would you like a salad with that?" the waitress said.

"Why would I want a salad?" Skeeter asked.

"Just asking. Anything to drink besides water?"

"Coffee."

"I'll put your order in and get you some fresh coffee."

The waitress left. Skeeter looked around. Besides himself, there were three other diners in the restaurant. An elderly couple in a booth ate slowly and avoided looking at each other. The third diner, on the other side of the room, was a blonde. Skeeter glanced at her and turned his attention to the ebb and flow of people outside the window.

The waitress brought him a cup of coffee and a handful of creamers. Skeeter tore open two creamers and poured them into his cup, creating a white swirl in black coffee. He glanced at the blonde again. She was attractive, but it was the many plates on her table that drew his attention. There wasn't an inch of bare surface to be seen. Maybe three other people had been eating with her and had to leave before she was finished.

The waitress took away some of her empty plates and then came right back with new plates laden with a T-bone steak, scrambled eggs, wheat toast, and hash browns. The blonde thanked the waitress and then dug into her food. Skeeter was intrigued.

Despite the enormous amount of food that she was consuming, the woman was not overweight. In fact, she was thin and muscular. She wore mirrored sunglasses, a cowboy hat, a Jamaican Bobsled Team T-shirt, paisley yoga pants, and combat boots.

She paused to gaze at Skeeter for a moment before putting a forkful of steak in her mouth. Skeeter froze. It was her. Nell. Straight from hell. It didn't matter what she was wearing. After what she had put him through, he would have known her anywhere.

The waitress came to Skeeter's table and placed his order in front of him.

"Can I get you anything else?"

Skeeter didn't respond.

"Let me know if you need something." The waitress walked away.

Skeeter told his body to take his phone out of his pocket, dial 9-1-1, and tell the police that the killer they're searching for is in a Denny's in Winslow, Arizona devouring everything on the menu. But his body refused. He couldn't move. He couldn't smell his food. He could barely breathe. He was too petrified to want a drink.

Skeeter's wrist was still red from where he'd rubbed the skin off trying to free himself from the power cords that Nell had used to tie him up. Just as he recognized her, soon she was going to recognize him. And then, she was going to kill him. Skeeter was sure of it. Just as he was sure that everything in his life eventually turned to shit. The funk he'd been wallowing in turned from blue to a soul crushing black.

His greatest regret was that he'd never see his ex-wife Edie again. Though Skeeter often claimed her nagging was the reason he became an alcoholic, the truth was their first years of marriage were the happiest days of his life. Despite all the terrible things she'd done to him and to be completely honest, all the terrible things he'd done to her, Skeeter had never given up hope that someday, somehow, he'd find a way to win her back.

"Damn it," Skeeter whispered.

He stole glances at Nell as she ate her scrambled eggs and wheat toast and decided that he was going to survive. Not just survive but live on to a greater glory. The young lady didn't know it yet, but Skeeter had something she needed. And in return, he was going to get Edie back.

Skeeter attacked his food as if it were his last meal. He had a plan. It was insanely dangerous, which just added to the thrill. He was sopping up the last of the pot roast gravy with a biscuit when he saw Nell ask the waitress for her check. Jumping out of his chair, Skeeter hurried to her table.

"Give me the lady's check along with mine," Skeeter said.

The waitress glanced down at the pile of empty plates on Nell's table.

"You sure about that?"

"Positive."

The waitress shrugged and walked away. Nell faced him but her mirrored shades prevented him from reading her eyes.

"Mind if I join you?" Skeeter asked.

"If you're trying to pick me up, I can tell you right now that it's not going to happen."

Skeeter sat in the chair opposite her.

"I am trying to pick you up. But not the way you're thinking."

"And what way is that?"

"You know. Not in a sexual way."

The waitress returned and handed two checks to Skeeter.

He gawked at the number on Nell's check. She held out her hand.

"Give it here. I'll pay it."

Skeeter shook his head.

"No. It's my treat."

He gave the waitress his credit card.

"If you're not looking for sex, then what exactly are your intentions?" Nell asked.

"I want to give you a ride in my truck."

Nell took her drink and sucked on the straw until she made the annoying slurping sound.

"I don't need a ride. I have a car."

"I don't believe you," Skeeter said.

The waitress returned with Skeeter's credit card and a receipt for both meals. He added a tip and signed it. Nell put her purse in her lap.

"Thanks for lunch, but this is where we say goodbye."

"You don't have a car," Skeeter said. "You never would have made it through the roadblocks in one."

Nell removed her sunglasses.

"Have we met before?"

Skeeter grimaced. He shouldn't have expected her to remember him, but he still felt insulted. After all, she had robbed and hog-tied him in his own truck. Seemed like something that was worth remembering.

"Wait a minute." Nell pointed her finger at him. "Now I remember. How could I forget after that intimate evening we shared in your truck? It's Scooter, right?"

"Skeeter."

"Like a mosquito. A buzzing annoying blood-sucking insect that I just might have to swat."

Skeeter had first-hand experience on how hard she could sway, but pressed on anyway.

"I know who you are. Nell Slagle." He leaned forward. "I know what you did."

"Everybody knows what I did. What do you want from me?"

Skeeter took a deep breath.

"I can take you anywhere you want to go. I can even get you into Mexico."

"I don't want to go to Mexico."

"I've got a hidden compartment in my truck. No lawman has ever found it. It's that damn good. The cops searched my truck twice today and they still didn't find my hidey hole."

"Is that what the kids are calling a vagina these days?"

Skeeter resisted the urge to cuss her.

"You won't get past the cops without my help."

"What's to stop me from tying you up again and taking your truck?"

"You can't hide and drive at the same time."

Nell leaned back in her chair and crossed her legs.

"Why would you help me? Like you said, you know who I am."

"There's something I want and I'm willing to make a deal with the devil to get it."

Nell smiled. Her smile made Skeeter relax a little bit. A teensy-weensy little bit.

"I'm intrigued," Nell said. "Tell me more."

Skeeter ran his hand through his long gray hair.

"Edie and I were married for twelve years. The first four were heaven. The last eight were hell. Then she got pregnant. I was thrilled. I'd always wanted to be a daddy and I figured a baby would save our marriage."

"I'm guessing it didn't work out like you planned."

Skeeter sighed.

"I never found out. I love Mexican food, but I didn't eat enough to make a Mexican baby."

Nell snorted.

"Are you saying a Mexican stole your job?"

"Needless to say, Edie and I got a divorce. She moved in with the baby's father. She had the nerve to tell me that she'd fallen in love with the guy."

"Maybe she did."

"She might think that but she's fooling herself. Nothing can match what we had. If that bastard hadn't filled her head with nonsense, Edie and I would still be together."

"You sure about that? You did say the last eight years were hell."

"We would have worked things out. Eventually."

Nell crossed her arms.

"Thank you for sharing your sad story with me. I don't see what it has to do with me."

Skeeter looked around the restaurant. The elderly couple had left, and the waitress was behind the counter chatting with another waitress.

"I'll take you wherever you want to go," Skeeter said. "If you agree to kill Rafael Vargas."

Nell's eyes widened. Skeeter could tell that she now saw him in a different way. She wasn't the only badass. He could be pretty damn badass too.

"I take it Rafael is the father," Nell said.

"I'd kill him myself. But then Edie would never forgive me."

"I won't do it."

"Come on. Nobody will suspect that you killed Rafael for me. Everyone will assume he was just another one of your victims."

Nell put her sunglasses back on.

"Find somebody else."

"What's the problem? You're a killer. It's what you do."

Nell shook her head.

"I'm not a killer. I'm an avenger. I kill specific people for a specific reason."

Skeeter held out his open palms.

"That's all I'm asking. Kill a specific person for a specific reason."

Nell looked out the window.

"Oh, shit."

An Arizona State Trooper cruiser had parked right outside the window. Two officers got out of the vehicle. Nell put her hand inside her purse and kept it there. Skeeter didn't need to ask what was in the purse.

"Don't panic. They could just be here to pay the water bill."

"Do what?"

"Use the bathroom."

"Why didn't you say so."

"I did. Come on. We can go out the side exit and get to my truck without them seeing us."

Nell tore her attention away from the window. Skeeter could see his face in her mirrored sunglasses. He saw a worried man.

"I'm not going with you," Nell said.

"There's nothing but open land all around this place. No trees. No mountains. No other buildings. There's nowhere you can run that the bears won't see you. I don't know how the hell you got here without anyone seeing you in the first place."

"I jogged from Flagstaff to Winona. Stole a car and drove the rest of the way."

Skeeter gawked at her.

"You really do have a car?"

"Why would I lie?"

"How'd you get past the roadblocks?"

"I don't know. Maybe they weren't set up yet."

"Hold on, Winona is fifteen miles from Flagstaff."

"I needed the exercise. Just my luck I stole a car that was low on gas. I barely made it here. Once I filled up, I decided to take a shower. The showers here are nice and clean. Plenty of hot water."

"I'll remember that the next time I come through." Skeeter looked out the window. "Which car is yours?"

"The blue Honda Civic parked near the road."

"The one the cops are checking out?"

The policemen stood next to the Honda. One officer studied the license plate while the other officer talked into his radio. Nell groaned.

"Fuck a dog. Okay, you win. I'll take that ride."

Nell took her empty hand out of her purse. Skeeter led the way to the side entrance. The sun blasted them, and the distant mountains shimmered from the heat. If the troopers did see them, Skeeter hoped they would assume he and Nell were an innocent couple and not a crazy man aiding and abetting a wanted criminal.

They made it to Skeeter's rig without anyone shouting for them to stop and raise their hands. Skeeter was sweating heavily as he reached under the dashboard and felt around for the hidden switch. He flipped it and a panel slid open in the floor of the sleeper. It led to a hidden compartment under both the cabin and the sleeper. Nell peered down into it.

"Why the hell do you have this?"

"Long story. Remind me to tell you when the cops aren't around."

Nell looked around the cab.

"I don't know about this. Maybe I could hide in the sleeper."

"They'd find you right away."

Nell took a gun out of her purse and pointed it at Skeeter's forehead. He peed a little. Why was it every time he was with this woman, he ended up wetting his pants?

"I don't like the idea of being trapped in a metal box," Nell said.

"People I've hidden in there said it was surprisingly spacious."

"I would still be at your mercy, and I have no reason to trust you."

Sweat poured down Skeeter's face. This was not working out at all like he'd hoped.

"I haven't told you about the hidey hole's best feature. It has a trap door."

"How did you manage to forget that?"

"I don't know. Gun to my head? Cops looking for you? Can't imagine why it slipped my mind."

Nell lowered her gun.

"Show me."

Skeeter reached down inside the hidey hole and pulled a lever on the side. The floor dropped open and they could see the asphalt below.

"I figured if a cop somehow found the door, then the

people inside would have an escape hatch in case they need to make a run for it," Skeeter said.

Nell put her gun back in her purse.

"You really put a lot of thought into this contraption."

"I take pride in my work."

Nell climbed down into the hidden compartment and lay on her back. Skeeter closed the panel and placed a rug over it.

"You okay in there?"

"Whoever was in here last had terrible body odor," Nell said.

Skeeter pulled out of the parking lot and eased onto the highway. As he drove east, police cars with flashing blue lights and sirens blaring flew past them in the westbound lane.

"By the way," Skeeter said. "Where do you want to go?"

"East," Nell said from beneath the floor.

"How far east?"

"Cleveland."

"Really? I never would have guessed you were from Ohio."

"I'm not. I want to go to Cleveland, Tennessee."

"What do you know? I'm from Valdosta, Georgia."

"So?"

"We're practically neighbors."

Nell groaned.

"I can tell already that this is going to be long trip."

CHAPTER SIXTEEN

After crawling through two roadblocks, Harry Pigott decided it would be a mistake to turn south onto I-17 in Flagstaff. The cops would have roadblocks all the way to the border. Instead, he stayed on I-40 and looked for an alternate route. In Winslow, Harry pulled into the Flying J Travel Plaza. The breakfast burrito he had in Vegas that morning was fighting him.

Coming out of the men's room, Harry searched for the coffee machines. Brightly lit and overloaded with endless varieties of junk food, the place was massive and the layout confusing. He walked into a dining room, realized the plaza included a Denny's, and was about to leave when he spotted her.

Nell.

The memory of her murdering two cops flashed into Harry's mind and chilled him to the bone. He turned on his heel and fled the dining room. He stood next to the hotdog roller machine until he calmed down.

"Damn it, Harry," he muttered to himself. "You're not some helpless wimp. They say she's a killing machine? So are you."

He went back to Denny's and stood outside the entrance

where he could observe her without being seen. He couldn't decide what annoyed him more; her lazy attempt at a disguise, or the fact that the disguise was working. All she did was put on different clothes along with a hat and sunglasses. Nell Slagle's photo was on every TV station and internet news site, and yet only Harry noticed her.

She was eating a lot of food. There were seven or eight plates on her table. As soon as she finished one, she moved on to the next. Harry took a moment to watch her, mesmerized by her voracious appetite. Taking out his phone, he called his sister, Kat.

"Commander," she said. "Is your ETA still the same?"

"Mama Kat. You'll never guess who I'm looking at."

Kat gasped.

"You located the target?"

"Affirmative."

"Looks like you won't need us after all."

"As Master Tzu says, 'When circumstances are favorable, one should modify one's plans'."

"Attack the enemy when he's unprepared. Appear where you're not expected."

"Damn right. I'll call back after the mission is completed."

As much as Harry wanted to take out his concealed Glock 43 and start shooting, he couldn't without endangering civilians. Also, taking a gun out in a crowded store might lead some idiot to think he was a lowlife scumbag trying to rob the place. A stupid assumption, because it was obvious just by looking at Harry that he was a good guy with a gun.

He could wait until Nell went outside and shoot her in the parking lot, but she was alone, and Harry was too hungry for revenge to wait. He was going to kill her now.

His plan was to approach her table, acting as if he were joining a friend. She would be confused. Who was this guy? He looked familiar. Then she would recognize Harry, see his gun, and know that her miserable life was about to come to an end right before he blew her head off.

"You don't have to wait to be seated," a waitress said. "You can sit anywhere you like."

Harry had been so focused on Nell that he hadn't noticed the waitress until she was in his face.

"Thanks. I see a friend. I'll sit with her."

"I'll fetch you a menu."

"That won't be necessary."

"Would you like to hear about today's lunch specials?"

"No. I would not."

"You sure? We got meatloaf and two vegetables for just twelve ninety-five. Includes a drink and a biscuit."

"I changed my mind. I'm not eating here after all."

"Okay. But if you decide to stay, you can sit anywhere you like. You don't have to wait to be seated."

Before the waitress scurried away, Harry noticed she had a decent rack. He looked back at Nell and was shocked to see that she was no longer alone. Even more amazing, the man with a gray ponytail sitting with her was Skeeter, the truck driver. Was it possible that he knew her?

An elderly couple walked by. Nell and Skeeter were the only customers in the dining room. They were having a conversation, though Skeeter was doing most of the talking. A different waitress than the one who had annoyed the hell out of Harry placed a credit card and a receipt on their table. Skeeter pocketed the credit card and signed the receipt.

This was terrible. Harry liked Skeeter. He had worked with

him on many gun shows and they'd always gotten along well. But seeing him pay for Nell's lunch gave Harry no other choice. He would have to kill both of them.

Harry removed the Glock from his IWB (inside the waistband) holster and was about to make his approach when Nell and Skeeter hurried out of the dining room. Harry followed but lost sight of them in the crowded truck stop. He put the gun back into the holster, headed for the front door, and bumped into an Arizona State Trooper. Stumbling back, the trooper grabbed Harry's arm before he fell on his ass.

"You okay, sir?" the trooper asked.

There were two of them, big beefy guys in crisp uniforms.

"Sorry," Harry said. "I wasn't looking where I was going."

"Anything the matter, sir?" the other trooper asked.

"Wife is waiting for me in the car. She gets really irritated if I take too long."

Harry had said the first thing that popped in his head. He'd been divorced for years.

The troopers glanced at each other.

"Do you drive a blue Honda Civic?" the first trooper asked.

"No, sir. A Land Rover Defender."

"That's a sweet ride."

"Yes, sir, it is indeed."

"Does your wife ever let you drive it?"

Harry chafed at the insult to his manhood, but he let it go. The longer he spent with them, the further Nell slipped away.

"If I remember to take out the garbage."

The troopers laughed and then left Harry to continue their search for the owner of the blue Honda. Harry could have told them that Nell Slagle was here, but she was his prey.

Harry left the store, putting on his sunglasses. Nell and

Skeeter must have seen the troopers coming and that's why they left in a hurry. If they had any sense, they'd climb into Skeeter's truck and get the hell out of here. Harry headed toward truck parking.

All the big rigs looked the same to Harry. He dashed from truck to truck, peering up at the cabs. If only he had pushed the waitress aside and shot Nell when he had the chance.

A truck's engine rumbled to life. Harry ran toward it and arrived in time for the eighteen-wheeler to roll past him. He peered into the cab. Skeeter was behind the wheel. There was no sign of Nell, but Harry would bet cash money that she was aboard.

He ran after the truck, his legs pumping as he crossed the parking lot. Too late he realized that he was in the path of an SUV. It screeched to a halt and honked at him. Harry jumped back and stared at the car, his heart racing. A family of four stared back at him.

"Watch where you're going!" the driver shouted.

"You watch where you're going."

Harry and the driver exchanged rude gestures and then Harry resumed chasing Skeeter and Nell. The truck idled at the edge of the parking lot, waiting for an opening in traffic. As he ran, Harry slipped his gun out. If traffic kept the truck waiting long enough, Harry could climb into the cab and shoot Skeeter. But Skeeter got lucky. Traffic thinned and he pulled onto the highway. Drenched in sweat, with his lungs burning, all Harry could do was watch the truck get smaller and smaller. He spat on the ground.

"You got away this time," Harry shouted. "But now I know how to find you."

CHAPTER SEVENTEEN

Special Agent John Easter stood at the edge of Northern Arizona University's football practice field. Two Flagstaff police officers stood on the other side. Yellow crime scene tape stretched around the edge of the field to keep the public away from the helicopter sitting on the fifty-yard line. It had been there for two days. The company that owned it was eager to retrieve their stolen property. The university also wanted the helicopter off their practice field.

A third police officer escorted a man past the police tape to Easter. The man had a Deluxe Helicopter Tours logo stitched into the fabric of his shirt.

"I'm here to fly this bird back to Vegas," the man said, jerking his thumb at the aircraft.

"You sure you have enough fuel?" Easter asked.

"Oh yeah. When it left the airport, it had enough to get to the Grand Canyon and back. That's our most popular trip. Nothing like seeing the canyon from a helicopter. Absolutely breathtaking."

"I'm certain it is. The helicopter is yours. We're done with it."

The pilot headed for the helicopter.

Nell's prints had been found on the helicopter. They'd also been found in a My Place hotel room, on a stolen Jaguar next to the North Las Vegas Airport, and on a carjacked Honda in the parking lot of a truck stop in Winslow. The trail went cold in Winslow. Nell had disappeared.

The helicopter lifted from the field. Easter and the officer turned away to avoid the debris blown toward them. Once the aircraft was out of sight, Easter took out his phone and called Zavala.

"Is the helicopter gone?" she asked.

"Just left," Easter said. "How'd the interview go with the couple at the hotel?"

"You mean Louis and Martha Roth, the world's most typical Las Vegas tourists? They said Nell was very nice."

"She didn't kill them. I suppose you could call that being nice."

"The hotel's security cameras show that Nell entered the hotel dressed as a maid."

"Got to hand it to her. Putting on a maid's uniform was a brilliant move. That's like putting on an invisibility cloak."

Easter heard the whirring of a helicopter overhead. The sound was deeper than the sound made by the one that had taken off earlier.

"Got to go. My ride's here." He turned to the officer next to him. "Once I'm gone, you can take down the tape and tell the university we're done."

The officer nodded and walked around the field toward the other two officers.

A military helicopter landed on the field and the door slid open. Lt. General Buck Carter was inside waiting. Easter climbed in, buckled into his seat, and the helicopter lifted off.

"How the hell did you manage to lose her?" Carter asked.

"I was about to ask you the same thing," Easter said.

Carter stared out the window. Easter did too. They had a wonderful view of the snow-capped San Francisco mountains. Not as glorious as the Grand Canyon, but still quite beautiful.

"We established a base of operations at Creech Air Force Base," Carter said. "Had a troop ready for deployment at a moment's notice. Drones on standby. But when it came time to capture her, it wasn't enough."

"We should have anticipated that Nell would disable the helicopter's GPS," Easter said.

Carter shook his head.

"That wasn't a factor. We followed the contrail. We had boots on the ground minutes after she landed. We patched into Flagstaff's surveillance cameras and had a drone in the sky. She still got away."

Easter thought back to his own military experience.

"Even with all the manpower and technology at your disposal, she was still a needle in a haystack. Flagstaff isn't Vegas, but it still has a good size population. You were looking for a Caucasian female in a college town that has dozens of Caucasian females. If that wasn't difficult enough, you didn't know what she was wearing or which direction she was headed."

"There were many times that night we thought we'd found her. But each time, it was the wrong woman."

If Carter hadn't jumped down Easter's throat, he might have almost felt sorry for him.

"Nell stole a car in Winona. A man was sitting in his vehicle with the engine running. He was so busy looking at his phone that she had the car door open and her hand on his arm before he realized she was there. She tossed him out, climbed in, and drove away."

Carter grinned.

"My wife hates it when people sit in their car with the engine running. She says that when she becomes queen she's going to make it a crime."

"We found the clothes she was wearing when she stole the helicopter. They were behind a donation box in Flagstaff. The box had been broken into. There are no security cameras around, so we have no idea what she's wearing now. And while the Winslow truck stop had plenty of security cameras, we weren't able to identify Slagle. There were dozens of women wearing hats obscuring their faces. Any one of them could have been her."

Easter could see the Las Vegas skyline ahead.

"What's your next move?" Carter asked.

"Every law enforcement officer in the country is on the lookout for Nell Slagle. Her face is everywhere. She'll turn up eventually. I just hope that when she does, it isn't because she murdered somebody."

Carter made a sour face. High ranking military officers were supposed to exercise great patience, but maybe that didn't apply when a top-secret weapon was on the loose killing civilians.

The helicopter landed on the Circus Circus helipad. Once Easter was out, the aircraft lifted off the ground and flew away. Easter took the elevator to the bottom floor of the parking garage where Zavala was waiting for him.

"I was afraid you and Carter might sneak off to catch a Cirque du Soleil show."

"I think he's in a hurry to get back to Creech Air Force Base to sulk," Easter said.

Zavala held up a plastic bag.

"I scored these at Walgreens."

Inside the bag were two paperbacks, *Amish You So Much*, a bonnet ripper, which was like a bodice ripper but with chaste Amish people, and *Touchdown There*, a football romance. Easter nodded his approval.

They got into the car and headed toward McCarran International Airport.

"Agent Driscoll briefed me on his visit to Morton Travel Plaza," Zavala said. "The truck driver who Nell allegedly attacked had left town, but Driscoll was able to talk to the manager who contacted the police. Her story hasn't changed. She says the truck driver identified his assailant as Nell Slagle."

"Even if it she did mug the truck driver, he may not be able to tell us anything we don't already know."

"Driscoll would like to stay on the truck driver even if it's a long shot."

The monorail passed by on its elevated track.

"I don't know," Easter said. "Should we be wasting time on long shots?"

"Going to Philly isn't a long shot?"

"It's Nell's last location before Honeydew took her to HARD-SOW."

Zavala scowled.

"Philly's a big city and she was homeless. She's not going to have a former address."

"She was an addict. She had to have been in Kensington. It was the Walmart of heroin. There might be some street people there who remember her."

"How about this? In exchange for going to Philly, we let Agent Driscoll contact the truck driver. That way we cover all the long shots."

Zavala took the airport exit.

"We're already going to Philly," Easter said.

"And I already told Agent Driscoll he could track down the truck driver."

CHAPTER EIGHTEEN

THE NIGHT WAS quiet except for Nell's combat boots scraping the asphalt road. She kept an eye out for a passing car or truck, though it rarely happened. She liked having the desert to herself. The evening sky's multitude of stars reminded of when her family used to go camping in Cherokee National Park.

Nell slowed to a walk when she reached an abandoned gas station. Skeeter's truck was parked behind it, obscured from vehicles passing by. Nell ran every night, and always waited until Skeeter was asleep before slipping out. She wondered if he ever woke up while she was gone or if he stayed asleep, completely oblivious to her absences. If he did know, he had apparently decided it wasn't worth bringing up.

She wiped sweat off her face with her T-shirt. The shirt was getting gross after running in it for days. Correction. It was gross. Her yoga pants were gross too. She didn't even want to think about her underwear.

Nell couldn't just walk into a Walmart and buy new clothes, not with her face all over the news. Perhaps she'd have Skeeter buy her new clothes, but there was no way she was going to have him buy her underwear.

Once she reached Skeeter's eighteen-wheeler, Nell crawled under the cab and climbed inside the truck through the escape hatch of the hidey hole. Skeeter's snoring echoed above her. Nell entered the cab through the secret door in the cab's floor. She took the water jug out of the mini-fridge and drank until it was empty. Wiping her mouth, Nell put the thin mat and blanket that she used for a bed over the secret door. Skeeter rolled over in the cab's bed, which only caused a brief pause to his horrendous snoring.

Nell took off her boots and got under the blanket. Before closing her eyes, she made sure her purse with the Glock in it was nearby. Her body had that good ache and exhaustion from strenuous exercise. Sleep came over her in less than a minute.

When Nell woke up, she could feel the truck moving. She had a sour taste in her mouth and her muscles were stiff. Opening the sleeper's heavy curtain, Nell was blasted by bright sunshine. She fumbled in her purse for her mirrored sunglasses. Once her eyes were shielded, she climbed into the passenger seat.

"Where are we?"

"New Mexico," Skeeter said.

"Can you be more specific?"

"Ass End of Nowhere, New Mexico."

The endless stretches of two-lane roads through the flat lands of New Mexico didn't look any different from the flat lands they'd just driven through in Arizona. They were taking the long way to Cleveland, Tennessee. The really long way. Skeeter avoided the major highways. As he explained it, sticking to back roads slowed them down, but gave them a much better chance of reaching their destination.

Skeeter was right. Before they turned off I-40, they went through three roadblocks. Each time, Nell had hidden in the cab's hidey hole, sweating and clutching her handgun. As officers searched the vehicle and their footsteps echoed above her, she had been sorely tempted to open the escape hatch and run like hell.

They hadn't come across a single roadblock on the back roads. They occasionally saw a police helicopter fly across the sky or a state trooper speed past them with lights flashing, but other than that they had seen no evidence of the nationwide search for fugitive Nell Slagle. She felt safe enough to ride shotgun.

Only once did Nell offer to share the driving. She had tried to explain her ability to operate any machinery just by touching it, but Skeeter reacted as if Nell had asked him if she could wear his penis.

"Why did you kill those people?" Skeeter asked.

"Why do you want to know?"

Skeeter shrugged.

"Just making conversation."

"That's how you start a conversation?"

"I'd like to know."

Nell shifted in her seat so she could face Skeeter. Some days he tied his shoulder length gray hair into a ponytail, and other days he let it hang loose. Today was a hang loose day. Nell wondered when old rednecks decided to look like old hippies. Or did old hippies just become old rednecks?

"I could use some conversation," Nell said. "So, I'm going to ask you a question."

"Ask away. I'm an open book."

"You haven't used your GPS for days. Do you have any idea where we're going?"

Skeeter sniggered.

"Don't need GPS. I know these roads like the back of my hand."

"Does the reason you know these back roads have anything to do with why you have a hidey hole?"

Skeeter glared at her.

"I don't like this conversation. Let's talk about something else."

"You can ask me why I kill people, but I can't ask you why you have a hidey hole?"

"Alright. On one condition. I'll answer your question if you answer mine."

"I don't know about that."

"My truck. My rules."

Nell looked out the window. The scenery didn't appear to be on the verge of changing any time soon.

"Okay. You go first."

"I'm an alcoholic," Skeeter said. "Been sober for ten years."

"I suspected as much. I'm a former addict."

"Let me guess. Pain pills?"

"For a while. Then I moved on to heroin."

"I could never do that shit. I hate needles."

"I snorted it."

"We could have our own little twelve-step meeting right here."

"Maybe later. Tell me about the hidey hole."

Skeeter groaned.

"My drinking got so bad that I started fucking up jobs. Got

fired. Nobody would hire me. Even after I got clean, I couldn't get work. Edie had a waitress job, but it wasn't enough to pay the bills. I needed work and driving a truck was the only thing I was good at."

"I can see where this is headed," Nell said. "When you couldn't find legitimate work, you added the hidey hole so that you could pick up some of that sweet people-smuggling money."

Skeeter shot her a sideways glance.

"What makes you think it was people? I could have been smuggling drugs."

"The first time you showed me the hidey hole, you said people who had hidden in there claimed it was surprisingly spacious," Nell said.

"I said that?"

"Yes, you did."

"Okay. I smuggled people. I'm not proud of it, but it kept food on the table and the bank from taking my home."

Nell reached into the food cabinet for a half-empty box of cheese crackers. She had asked Skeeter to get the regular kind, but he had gotten some kind of spicy flavor. She ate them anyway.

"How'd you get started?" Nell asked. "It's not like you could just put an ad in the paper. *Truck available for hauling illegal immigrants. Call this number and ask for Skeeter.*"

"There's a big chicken plant up the road from Valdosta. Back in the day, I'd hauled frozen chickens for them whenever their regular fleet was maxed out. I still had friends at the plant. They told me how they were always in need of cheap labor and nobody's cheaper than an undocumented worker. They hooked me up with the coyotes on the border."

"What was it like, sneaking people into the country?"

"Scary. Depressing. Terrible. Don't know how I managed not to fall off the wagon. Was a huge relief when I finally started getting honest work again."

Nell finished the cheese crackers and stuffed the empty box into the plastic bag they used for garbage. She looked over her shoulder at the sleeper floor and wondered if she was the first person in the hidey hole who wasn't Hispanic.

"This guy you want me to kill," Nell said. "Rafael. Is he one of the people who hid in your hidey hole?"

Skeeter ground the gears. The truck made an angry sound.

"You better kill that goddamn son of a bitch."

"You didn't answer my question."

"I could tell right away that Rafael was different from the others. Most of them stared at me with big, watery eyes. It was like I was hauling cattle instead of people. But not Rafael. He already knew English. He was smart and funny. Funny comes in handy on a long dangerous trip. Helps you deal with the tension."

"I'm trying, but you never laugh at my jokes."

"That's because they're not funny."

"Ouch. Go on with your story."

"Rafael was good people. Or least, I thought he was. Instead of dropping him off at the chicken plant with the other beaners, I took him with me to Valdosta. Edie was pissed at first, but he charmed her. It was her idea that he enlist in the army to get his citizenship. After four years, most of it spent in Iraq, Rafael was able to get a green card. He came back to Valdosta and started a home repair business. By that time, I'd started to get legitimate jobs that kept me away from home for weeks at a time. I asked Rafael to check in on Edie for me. You can guess what happened after that."

"The baby kind of gives it away."

"Edie and I were going through a rough patch and the sneaky bastard took advantage. After all I did for him."

Nell had more questions for Skeeter. Was he more upset that Edie cheated on him or that Rafael betrayed their friendship? Did Edie give birth to a boy or a girl? Once Rafael was out of the way, did Skeeter plan to raise this child as his own?

With such a long trip ahead of them, she decided to save the questions for later.

There were few billboards to break up the monotony. But then, a sign on the side of the road caught Nell's attention. It was a hand-painted wooden sign white with black lettering, the kind of sign that let drivers know about a fruit stand up ahead. But this one was the first line of a poem. About a half mile later was the next verse. Two more signs completed the poem.

ROSES ARE RED

MY GUN IS BLUE

I AM SAFE

HOW ABOUT YOU?

Nell wished that she could meet the poet so that she could kick his teeth in.

"Your turn," Skeeter said.

"You really want to know why I attacked the WAR Show?" Nell asked.

"I do."

"Do you remember the shooting at Red Clay Middle School."

"There are so many of them it's hard to tell them apart."

Nell took a deep breath.

"My little brother Carson loaded my mother's car with a semi-automatic rifle and two handguns. He drove ten miles from my mother's house to Red Clay Middle School. He went inside and started shooting. His final body count for the day was twenty-five dead, and three wounded."

Skeeter scowled.

Damn," he said.

"Yeah," Nell said. "Damn."

"I'm sorry. I don't remember that shooting."

"It's okay. A lot of people don't remember Red Clay. It happened right after Sandy Hook and the two shootings were almost identical. Both had a gun-loving mother, a mentally ill loner, and nearly the same number killed. On top of that, Adam Lanza used a Bushmaster at Sandy Hook and Carson used a Beastmaster at Red Clay."

They came upon another gun poem.

CASTLE OR CABIN

OR GEODESIC DOME

HOMELAND SECURITY

STARTS AT HOME

"Any idea why your brother did it?" Skeeter asked.

Nell shook her head.

"Not really. Carson needed professional help. Therapy and medication. But our mother, Peggy, refused to acknowledge it. She coddled him and insisted he'd grow out of it. To make matters worse, Peggy loved guns. She started taking me and Carson to the gun range as soon as we were old enough to hold a handgun. When Carson started hiding from the world, she thought if he had a hobby other than sitting in his room playing video games and surfing for creepy shit on the internet, he'd start acting normal. She encouraged him to get into guns as much as she was into them."

"Didn't anybody tell her that was a bad idea?"

"God knows I tried. But Peggy wouldn't listen to me. She believed that guns protect us. Guns are a shield not a weapon. Guns are our God given right. You want my guns, try and take them. Second amendment. Second amendment. But guns didn't protect her. Carson took one of her precious guns and pumped three bullets into her brain while she was sleeping."

They passed a third gun poem.

TYRANTS AND CROOKS

LOVE GUN CONTROL

UNARMED VICTIMS

ARE THEIR GOAL

"That's fucked up," Skeeter said.

"I know, right? What kind of nut roll writes these poems and then goes to all the trouble to put them out on the highway?"

"I mean what happened to your mother."

"You think? On the day of the shooting, I went to her house to once again try to talk her into getting Carson some kind of treatment. But I was too late. I found her in her bedroom with her brains blown out. I was about to call the police when I saw Carson standing at her door. He smiled at me and said, 'You can't be the Beastmaster forever. But I'm the Beastmaster today'."

"What the hell does that mean?"

Nell sighed.

"I'm partly responsible," she said. "When I was sixteen, which would have made Carson thirteen, we were at the firing range. Carson was about to shoot his Beastmaster, his favorite rifle, and he said, 'I'm the Beastmaster.' I thought that was lame and decided to tease him. I said, 'You can't be the Beastmaster forever. Eventually, you have to go back to being Creepy Carson.' That was my mean big sister nickname for him. Creepy Carson. Instead of feeling the burn of my insult, the little idiot said, 'You can't be the Beastmaster forever. But I'm the Beastmaster today.' From then on, he said it every time he fired his favorite rifle. I think in his mind when he fired the Beastmaster, he became a Beastmaster, an instrument of destruction."

"That kind of makes sense."

"It's why I said the same thing before I started killing people in Vegas. When I walked onto the convention floor with a Beastmaster, I was the weapon. I was death."

Skeeter glanced at Nell and then stared ahead at the road.

"When Carson said those words to me," Nell said, "I knew he intended to shoot me dead."

"You're lucky you're still alive."

"I guess you could call it lucky. He shot me but he didn't kill me. He could have easily put a bullet in my brain like he did Peggy. Maybe he figured I would bleed out, so why waste the ammo?"

"You're an avenger because your little brother killed your mama. Sure. I get it."

Nell stared out the window.

"I don't think you do. After Carson killed those kids, the government should have changed the laws so that it would never happen again. All we got was thoughts and prayers."

"I remember the NRA saying we should do something about mentally ill people," Skeeter said.

Nell rolled her eyes.

"But not if that something meant keeping guns out of their hands. If the NRA put a penny of their blood-soaked profits into medical care for the mentally ill, I might take their concern seriously. Instead, they used the Red Clay shooting as another way to scare gun nuts into buying more guns."

Skeeter flinched from her intensity.

"You'd think dead kids would convince people not to buy a gun."

"Every school kid in America is scared some crazed loner is going to shoot them," Nell said. "Nothing is going to change until gun makers and gun lovers are just as scared as them."

"That don't make no sense. Gun lovers have guns. If a crazy person comes at them, they'll kill the wackadoodle."

"Guns didn't save Peggy from the wackadoodle."

They passed a fourth gun poem.

TELL YOUR SENATOR

WHEN HE RUNS

BAN THE CRIMINALS

NOT THE GUNS

"Those who profit from the sword should die by the sword," Nell said. "But they don't. They just keep making a profit while the rest of us live in fear. It's time for them to be afraid."

"Oh shit," Skeeter said. "I see where this is going."

"I want to scare the bejesus out of every gun maker and gun lover in America. I want them to know what it's like when a crazy loner comes to *their* place and starts shooting at *them*. And they can't stop me. Their guns won't save them. Because this bitch is bulletproof."

Skeeter groaned.

"So, Las Vegas. That was just the beginning."

"That's right. I plan to keep avenging every chance I get between here and Cleveland."

Skeeter pinched the bridge of his nose.

"You didn't tell me about this before you got in my truck."

"You only thought about Rafael. You didn't even consider my plans."

"I didn't agree to be party to a killing spree."

"You don't have to. You can drop me off right now and we'll go our separate ways."

Skeeter's knuckles were white from gripping the steering wheel.

"Let me think about it."

"Sure. You do that."

CHAPTER NINETEEN

FEW PEOPLE WOULD choose to prowl the Sonoran Desert at night. Especially if they were weighed down with military gear, carrying a fully loaded semi-automatic rifle, and facing potential danger with every step. Harry Pigott was one of those few people. He missed patrolling the border in search of illegal immigrants the same way some men miss complimenting a co-worker's breasts without having to worrying about her calling human resources.

The desert was colder than his ex-wife's heart, but Harry was sweating under his combat uniform, tactical vest, boots, and patrol cap. He held up his right hand. His squad of four militiamen stopped at his command.

"See something, Commander?" Kat asked.

When they were on duty, RAFF militiamen addressed Harry as Commander, and Kat as Mama Kat.

"Negative, Mama Kat," Harry said. "But I can feel them. They're nearby."

Harry swept the area with his flashlight. He passed a ravine and then brought the light back. A man wearing a ball cap rose like a gopher popping out of his hole.

Kat playfully punched Harry's shoulder.

"Haven't been on patrol in over a year and you can still sniff out the enemy like a hound dog."

More heads popped out of the ravine.

"Hey!" Harry shouted. "Get over here. *Ándale!*"

A group of brown-skinned men, women, and children trudged toward the RAFF militiamen.

"You getting this, Spider?" Harry asked.

Militiaman Grover Webb, addressed as Spider, followed the people with his camcorder. One of Grover's duties was to videotape the squad's patrols. Later, Grover would edit out the boring parts and download the video to RAFF's YouTube channel.

"Yes, sir," Grover said. "Got the whole family."

Armpit sweat stains on Grover's camo shirt spread to his man tits, and his face was shiny. He was overweight and sweated profusely even in air-conditioned spaces. But Harry overlooked his physical condition, because in civilian life, Grover was an engineer. The man knew a little something about everything and could fix just about anything.

When the thwarted fence jumpers got to the RAFF squad, Harry ordered them to sit on the ground. They always followed orders. Harry figured it was because the illegals saw RAFF militiamen, English-speaking Americans wearing combat uniforms with American flag patches on the sleeves carrying semi-automatic weapons, and assumed they were part of the U.S. border patrol.

Harry turned to Ron Murphy, addressed as Dutch.

"Dutch," Harry said. "Contact border patrol so that they can pick up these illegals."

"Yes, sir, Commander."

Ron was a seventy-eight-year-old Vietnam vet, making him RAFF's oldest militiaman. While he called the Tucson Sector of the United States Border Patrol, Kat spoke directly to the camcorder.

"Look at these kids here." She pointed at two boys wearing dirty T-shirts and jeans. "They aren't dressed properly for the rugged terrain. What kind of parent drags their children into a dangerous situation like this?"

A RAFF soldier moved next to Kat and glared at the camcorder. His name was Dale Klug and was addressed as Boomslang. Dale was a meathead, but he was young and in outstanding physical condition.

"The kids probably don't even belong to these people. They're probably using these kids as props."

One of the boys sneezed and wiped his nose with his sleeve.

"Did you see that?" Kat said. "They're not just bringing kids into a war zone, they're bringing sick kids. These boys could be carrying a disease that we've never seen in the United States."

"You mean, like we wouldn't have a cure for whatever is ailing them?" Dale asked.

"Exactly. This could be evidence of germ warfare by the drug cartels. Same as when the Colonists gave smallpox-infected blankets to the Indians."

Harry stifled a laugh. The sneezing kid most likely caught a head cold while hiking through the desert at night, but it was a decent scare tactic. Some of their viewers would buy it, but Harry doubted any of them would catch the unintentional irony of Kat comparing white people poisoning brown people with brown people poisoning white people.

"At ease, men," Harry said. "Let's take a breather while we wait for border patrol to arrive."

"Should I keep recording?" Grover asked.

"No. Turn it off. Save the battery."

Grover shut off the camcorder. Ron lit up a cigarette. Harry drank water from his canteen. Dale placed his hand on Kat's shoulder, wiggled his eyebrows, and jerked his head toward the ravine where the illegals had been hiding. She shook her head. He tried to put his arm around her waist, but she removed his hand and scowled at him. He got the message and bummed a cigarette from Ron. Kat stood in front of Commander.

"May I have a word in private with you, sir?" Kat asked.

"Certainly," Harry said. He turned toward Ron. "Dutch. Keep an eye on the illegals."

Ron blew out a cloud of smoke.

"Yes, sir, Commander."

Harry and Kat trudged three yards away from the others and clicked off their flashlights. It was so dark Harry could barely see Kat, but he could see millions of stars above them, another thing he missed about desert night patrols.

"Do these men meet your approval?" Kat asked.

The purpose of the recent night patrols wasn't just to hunt for immigrants trying to sneak into the country instead of getting in line and doing it legally. Spider, Boomslang, and Dutch were in Kat's opinion RAFF's best soldiers. But Harry wanted to evaluate them himself.

"Before I answer your question," Harry said. "I need you to answer mine."

"Certainly, Commander," Kat said.

"Did you choose Boomslang because he's one of RAFF's best soldiers, or because you're screwing him?"

Harry wished he could have seen Kat's expression.

"Can't he be both?" she asked.

Harry laughed.

"I suppose he can."

According to the RAFF rules Harry had written when he started the militia, sex between officers and enlisted personnel was forbidden. On the other hand, *The Art of War* states that a good leader bestows rewards without regard to rules. Besides, it was obviously too late for Commander to forbid Kat from sleeping with a man under her command.

"Does that mean Boomslang meets your approval?" Kat asked.

"That depends," Harry said. "What does Nancy Klug think about you sleeping with her husband?"

Kat hissed.

"It's not like we planned on hooking up. But things happen during wartime."

"I seem to recall Boomslang and Nancy have a young daughter. I can't remember the girl's name."

"Belle."

"I didn't happen to see her at base camp."

"Nancy left with Belle three months ago. Took Boomslang's car. I've been doing my best to keep him from worrying about them."

"I bet you have. Boomslang's in."

"Thank you, Commander!"

"Spider too. But not Dutch."

"Why not Dutch? He's the toughest bastard I know."

"He's too old and he smokes like a chimney."

As if on cue, Ron began to cough.

"We're already taking a chance with Spider," Harry said. "The man is one doughnut away from a heart attack."

"I did the best I could with what I had."

"I know you did."

Headlights came toward them. Border patrol had arrived. Harry and Kat rejoined the rest of the RAFF squad. Border patrol agents packed the illegals into the back of their vehicle.

"Hey, Commander," an agent said. "Good to see you again."

"Glad to see you too," Harry said.

After border patrol drove away, Harry ordered his men to return to base camp.

RAFF Base camp was a small village of tents, prefab cabins, yurts, and mobile homes. The air was smoky from campfires and cigarettes. The diesel-powered generators that provided the camp's electricity rumbled steadily. As Commander followed well-worn dirt paths, he was reminded of how much the RAFF Base Camp had shrunk. There were empty spaces between tents and cabins. Ruts in the ground, dirty clothes, and broken toys marked where a soldier's home had been.

"Stow your weapons and get cleaned up," Harry said to the squad. "We'll meet in the mess tent for chow."

The mess tent was the largest structure in the camp. The kitchen and serving line covered half the area and the double row of picnic tables covered the other half. Harry sat at the head table with Kat and Dale. As a Bulard Arms sales rep, Harry had been to many fancy four-star restaurants. But none of those meals could compare with the simple down-home-all-American goodness of tonight's hot dogs, baked beans, and homemade coleslaw. Something about being with fellow patriots, his true family, made everything taste better.

Harry washed down the last of his meal with a cold Budweiser and then stood. All talk stopped and everyone focused on him.

"It seems like only yesterday I first came to the Arizona border with camping equipment, a cache of weapons, twenty-one true patriots, their assorted family members, and a dream. A dream to restore the Constitution and stop the invasion of illegal immigrants pouring across the border into this blessed country of ours."

The diners applauded. Ron shouted, "Boo yeah!"

"There is nothing I'd rather do than stay here with you and continue making that dream come true. Sadly, I can't. I can't because recently I came face to face with evil. Not from over there." Harry pointed toward Mexico. "No. This evil came from within. It was disguised as a cute girl with a magnificent ass, but I wasn't fooled. She was pure evil. The evil one's name is Nell Slagle."

The diners grumbled and cursed the evil one's name.

"Nell Slagle is the reason I can't stay here with you. As long as she's free, our gun rights are in peril. We can't protect our border, our homes, or our freedom without our guns."

"Hell no!" Ron shouted. "They can have my gun when they pry it from my cold dead fingers."

"Nell Slagle is the reason I have a new mission. Mama Kat and I are going to track down that evil woman who almost killed me and show the nation what a good man with a gun can do."

Harry beamed as the diners hooted and hollered.

"Uh, Commander," Ron said, "if you and Mama Kat are leaving on this mission, then who's in charge while you're gone?"

"You are, Dutch," Harry said.

"Me?"

"I wouldn't give you this awesome responsibility if I didn't think you could handle it."

Ron puffed out his narrow chest and then had a coughing fit. When the cough subsided, militiamen shook his hand or saluted. With dinner over, kitchen staff gathered paper plates and cups. Cases of beer and bottles of booze were brought to the table. Maybe it was to wish Harry a successful mission or to celebrate Dutch's promotion, but one way or another RAFF was going to get drunk tonight.

The next morning, Harry stood next to his car and sipped hot coffee as he watched the sun rise over base camp. Kat stood beside Harry with her own cup of coffee. She wore a black tank top and tan cargo pants. Her short black hair was the same color as her tank top. Along with Kat's HISS and PURR knuckle tattoos, Harry could see the tattoo of a leaping cat holding a gun on her right forearm, and "We The People" over an American flag tattoo on her left. Her shirt covered her crossed pistols tramp stamp.

Harry had made sure not to overindulge last night. He had no desire to start the mission with a hangover. Kat had also limited her intake of alcohol. Dale and Grover had not taken the same precaution. They stumbled out of camp with bleary eyes and forlorn expressions. They dropped their duffel bags next to Harry's car.

"Izzat a Land Rover?" Dale asked.

"It's a Land Rover *Defender*," Harry said, placing his hand on the hood.

Grover wove toward Harry and faced him on unsteady feet.

His sweaty face had a greenish tint. If Grover puked on the interior of Harry's car, Harry was going to take out his hunting knife and gut the fat boy like a trout. He wouldn't really do it, but he would make Grover clean up his mess.

"I just want to say what an honor it is that you chose me to be on this special mission. I will not let you down," Grover said.

"Did you remember to pack the video gear?" Harry asked.

"Yes, sir. It's just, it's the only camera we have."

"Don't worry. If it breaks, we'll buy a replacement."

"Yes, sir. But what's Dutch going to do? He won't be able to make videos of his patrols."

"This mission has top priority and needs to be documented for prosperity. We'll return the camera after we have achieved our goal."

"Yes, sir."

Harry opened the Defender's trunk.

"Everyone gather 'round."

Kat, Grover, and Dale joined Harry. He slid four rifle cases out one at a time from the back of the car. Inside were Bulard Model 601 semi-assault rifles, Beastmasters, nestled in foam padding.

"Everybody take one," Harry said.

They removed the rifles from the cases and ran their hands over the cool metal.

"Hot damn!" Dale said. "A brand new Beastmaster."

"Wasn't there a movie by that name?" Grover asked.

"You got your phone. Look it up."

A quick search had Grover nodding his head.

"Yep. *The Beastmaster*. Came out in 1982. Marc Singer and Tanya Roberts."

"Oh yeah," Dale said. "I saw it on cable late at night. Tanya did a topless scene. Nice rack."

"I think she was a Bond girl." Grover consulted his phone. "Yep. A Bond girl and a Charlie's Angel."

"Excuse me," Harry said. "If you two are done playing Trivial Pursuit, can we get back to work here?"

Grover quickly put his phone back in its holster.

"Yes, sir."

"Yes, sir," Dale said.

"Spider," Harry said. "Get the camera out and set it up on the tripod. I want to record the mission's inaugural video."

Grover got to work. Dale sat on the ground and rested his back against the car. He soon dozed off. Kat gestured for Harry to step aside with her.

"Why did you get Beastmasters?" Kat asked. "There are other long guns just as good."

"Two reasons. One: my Bulard employee discount. Two: Nell's hot for the Beastmasters. I want her to die by her favorite gun."

"Speaking of Bulard, do they know about our mission?"

Harry spit on the ground.

"Hell, no."

Kat gnawed on her knuckle. Harry laughed.

"Don't worry about Bulard. They insisted on giving me six weeks FMLA leave to deal with my PTSD. Six weeks should give us plenty of time to find our target and eliminate it."

"But if Spider post videos of us hunting her on the RAFF YouTube channel, they're liable to find out."

Harry shook his head.

"Only true patriots watch us. I love working for Bulard,

but they are first and foremost a corporation. The only freedom they care about is the freedom to make money."

"But Commander, they will eventually find out."

"Yeah. When I put a bullet in Nell's head." Harry pointed his finger at his temple. "And then, they'll be offering me a promotion because I'll be a hero for stopping a crazed killer. With a Bulard gun."

Kat crossed her arms.

"You're taking a big risk, Commander."

Harry chuckled.

"Don't worry. It's better to beg forgiveness than ask for permission."

"I don't remember that being in *The Art of War*."

Harry put his arm around Kat's shoulder.

"Mama Kat, don't you trust me?"

"You know how much I trust you, Commander. But I can't help wondering…"

"How the hell are we going to find a fugitive when every cop in America can't find her?"

"Exactly."

Harry grinned.

"Because I know where the bitch is hiding."

Kat's eyes widened.

"Where? How? What the fuck?"

"Remember when I called you from the truck stop?"

"You were about to take Nell out, but then you said troopers detained you and she escaped."

"I didn't tell you the rest. I saw her leave with a truck driver named Skeeter Foote."

Kat stepped away from Harry.

"How do you know his name?"

"Bulard's been using Skeeter for years. He's reliable. I liked working with him and even broke bread with him a few times. When one of the other truckers told me that Skeeter used to smuggle illegals across the border, I didn't believe them. Not a good guy like Skeeter. I believe them now. I think he's got a hidden compartment in his truck."

Kat nodded.

"It makes sense. But wait. How are we going to find Skeeter? He could be anywhere."

Harry took a phone out of his pocket and showed Kat the GPS tracer app that he'd downloaded.

"See that moving dot? That's Skeeter. He's got a head start on us, but if we haul ass, we'll catch up with him in no time."

"How did you get this?"

"I got the Bulard truck dispatcher to give me Skeeter's GPS identification."

Kat looked around as if she expected a government agent to leap out and grab the phone.

"He just gave it to you?"

"The dispatcher is a member of RAFF. You remember Pops?"

Kat grinned.

"Good old Pops. How the hell is he?"

"He's finally gotten his diabetes under control. I gave him a direct order to give me Skeeter's GPS and to keep his mouth shut. Here. Take the phone. You're the navigator."

Kat took the phone from Harry and slipped it into her pocket.

"Commander," Spider called out. "Camera's ready."

"Excellent," Harry said. "Somebody wake up Boomslang."

Grover woke Dale up. He struggled to his feet, scratched

his stomach, and yawned. He joined Harry and Kat in front of the Land Rover. Grover started the video recording and hurried to stand next to Dale. All four cradled their Beastmasters in their arms.

Harry glared at the camcorder.

"I'm Harry Pigott, but you can call me Commander. I'm the commander of Real American Freedom Force. There is a mass murderer on the loose. The government would love to use the senseless spilling of innocent blood to take away our sacred Second Amendment rights. I will not stand by and let this happen. That isn't to say I'm not concerned about this monster on the loose. Quite the opposite. As a United States citizen with the legal right to carry a firearm, I plan to protect myself and my fellow countrymen and women. Me and my fellow members of RAFF are joining the hunt for Nell."

Kate, Grover, and Dale nodded vigorously. Harry continued.

"When we find her, we will not take the law into our own hands. If necessary, we will stand our ground and protect ourselves. The rifle we carry is not a weapon. It's a shield. A shield against killers and against tyranny. We don't take this mission lightly. But the saying is true. It takes a good man with a gun to stop a bad man with a gun. Or in this case, a bad girl with a gun."

"That's right," Dale said. "We're going to spank that bitch."

Harry pinched the bridge of his nose.

"Bees and scorpions carry poison."

"What does that mean?" Dale asked.

"Even a puny opponent shouldn't be treated with contempt."

"Huh?"

Kat put her hand Dale's shoulder.

"It's a lesson from *The Art of War*. Remember? I told you to read it."

"I'm not much of a reader," Dale said.

"I'll download the audiobook. You can listen to it in the car."

Grover held up his hand.

"I can edit that part out, Commander. You can pick up after 'bad girl with a gun.'"

"Okay," Harry said. "Picking up where I left off. Only this time, I talk and everybody else keeps their mouth shut." Harry pointed at the camcorder. "Nell Slagle. If you're watching. I'm coming for you. You might want to turn yourself in before I find you. That's all for now. God Bless America."

Harry and his squad continued to stare at the camcorder for a minute.

"Okay," Harry said. "That's a wrap. Let's load up. We got a killer to track down."

CHAPTER TWENTY

Easter and Zavala arrived in Philadelphia with cautious expectations. Drug addicts weren't known for their longevity. There was a chance that everyone who knew Nell when she'd lived here was deceased.

The special agents concentrated their search in the Kensington neighborhood. Despite the city's efforts to shut down the flow of drugs with more police patrols and more homeless shelters, there was no shortage of opioids, addicts, and despair in the neighborhood. Homeless people huddled under dirty blankets on the sidewalks. After a few fruitless inquiries, Easter and Zavala turned to the local police.

More than one patrolman told them that if anyone would remember a homeless person from years back, it would be Dolores Wilson. Her street name was Mother Hen because of the way she watched over her fellow addicts. Mother Hen had proved harder to kill than a cockroach, having survived living on the streets of Kensington for over a decade. An officer they spoke with knew Mother Hen was currently living in one of the city's homeless shelters but wasn't sure which one.

The shelters were protective of their residents' identities. Easter and Zavala couldn't simply call and ask if Dolores was staying there. They had to go to the shelters and show their FBI badges to whomever was managing the facility. Starting with the shelters in Kensington proper, they worked their way out.

They found Mother Hen at the ninth shelter they visited. Mercy Hospice was in Washington Square West near an Episcopal Church and red brick row houses. The door was locked. They rang the doorbell. A minute later, a woman with short spiky hair answered. Easter and Zavala's dark suits made it obvious that they weren't looking for a hot meal and a clean room.

"Can I help you?" the woman asked.

"We'd like to speak to the shelter director," Zavala said.

"Is there a problem?"

The special agents had been dealing with this kind of paranoia from shelter workers all day. They assured her that there was nothing to worry about, and she led them to a small office where a woman was talking on her phone. She covered the receiver with her hand.

"I'll be right with you."

Easter and Zavala sat on plastic chairs. A name plate on the desk told them that the woman's name was Jennifer and that her title was program director. She continued talking as if they weren't there. Easter picked up that the conversation had something to do with an upcoming fundraiser. He'd heard similar conversations at some of the other shelters they'd visited. When it appeared that this discussion wasn't going to end anytime soon, Easter took out his FBI badge and held it in front of Jennifer's face. To her credit, she didn't panic.

"I have to go," Jennifer said. "I'll call you back later."

She hung up the phone and stared at them.

"I'm Special Agent Easter and this is Special Agent Zavala," Easter said. "We need to ask you a few questions."

"Is there a problem?"

"Do you have a Dolores Wilson staying here?"

Jennifer chewed her lower lip as if she were trying to prevent any words from escaping her mouth.

"Is Mother Hen in trouble?"

"We just want to ask her some questions," Easter said.

Jennifer's gnawed on her lower lip some more.

"She's here."

"We've been all over the city, so don't tease me," Zavala said. "Is she's really here?"

"She's been here for three months and has been doing quite well. We're helping her transition to a more permanent home."

"Our questions will have no impact on her plans."

The phone rang, but Jennifer ignored it.

"Mother Hen is in her room."

"Good," Easter said. "We won't be long."

"The thing is…she's not alone."

Easter and Zavala glanced at each other.

"A roommate or a lover?" Zavala asked.

Jennifer giggled.

"Neither. A reporter. Seems everybody wants to talk to Mother Hen today."

"You left her alone with a reporter?" Easter asked.

Jennifer scowled.

"Normally, we wouldn't. But Mother Hen is a special case."

"Meaning you trust her," Zavala said.

"Completely."

"How long has the reporter been talking to her?" Easter asked.

"I'm not sure. Fifteen, twenty minutes. We can go up there and see if she's done."

Jennifer led them through the house. The place was tidy and brightly lit as if they were visiting a nice family home. They passed a living room where children of various ages watched cartoons. They climbed a staircase to the second floor and followed a narrow hallway to the last room. The door was open. Inside were two beds and a dresser. Sitting on the bed closest to the window was a thin woman wearing a gray sweatshirt and jeans. Sitting on the other bed was a Black woman wearing stylish eyeglasses. She had an open notebook on her lap. Jennifer knocked on the door. Both women looked up.

"Hello, Ms. Jennifer," the thin woman said. "Don't tell me these people are also here to see me?"

"You're very popular today, Mother Hen," Jennifer said. "This is Mr. Easter and Ms. Zavala. They're with the FBI."

"Dani?" Zavala asked. "Dani Lewis?"

The Black woman smiled.

"Why if it isn't Agent Zavala and Agent Easter. I'm surprised you remember me. I know you two talk to a lot of reporters."

"What are you doing here?" Easter asked.

"Same thing you're doing. Getting background information on Nell Slagle."

Easter did his best to hide his annoyance that a reporter had located a potential source before the FBI did.

"We're sorry to interrupt, but we need to speak with Ms. Wilson," Easter said.

Lewis closed her notebook and stood.

"That's okay. We were just finishing our conversation." She turned to Wilson. "Thank you for your time, Mother Hen."

"Have a blessed day," Wilson said.

As soon Lewis left the room, Easter and Zavala entered.

"Do you prefer to be called Dolores or Mother Hen?" Easter asked.

"Only my friends call me Mother Hen," Wilson said. "You can call me Dolores."

Despite the less than friendly response, Dolores never lost her smile.

"Okay, Dolores," Easter said. "We'd like to ask you a few questions."

"Let me see your badges."

Easter and Zavala showed Wilson their badges.

"My roommate won't be back for a while," she said. "You can sit on her bed."

Zavala turned to Jennifer.

"Thank you for your help. We'll take it from here."

Jennifer left. Zavala closed the door. As the agents sat side by side on the roommate's bed, Easter noticed that the beds were perfectly made with the corners tightly tucked in. The two pairs of shoes on the floor were lined up neatly and brightly polished. Dolores sat with straight posture. Some habits were hard to kill.

"What branch were you in?" Easter asked.

Dolores's smile disappeared. She looked at Easter as if he'd just unleashed a big smelly fart in her personal space. He didn't think it was because of the fierce rivalry between the Army and the Marines. More likely she didn't care to discuss her military service.

"Army. 528th Brigade."

"How long?"

"Eight years. And you?"

"Marines. Third Battalion. The Thundering Third."

Zavala jammed her elbow into Easter's side and pointed at a tattered paperback on the dresser.

"Look!" Zavala said.

Easter glanced at the book and did a double take. It was a cowboy romance novel. On the cover, a hot woman wearing a black lace bra and tight jeans embraced a hunk wearing tight jeans, a cowboy hat, and a denim shirt. The shirt was unbuttoned to show off his washboard abs. His face was covered with red and white greasepaint, he had a red rubber ball on his nose, and he wore a bright red cowboy hat. The title was *Not My First Rodeo Clown*.

"Somebody donated a big box of romance novels to the shelter," Wilson said. "I've been eating them up like candy."

"I've read that one," Zavala said. "It's by my favorite author."

Wilson's smile returned.

"Katie Kemp is the best."

"I could spend the whole day talking about her books," Zavala said.

"But we can't," Easter said. "We need to ask you about Nell Slagle."

Wilson nodded. Though her skin was rough and creased from years living outdoors, she had a fierce beauty.

"I saw on the news what she did in Las Vegas."

"How did you know Nell Slagle?" Easter asked.

"We were both in Emerald City."

"That's a homeless camp, right?"

"It was, until the city tore it down."

"What can you tell us about her?"

Wilson closed her eyes, breathed in, and held her breath. Then she exhaled and opened her eyes.

"She was high most of the time, slumped in her wheelchair like a boneless chicken."

"What about when she wasn't high?"

"Sweetest girl I've ever known. Never had a mean thing to say about anybody. I liked her. Tried to keep an eye on her best I could."

"Did she ever talk about herself?"

Wilson gazed out the window.

"Not at first. Whatever happened in her life hurt so bad she couldn't put it into words."

"But she started talking eventually," Easter said.

Wilson faced the special agents.

"She told me her daddy died in a car wreck."

The death of Nell's father, Russ Slagle, was not news to Easter and Zavala. It was in their briefing. Because Russ was the father of a mass shooter, his obituary made national news along with editorials about how much he knew about his son's mental illness and steps he should have taken.

"Was Nell close to her father?" Easter asked.

"I don't think so," Wilson said. "She said before her daddy died, she got her pills through his insurance. Then after he died, she had to pay for them on her own. That's how she ended up spending her life savings chasing her next fix."

"What about her mother?"

"She told me what her brother did in Cleveland. She felt bad about not doing enough to stop him but what really broke her heart was that she wasn't able to save her momma. I could see it in her eyes, the guilt was eating her up."

"She blamed herself for her mother's death?"

Wilson nodded.

"She wished she had taken her mother's guns away and buried them before they could be used to put somebody in a grave. That's why her killing those people in Las Vegas makes no sense. Nell hated guns. She hated gun makers. She said they buy politicians to make sure people like Carson can shoot people like those poor kids."

Zavala leaned forward.

"It sounds like Nell really opened up to you."

Wilson shrugged.

"Not really. She only talked about guns once and only because I tried to give her one."

"Is that something you did often?" Easter asked. "Give guns to homeless people."

Wilson shook her head.

"It wasn't like that. Nell had some trouble. I wanted her to be able to protect herself in case trouble came around again. But she turned me down."

"What sort of trouble did Nell have?" Zavala asked.

"When people live like animals, they tend to act like animals. That's all I have to say about it."

"Do you remember the last time you saw Nell?" Easter asked.

"Yes, sir. I do. Men in white coveralls were putting her on a bus along with nineteen other homeless people from Emerald City. All of them were my friends and when the bus drove away, I knew I'd never see any of them again."

"Did the men in white coveralls say where they were taking them?" Easter asked.

Wilson glared at him.

"Hell no. The government is always trying to make the homeless go away. So, when some company shows up with a line of bullshit about how they need volunteers for a clinical trial, it's pretty damn obvious that Philly gave them permission to use us as lab rats."

The room felt stuffy. Easter wished he could open a window.

"You're right. That's exactly what they did."

Wilson leveled her eyes at Easter.

"Thank you for being honest."

"I'm sorry I can't tell you more."

"I begged Nell not to go. But she was promised room and board. A chance to get clean."

"Did they make the same offer to you?"

"I turned them down. In the Army, you learn to never volunteer for shit."

Zavala nudged Easter. It was her signal to let him know that she felt they had gotten all the information they could possibly get from Mother Hen. He agreed.

"Thank you for your time," Easter said. "We won't intrude on you any longer."

"You can get back to your book," Zavala said. "Though I could tell you how it ends."

"Don't you dare," Dolores said.

CHAPTER TWENTY-ONE

WHEN EASTER AND Zavala stepped out of Mercy Hospice, Dani Lewis was across the street waiting for them.

"Just pretend she isn't there," Zavala said.

"That's going to be hard to do," Easter said. "She's waving at us."

"I'm sure Mother Hen told Dani how Nell left Philadelphia. Dani's a reporter. She's not going to give up until she finds out who took Nell, where they took her, and how it connects to what Nell is doing now."

"If and when she finds out it won't be because we told her."

"In that case, let's go say hello."

Zavala waved at Lewis. The reporter crossed the street.

"Have time for a cup of coffee?" Lewis said. "There's a coffee shop a block from here."

"We can't tell you anything pertaining to Nell Slagle," Zavala said. "And anything we say about anything is off the record. If that's okay with you, then sure, we'd love some coffee."

Lewis pointed north. "The coffee shop is that way."

"I'm impressed the Cleveland Daily Banner sent you to Philadelphia for this story," Easter said.

Lewis made a face that was somewhere between a grin and a grimace.

"I'm not with the Banner anymore. I work for the Washington Post."

"The Post!" Zavala said. "I'm impressed."

Lewis shrugged.

"My series on the Red Clay Middle School shooting was nominated for a Pulitzer for investigative reporting. I didn't win, but the nomination caught the attention of the Post."

The coffee shop was a hipster's paradise, with graffiti-covered walls, tables with mis-matched chairs, and vegan baked goods. The sour scent of coffee dominated the place. There were only few customers scattered about hunched over their laptops. Easter, Zavala, and Lewis got coffee in fat ceramic cups and settled at a corner table.

Lewis emptied two packets of sugar into her cup.

"Is there any truth to the stories that were obviously planted on social media?"

"Which stories?" Easter asked.

Lewis stirred her coffee and took a sip.

"The ones where either China, Russia, or North Korea removed the bullet from Nell's back, trained her to be an America-hating assassin, and then let her loose in Las Vegas to start a race war."

"We already said we can't talk about Nell Slagle."

"That doesn't mean we can't talk about what other people are saying about her."

Easter glanced at Zavala.

"I believe those stories are just conspiracy theories," Easter said.

Lewis grinned.

"I just won a bet at the office. What about the bullet moving on its own, Nell doing self-physical therapy to walk again, and suffering whatever mental illness plagued her brother?"

"I suppose it's possible."

"Is it possible to give me some clue as to where the men in white coveralls took Nell along with the other homeless people? Or who removed the bullet from her spine and got her walking again? Or where the hell she got the body armor?"

Easter sipped his coffee. It was strong, just the way he liked it.

"What part of we can't talk about Nell Slagle did you not understand?" he said.

"Admit it," Lewis said. "The Pentagon is behind this."

Easter almost reacted but managed to keep a neutral look on his face. Zavala looked out the window.

"Is it clouding up?" Zavala asked. "I hope it doesn't rain."

Lewis crossed her arms.

"The last time I saw Nell, she was an emotional and physical wreck. I tried to get her some help, but her addiction was too strong. The young lady who showed up in Las Vegas was in top physical condition and could drive a tank. She had to have had military training."

Easter was impressed. Lewis had almost figured everything out. The main thing she missed was that Nell was bulletproof.

"Sounds like you have your own conspiracy theory," Easter said.

Lewis glared at the special agents.

"Give me time. I'll prove it's more than a conspiracy theory."

The sun streamed through the shop windows. There was no sign of rain. Americana music played softly in the background.

"How did you know about Mother Hen?" Lewis asked.

"I was going to ask you the same question," Easter said.

"I tried to keep in contact with Nell after the shooting. I knew she moved here, and I meant to come check on her, but I never did."

"I didn't realize that journalists stayed in touch with the siblings of mass shooters."

"It's not unusual to check in on those affected by the shooting from time to time to see how they're adjusting. But Nell was a special case because the world didn't want anything to do with her. I intended to do an in-depth profile of her as the forgotten victim."

One of the reasons the Bureau assigned this case to Easter and Zavala was because they had handled the Red Clay shooting. The Bureau assumed that the special agents' prior experience with Nell Slagle gave them a better perspective on how to track her down. But Easter and Zavala barely remembered Nell. They had dealt with so many mass shooting survivors with shattered lives that they all blended together.

"You said you intended to write the profile," Zavala said. "That implies you never wrote it."

"My editor turned it down." Lewis frowned. "Maybe you can't talk about Nell, but I can. Two months after the shooting, the city of Cleveland held a candlelight vigil for the nineteen students and four adults that Carson murdered. I covered the story for the Banner."

Candlelight vigils. Easter had never attended them.

"Please don't tell me that Nell went to the vigil," Zavala said.

Lewis cut her eyes at Zavala.

"Don't get ahead of me. Nell tried to attend. She should have known better. I blame the pain meds. She wasn't thinking clearly at the time."

"She would've needed help getting to the park," Easter said. "Who took her?"

"A hospital volunteer named Mavis Gathercole. She believed that the powerful love of Jesus healed all spiritual wounds, and she convinced Nell to go."

"How did she get permission to take Nell out?" Zavala asked.

"She didn't. Nell was in a busy hospital. Nobody noticed what Mavis was doing."

Easter had met plenty of people like Mavis Gathercole during his years with the FBI, people with loads of good intentions and zero common sense.

"Mavis got there late," Lewis said. "I was talking to attendees, getting their reactions to the speeches, when I spotted Mavis and Nell at the back of the crowd. Turned out the vigil's organizers saw them too. They sent a woman named Valerie to deal with it. Valerie and I got to them at the same time."

"How ugly was it?" Zavala asked.

"Maybe it would have been better if Valerie had demanded that they leave at once. Instead, Valerie was very polite. She explained that the people at the vigil were honoring loved ones they'd lost to senseless violence."

"That would include Nell, since she'd lost her mother."

"Yes. And no. Valerie told her that having the sister of the man who killed their children there was too upsetting. She asked Nell to leave out of respect to the victims' families."

"She must have wanted to curl up and die."

"I dropped by the hospital after the vigil. Nell refused to

talk about what happened. As for Mavis, the hospital dismissed her for taking a patient out without authorization."

"What's the moral of the story?"

"Nell got screwed by everybody. And nobody bought her dinner."

"There's her motive for the convention center shooting."

Lewis shook her head.

"I don't buy it. No matter how much hurt or rage Nell is carrying inside, the last thing she'd want to do is become a murderer like Carson. Somebody did something to her brain that turned her into a killing machine."

Easter realized that he hadn't completely understood Nell's reason for killing until now. Maybe he expected something more complicated, but it was really quite simple. In fact, she had stated her motive to Kassie Arrowsmith.

"Nell believes that those who profit from the sword should die by the sword," Easter said.

Lewis wrinkled her nose.

"I remember reading that in the police report. I think Nell was just being flip."

"I think she meant it," Easter said. "Nell blames gun makers and gun lovers for ruining her life."

"Peggy loved guns. Does that mean Nell blames her mother as well?"

"Maybe."

Lewis scowled.

"No way. Nell was crushed that she wasn't able to go to Peggy's funeral. In fact, the last time I spoke to her she said she felt bad that she never visited her mother's grave."

Easter felt the penny drop. He had no idea where Nell was at this moment, but he knew where she was going.

CHAPTER TWENTY-TWO

With shears in hand, Nell gazed at her reflection in the bathroom mirror. The ideal American girl; long blonde hair, blue eyes, button nose, and a few stray freckles, stared back at her.

"Goodbye, ideal American girl."

Nell snipped off a strand of hair and dropped it into the sink. The last time she'd tried to cut her own hair she was nine years old and created bald spots on the side of her head. Peggy had freaked. An emergency trip to a beauty salon couldn't repair the damage, and Nell was forced to wear a hat for weeks.

This time, Nell wet and combed her hair. She used her fingers to determine a straight line and checked the results with each snip of the shears. When she was done, she had a chin length bob that wasn't quite even all over but close enough, and a sink full of damp blonde hair. She was pleased at how different she looked, and she hadn't even gotten to the coloring.

On the bathroom counter were a hair dye kit, an eyebrow tinting kit, Vaseline, shampoo, and towels. She still couldn't believe that Skeeter had gotten everything she asked for. Not only that, he'd given her one of his old T-shirts to wear during the dyeing process. It had a few holes, and the bottom hem came down to her knees. He claimed he was going to throw it out, so this way Nell wouldn't ruin her only shirt by getting hair dye on it.

Nell wished she could destroy her only shirt. She was sick of wearing the same thing every day. She thought she'd have an opportunity to steal or buy more clothes as she made her way to Cleveland. But it didn't work out that way. All that would change once she dyed her hair. Different hair was as almost as good a disguise as a maid's uniform.

Nell rubbed Vaseline around her forehead, neck, and ears. She slipped on the clear plastic gloves that came with the kit before squirting the tube of hair dye into a dispenser bottle that already contained a white substance. After a few shakes of the bottle, Nell squirted the black goo down the roots of her hair. She mashed it in and then continued squirting and mashing until her hair was black sticky spikes.

The color would take thirty minutes to set, so Nell took off the plastic gloves and left the bathroom. Sitting still in a hotel room by herself was a luxury after days of traveling.

There was a box of hot and spicy cheese crackers on the bedside table. While Skeeter had remembered everything on Nell's hair dye list, he had forgotten to get her regular flavor cheese crackers. When she asked him why he always got the flaming hot crackers, he'd replied that he liked crackers with a bite to them.

Nell's stomach growled. She snacked on the crackers and picked up where she'd left off in her romance novel. On the cover was a muscular carpenter holding a hammer over his crotch. The title of the book was *You Got Nailed*.

Skeeter had given her the paperback. They had been at a

truck stop with a laundry room. As Skeeter gathered his dirty clothes, he offered to clean Nell's clothes as well.

"All I have are the clothes on my back," Nell said.

"Which are starting to get pretty rank."

"You're not freaked out about having to handle my underwear?"

"I used to do the laundry when I was married to Edie. Handling bras and panties was just part of the job."

Nell had covered herself with a blanket before stripping off her sweat-stained clothes. She hadn't cared if Skeeter had seen her naked. She could have easily broken his arm if he tried to touch her. But there was no reason to give him any ideas.

Skeeter was only gone for ten minutes when he returned.

"You're done already?" Nell asked.

"I found this in the laundry room." Skeeter handed her the romance novel. "There's nobody in there, so it was probably left behind. I thought you might want it. To help pass the time."

"Thank you, Skeeter. That was mighty thoughtful of you."

"It's just a book."

It wasn't just a book. Or an old T-shirt. Or stopping for the night at a hotel in Trinidad, Colorado so that Nell could dye her hair in private. Skeeter had been mighty considerate toward Nell ever since she told him of her intentions to continue terrorizing those who profit from the sword. She worried that he was softening her up to say goodbye.

When thirty minutes had passed, Nell went back to the bathroom, got into the shower, and washed out the dye. She was afraid her hair would smell like chemicals, but something in the formula gave it a clean scent. She dried her hair, leaving black splotches on the towel. In the mirror, a woman with short black hair stared back at her.

"Hello, stranger. You new in town? Have you seen that horrible Nell Slagle around? If you do, run away."

Nell reluctantly put on her T-shirt and paisley yoga pants. At least now she could go into a store and buy something new. She stepped out onto the walkway and knocked on the door to the next room. Skeeter answered. She could tell from his expression that he didn't recognize her at first. That was exactly the response that she had hoped for. Nell ran her hand through the shortened strands.

"My new disguise. What do you think?"

"It's really black. Like punk rock black."

"I'll take that as a compliment."

The Andy Griffith Show was on the TV in Skeeter's room. Deputy Barney Fife threatened to put his single bullet into his gun. Skeeter picked up the remote and turned off the set.

"With your hair like that," Skeeter said, "we could go out to dinner."

The idea of eating in a restaurant with real utensils, and not huddled in the cab scarfing food from a Styrofoam clamshell like a squirrel eating nuts inside a tree filled Nell with joy.

"Let's do it."

Skeeter pouted, which was very unattractive on a man of his advanced years.

"I don't want to take the truck out tonight. It was hard enough getting to this place in full daylight."

They were at a Days Inn at the end of a dirt road in a hilly residential area on the outskirts of downtown Trinidad. Most of the rooms faced a lovely mountain range which Nell couldn't name if her life depended on it. Skeeter had chosen the hotel because they gave him a trucker's discount and provided parking for eighteen wheelers.

The hotel must have been aware of how hard it was for trucks to get here because there was a stack of take-out menus next to the TV. Skeeter flipped through them and held up two menus.

"Tex Mex or pizza?"

"Before we decide on dinner, there's something we have to talk about," Nell said. "Something we've been putting off that we can't put off any longer."

Skeeter sat on the bed. He looked deflated.

"I suppose you're right."

"When you were doing the laundry the other day, you left your phone in the truck. I used it to search the internet."

Skeeter gawked at Nell.

"How'd you figure out my pass code?"

Nell rubbed her fingers together.

"I told you how when I touch a machine, I can instantly operate it. It's like the machine tells me all its secrets. Including pass codes."

"You shouldn't have done that."

"On the list of things I should not have done breaking into your phone is near the bottom. I found a gun show that's happening three days from now in Longview, Texas."

"Did you, now?"

"It's on the way to Tennessee."

Skeeter stared at the two menus as if the answer he was looking for was listed among the entrees.

"I told you this is what I was going to do," Nell said.

"That you did."

"You still haven't made up your mind, have you?"

"I said I'd think about it."

"In three days, I'm going to be at the gun show in Longview whether you take me there or not."

Skeeter put the menus on the nightstand.

"You already killed a lot of people in Las Vegas."

Nell carried a straight back chair over so that she could sit facing Skeeter.

"It wasn't enough. Honeydew turned me into a weapon. Instead of them pointing me at their enemies, I have an opportunity to point myself at *my* enemies."

"You got a right to be angry, but that doesn't mean you get to decide who deserves to die."

Nell looked into Skeeter's eyes.

"You decided that Rafael Vargas deserves to die."

Skeeter looked away.

"I know where Longview is. We got time to go to Austin first."

"Why Austin?"

"I figured you'd want new clothes to go with your new hair. It's a good place for that. And I should have an answer by then."

"Okay. Let's go to Austin. But first, let's order Tex Mex."

CHAPTER TWENTY-THREE

Easter and Zavala returned to Las Vegas and checked back into Hampton Inn near McCarran International Airport. With no fresh leads on Nell's location, the special agents intended to go over the case from the beginning to see if they had missed anything.

Easter put his suitcase and briefcase on the bed, turned on the TV and surfed until he found a news channel. Handsome news anchor Walt Williams stared at the camera with practiced gravitas.

"As the hunt for Nell Slagle continues, the debate over gun control heats up," Williams said. "The longer Slagle remains at large, the more demand there is from gun control groups for new gun legislation."

Video of a gun control rally marching down a city street came on the screen. Marchers held signs with anti-gun slogans like "Remove Guns Reduce Death" and "How Many More?"

Williams came back on the screen.

"While anti-gun groups point to Slagle and other mass shooters as proof of the need for more gun restrictions, in an odd twist, phone videos of Slagle from the Las Vegas shooting have gone viral and have turned her into a sort of bizarre folk hero for some anti-gun supporters. Here are those amateur videos. You can decide for yourself. Warning. Some of the content is disturbing."

Easter turned up the sound as the screen cut to a cellphone video. Nell burst through double doors onto the convention floor with a rifle in her hands and another rifle slung over her shoulder.

"You can't be the Beastmaster forever!" Nell shouted. "But I'm the Beastmaster today!"

The way Nell opened fire on the convention crowd, it was a miracle the person who recorded the video survived. The video ended and a second one began.

Nell stalked past dead bodies. She stopped and swung the rifle directly at a woman crouched behind a booth. Easter recognized Kassie Arrowsmith, the Bulard Arms booth model.

"Please don't shoot me!" Kassie yelled as she held hands over her head.

Nell pointed the rifle away from Kassie.

"Damn it, Kassie. I almost shot you."

"What the hell are you doing?"

"I'm making sure people who profit from the sword die by the sword."

The person recording the video panicked and the scene shook as they ran away. The screen cut back to Williams.

"We spoke to some individuals who claim they were inspired by the video."

The screen cut to a reporter at the anti-gun rally talking to a protester who looked to be in her twenties, had purple hair, and many tattoos. A graphic at the bottom of the screen identified her as Saffron Winer.

"The gun lobby is a terrorist organization," Saffron said. "Gun lovers give the gun lobby money, so that makes them terrorists too. Nell is fighting terrorism."

"But she's killing innocent people," the reporter said. "How do you justify that?"

Saffron shrugged.

"Nell said it perfectly. Those who profit from the sword should die by the sword. The people at that death merchant convention, the ones she killed, they weren't innocent. They got what they deserved."

Easter's phone rang just as the screen cut to a reporter talking to a young man with an elaborate beard and a wool cap. He too was inspired by the viral video. Easter muted the sound. He looked at his phone and saw that it was Zavala.

"I was watching the news and saw videos of Nell."

"Me too. How it is that we're just now seeing them?"

"People would rather get their video on TV than help the police."

"That thing she said about the Beastmaster. Those were the exact words Carson Slagle said before the massacre at Red Clay Middle School."

"Those who profit from the sword die by the sword. She didn't get that from Carson."

On the TV, the Nell-loving hipster dude interview had been replaced with footage of a pro-gun rally. People stood in front of a government building holding signs with pro-gun slogans like "Keep American Armed" and "With Guns We are Citizens. Without Them We are Slaves."

"Come to my room when you're ready then we'll go to lunch," Easter said.

He hung up and turned the sound back on. Walt Williams was interviewing a pro-gun protester who claimed Nell Slagle was a Democrat socialist who wanted to take away his guns and his freedom. Zavala arrived at Easter's room just as the network went to a commercial for Life Insurance.

"How did the sweet, non-violent Nell described by Dolores Wilson and Dani Lewis become the avenging, fully armed Nell we saw in those viral videos?" Zavala asked.

"The Nell that Wilson and Lewis knew was powerless. When a person doesn't have power and then gets power, they tend to use it a lot. Often, they revel in it."

"By that logic, Las Vegas was just the beginning. She's going to strike again."

"And there's nothing we can do but wait until she does."

Zavala rubbed her chin.

"I don't think she's lying low. She's on the move."

"How? Every trooper in the country is on the lookout for her."

"Somebody is helping her. Once we find out who it is, they'll lead us to Nell."

CHAPTER TWENTY-FOUR

Harry Pigott had planned to avoid alcohol. He had wanted to stay sharp and focused on RAFF's tracking down and obliterating the demoness known as Nell Slagle. But here he was in a Quality Inn's hotel bar with a gin and tonic in his hand. It was Kat and Dale's fault. And partly Harry's. He had booked three rooms, and had taken the room next to theirs. After a delightful dinner at the Tequila Family Mexican Restaurant, Harry had given the squad orders to retire early so that they would be fresh and rested when they hit the road in the morning.

Kat and Dale had disobeyed Harry's orders. As soon as they were in their room, they started having sex. After listening to hours of banging and squeaking, moaning and groaning, and shout outs to God and Jesus, Harry gave up trying to go to sleep and decided to get a drink. He could have knocked on Kat and Dale's door and ordered them to stop but decided that there must be something in the *Art of War* about a leader allowing his troops to copulate like crazed weasels.

The bar was close enough to the hotel's indoor pool that chlorinated water burned Harry's eyes and shouting children scorched his ears. Harry was determined to enjoy his beverage, so he ignored these distractions as best he could and savored the smooth taste of gin.

Another distraction to ignore was Grover. He was supposed to be in his room asleep same as Kat and Dale. Instead, he was in the jacuzzi next to the pool wearing only a pair of denim shorts, his mounds of pale skin making him look like a giant dumpling boiling in water.

Even though Harry's soldiers had disobeyed his orders, he wasn't going to punish them for their insubordination. They'd had a rough start to their journey, which was why Harry had decided to stay at a hotel for the night. They needed a moment to recuperate.

Following Skeeter's GPS signal had proven harder and more time consuming than Harry had anticipated. Skeeter took back roads through remote areas of the country that Harry never dreamed existed. As Harry's Land Rover climbed over treacherous mountains and rumbled down dirt roads, he wondered how in the hell Skeeter's eighteen-wheeler managed to get through these parts.

And then there were the numerous times that Skeeter's GPS signal simply disappeared, because after all they were in middle of fucking nowhere. Harry had to keep going on faith that a satellite would pick up his signal again, and often when it did, he discovered that Skeeter had taken another side road and Harry had to double back.

They rolled into Trinidad mere hours after Skeeter left town. Harry thought about pushing on, but part of staying sharp and focused included getting some decent rest. Which he had had every intention of doing until Kat and Dale's rutting had driven him down here to the bar.

He swallowed the remainder of his gin and tonic and ordered another one. A baseball game on the TV mounted over the bar drew his attention. A batter struck out and glared at the pitcher on his way to the dugout.

His phone rang. It was a number he didn't recognize. He would have ignored the call, but it might be a RAFF soldier calling to inform him that Dutch had dropped dead.

"Harry Pigott?" It was a woman's voice.

"Yeah. What do you want?"

"My name is Dani Lewis. I'm a reporter with the Washington Post."

"How'd you get my number?"

"I'm a reporter with the Washington Post."

The waiter placed a fresh drink in front of Harry and took his empty glass.

"I don't talk to the lamestream media."

Dani laughed.

"Of course, you do. Otherwise, you would have already hung up on me."

Harry took a sip of his gin and tonic. And he didn't hang up.

"I've already told you vultures that I don't want to talk about what went down at the convention center."

"That's not why I called."

"Really?"

"I recently discovered Real American Freedom Force's YouTube videos pertaining to your hunt for Nell Slagle."

Harry groaned. Kat had warned him this might happen, and now she was going to give him no end of shit for it. Of course some reporter stumbled across his videos. They were online where any fool could find them.

"How did I look? Did I remember to stand up straight and speak clearly?"

"You have excellent screen presence, Commander," Lewis said. "May I ask you some questions?"

As Harry downed the rest of his drink, he considered his options. He could end the conversation now. But that wouldn't stop Lewis from doing a story about his mission and using RAFF's YouTube videos as source material to advance her liberal agenda against true patriots like himself.

"Depends on the question."

"You only have to answer what you're comfortable answering."

Then again, if Harry answered a few questions, maybe he could get her to see that he and his men were concerned citizens helping the cops catch a dangerous criminal and not a bunch of inbred hillbillies.

"Okay. Let's do this thing."

"Do I have your permission to record our conversation?"

"You have a nice voice. You ever consider doing radio?"

"Thank you. Do I have your permission?"

"Sure."

"How's the search going?"

Harry watched a young mother and her daughter walk away from the pool in wet bathing suits with towels wrapped around their waists. The mother's breasts were almost as big as Jolene's.

"Don't you want to ask me why we're willing to get off our couches, spend our own money, and hit the road to find this killer who's terrorizing our nation?"

"You stated your reasons in your first video. In later videos, you always state where you are and how close you are to Nell."

The waiter came by and pointed at Harry's empty glass. Harry nodded.

"I like to keep the viewers abreast of our progress."

"I'm sure they appreciate it. Mr. Pigott, this is a big country. Nell could be anywhere. Yet you give the impression that you know exactly where she is at all times. Do you really know, or are you just telling your viewers that to keep them watching your YouTube channel?"

The young mother and her daughter passed by again, this time headed toward the pool. They each carried soda cans and bags of chips. Harry noticed that the mother's ass was wider than Jolene's, but that wasn't necessarily a bad thing.

"Are you suggesting that I'm lying to my viewers?"

"Not lying. But maybe exaggerating a bit?"

"Now, lookie here, Miss Bigshot Reporter. I'm sure you did a Google search on me and know that when I'm not saving America, I sell guns. I'm damn good at my job. I could sell shit to an asshole. But on those RAFF videos, I'm not selling anything. I'm telling the God's honest truth to my fellow patriots."

"So, you do know Nell's location? And if you do, why haven't you shared this information with law enforcement?"

The waiter brought Harry his third gin and tonic. This had to be the last one if he was going to be in any shape to drive first thing in the morning.

"You know I was in the room when she killed those two police officers."

"You said earlier that you didn't want to talk about that day at the convention center."

"I feel like talking about it now."

"If you're willing, I would love to hear about it. Please continue."

Harry sipped his drink. The alcohol was buzzing in his head.

"She used my shirt to wipe the officers' blood off her face."

"I know. I read the police report."

"Did the report mention that the security guard shoot her four times point blank in the chest and that she shook it off like it was nothing?"

"It did. There's been a lot of speculation about how she managed to survive, but nobody knows for certain. Since you were an eyewitness, do you know how she did it?"

Grover walked toward the bar, leaving a trail of watery footprints behind him. He saw Harry and his mouth formed a surprised O. He turned and hurried in the opposite direction. Harry shook his head and took another sip.

"The military has technology that's decades ahead of what the public knows. I think Nell seduced someone high up in the military, and through that person, she stole an advanced skintight body armor."

"That's a good theory," Lewis said. "Any clue as to the identity of this high-ranking military person?"

Harry shrugged.

"My guess is he works for the Pentagon and is at least a Lieutenant General. He was probably attending the WAR Show, had the body armor in his room, and ordered a prostitute."

"Are you suggesting that Nell is a prostitute?"

"It is politically inappropriate to say a woman is a prostitute if she has sex for money?"

"But this situation with the Lieutenant General is completely speculative. Never mind. Why do you think she killed the police officers and the people at the convention?"

"It's obvious. PMS."

Harry finished his drink. The waiter came by and asked if he wanted a fourth. Harry shook his head and asked for the check.

"Going back to what we were discussing earlier," Lewis said. "How exactly are you tracking Nell?"

"Hunter's instinct."

"What is hunter's instinct?"

"It's how I'm going to catch Nell Slagle."

CHAPTER TWENTY-FIVE

THE MAN STARED at Nell like she was some kind of freak, but she continued to hug the jumbo box of cheese crackers anyway. These weren't the spicy hot flavored crackers that Skeeter always bought. They were regular cheese flavor the way God intended. Nell kissed the box.

"Hey! Pay first," the man said. "Then you can do whatever you want."

"Sorry," Nell said.

She peeled a hundred-dollar bill from the money roll in her purse and handed it to the man. If he was fazed by the large denomination, he didn't show it. The man gave Nell her change and she walked away with the cheese crackers tucked under her arm.

With her hair cut short and dyed black, Nell no longer had to hide in Skeeter's truck. Eager to do some much-needed shopping, she had suggested they stop at the first Costco or Walmart they came to, but Skeeter insisted they wait until they got to the Austin Country Flea Market.

Nell had been skeptical. Her past experiences with flea

markets had meant driving to a desolate part of town to wander around a few folding tables laden with dusty antiques, broken toys, used gardening tools, and packs of tube socks. This flea market had those items, but a hell of a lot more. It was the biggest damn flea market Nell had ever seen. The open-air buildings seemed to stretch on forever. Nell was dazzled by the sheer volume and variety of stuff for sale.

"This is amazeballs," she said.

"You saw the sign coming in," Skeeter said. "Five hundred vendors. If you can't find what you're looking for here, it don't exist."

Skeeter had suggested they split up and regroup at the market's entrance in two hours. Nell had readily agreed. After so many days cooped up together in the cab, they needed some time away from each other.

Nell put Skeeter out of her mind and concentrated on shopping. An hour later, she had bags filled with clothes, underwear, running shoes, and more snack food. She paid for them with bills from her money roll, but the prices were so low that she barely made a dent. With her enhanced strength, she had no problem carrying the heavy bags, but they were bulky and that was a pain in the ass. And she was hungry. Her stomach growled like an angry dog. Searching for a food stall, Nell passed a booth selling women's clothing, stopped, and doubled back.

The booth had a Nell Slagle for sale; a mannequin with a blonde wig dressed in a skintight camo t-shirt, camo booty shorts, a ball cap with a Bulard Arms logo, and combat boots. The clothes were identical to what she wore at the WAR Show when she mowed down half the attendees. The woman operating the booth, a Latinx woman who looked to be in her forties wearing skinny jeans and a sparkly blouse, came over to Nell.

"Can I help you?" she asked.

"Do you realize who this looks like?" Nell asked, nodding at the mannequin.

The woman glanced at the mannequin, shook her head, and stepped out of the booth.

"*Lo siento*. The sign fell down."

She picked up a handwritten sign off the ground and placed it in the mannequin's outstretched arms. The sign read, "Nell Slagle Halloween Costume."

Nell laughed. The woman giggled with her.

"Kind of early to be thinking about Halloween," Nell said.

The woman raised an eyebrow.

"Never too early to think about Halloween."

"Good point. But honestly, who would wear this?"

"You kidding? Lots of women going to be Nell Slagle this year."

Nell stared at the mannequin as she tried to process the idea of people dressing as her.

"You really think so?"

"Sure. Whether you think she's hero or monster, she's sexy badass."

Nell felt a surge of pride and was almost tempted to tell the woman that she was the real deal.

"You really think Nell is sexy?"

"Yeah. But her butt's too small."

Nell wasn't sure if she should feel pleased or insulted.

"If everybody wants to be Nell on Halloween, then why haven't you sold this outfit?"

The woman gestured at the mannequin.

"This just for display. We have clothes, hats, and boots in

different sizes. If you're interested, you'd better buy now. I've sold a lot of Nell Slagle costumes today."

It was an absurd notion. Nell had recently gone to a lot of trouble not to look like this sexy blonde badass. Then again, her plan was to continue making sure that those who profit from the sword die the sword by attacking as many gun shows between here and Cleveland, Tennessee as she could. If she attacked a gun show looking like she did now, then she'd have to alter her appearance again. There were only so many things she could do with her hair.

But if she showed up dressed like Halloween Nell Slagle, then she could take the costume off after the attack and disappear in plain sight.

"Would you be willing to sell me the blonde wig as well?" Nell asked.

The woman went back into the booth and returned with a cardboard box. She placed it on the display table. It was filled with blonde wigs in clear plastic bags. She took one out and handed it to Nell.

"The wig is part of the costume," the woman said.

The hair was a lighter blonde than Nell's natural color, but she doubted anyone would notice the difference.

"I'll take it," Nell said.

"Great," the woman said. "I can tell you're going to make a great Nell Slagle this Halloween."

Nell liked to think she made a great Nell Slagle every day.

CHAPTER TWENTY-SIX

SKEETER GLANCED AT his watch repeatedly as he waited outside the entrance to the flea market. Nell was fifteen minutes late. Knowing that she didn't own a watch or a phone didn't make the wait any easier. It was if he'd made a date with a caveman.

His phone rang. He didn't recognize the number and couldn't imagine who would be calling him. It certainly wasn't Nell. For one thing, he heard a man's voice.

"Hello?"

"Is this Terry 'Skeeter' Foote?"

"Yeah."

"Are you the owner and operator of a Freightliner Semi-truck?"

The man recited Skeeter's license plate number. Even though it was a warm day and he was standing in the sun, Skeeter felt a chill so deep he shivered.

"You seem to know a lot about me, but I don't who the hell you are."

"I'm Agent Wayne Driscoll with the FBI. I'd like to ask you a few questions. Is now a good time?"

Skeeter looked around. He half expected a team of FBI agents to come running out and tackle him.

"Now's as good a time as any. What do you want to know?"

"There's a LVMPD police report stating that last Monday night you were assaulted and constrained in your truck while parked at the Morton Travel Plaza in North Las Vegas."

"I didn't call the cops."

"The manager of the truck stop did. According to the report, she rescued you."

Skeeter watched two boys laughing while they chased each other.

"I'm not saying it didn't happen. But I didn't see any reason to involve the police."

"Were you assaulted last Monday night?"

Skeeter dug a hole in the dirt with the toe of his boot.

"Yeah. I was."

"Was the assailant a woman?"

Skeeter wanted to kick himself for being such a goddamn blabbermouth with the truck stop manager. Sure, he wasn't thinking straight at the time and was glad to be alive, but if only he could go back in time and tell himself to shut the fuck up.

"Yeah. She kicked my ass."

"Can you describe the woman who attacked you?"

"It was dark. I couldn't see her clearly."

"How did she gain access into your truck?"

Skeeter had dealt with the police enough times to know that if he lied, he was like a fly buzzing around a spider web. Sooner or later, he was going to get caught.

"Are you still there, Mr. Foote?" Driscoll asked.

"Give me a minute," Skeeter said, rubbing his forehead.

"This happened a week ago. When you drive a truck, the days tend to blend together, and a week can feel like a month."

There was only one possible reason why the FBI would be calling Skeeter about what happened in his truck last Monday night. Either they knew for certain that Nell was the female who had handed him his ass, or they strongly suspected it.

The million-dollar question was whether the FBI suspected that there was a connection between Skeeter and Nell.

Skeeter could tell the truth. He could tell the FBI that Nell Slagle was at a flea market in Austin, Texas. He knew this to be true because he brought her here.

Or he could keep lying and hope he didn't get caught in a web.

"Sorry to keep you waiting," Skeeter said. "I'm sure you're busy."

"It's okay. Take your time."

"It's just that I'm not comfortable discussing this with an officer of the law because I engaged in what could be considered illegal behavior."

"Don't worry, Mr. Foote. I'm only interested in the woman who was in your truck that night."

"I saw her walking through the lot and called out to her. I don't normally have anything to do with lot lizards, but that evening I suffered a moment of weakness."

"A lot lizard?"

"That's what we call whores that peddle their asses in truck stops. As you can imagine, it doesn't attract the most high-quality prostitutes."

"I see. Can you describe the woman?"

The two boys Skeeter had noticed earlier were still chasing each other. A woman shouted at them. From the way they immediately stopped running and walked to her, she had to be their mother. Instead of giving Agent Driscoll a description of Nell, Skeeter described the boys' mother.

"Short and chunky. Long black hair tied into two braids. Brown skin, brown eyes."

"Are you certain?" Driscoll asked. "Earlier, you said it was dark."

"Well, I said it was dark because I didn't want to admit that I was mugged by a skanky whore. I saw her clearly. She was a native-born Mexican. No Europeans in her family's woodpile."

"I see. Thank you for your time. I have no further questions."

The FBI agent hung up. Skeeter felt the tug for a drink.

Nell appeared out of the crowd. She carried a bunch of shopping bags and had a big grin on her face. For a cold-blooded killer, she had a nice smile.

"Sorry I'm late," Nell said. "I got held up."

"I see you did a little shopping." Skeeter nodded at Nell's bags.

"You were right. They've got everything here."

"It's getting late. We should go."

Skeeter turned and headed toward the parking lot. He'd gone about a yard before he realized that Nell wasn't with him. She stood at the flea market entrance, people flowing around her like a boulder in a stream. Skeeter walked back.

"What?" he said.

"We left Trinidad with unfinished business. Before we go any further, I need to know. Are you taking me to Cleveland or are we about to go our separate ways?"

Skeeter wanted to talk about this in the truck, but here was as good a place as any.

"That depends. What are your plans?"

"I told you."

"You never told me *why* you want to go back to Cleveland."

Nell stared at the highway. The afternoon sun gave her a golden glow.

"I never got a chance to say goodbye to my mother. I was still in the ICU when they buried her. Later, I was too depressed to go to the cemetery, and then I was too strung out to even think about it."

"Family's important," Skeeter said. "You should visit your mama. But the trip to her grave will take an afternoon at most. Then what are you going to do?"

"Disappear."

Skeeter bent the edge of his ear.

"Did you say 'disappear?'"

"Back before my parents split up, we used to go camping in Cherokee National Forest. The park is right outside Cleveland."

"You're planning on living in the forest?"

"Hell no. I hated those camping trips. But the Appalachian Trail goes through Cherokee. I'm going to hike the trail up to Maine and then cross the border into Canada."

Skeeter had to admit it wasn't a bad plan. He remembered reading a story about a fugitive who hid from the law by hiking the trail. He managed to stay on the run for six years before Johnny Law finally caught up with him.

"The weather is nice now," Skeeter said. "But by the time you get to Maine, it's going to be cold as hell and the snow's going to be up to your tits."

Nell snorted.

"Excuse me. Have we met? Or did you forget that I'm invulnerable? Snow's not going to stop me."

"Alright. But what about what you said the other day?"

"I'm going to the gun show in Longview. After that, I'm going to find more gun shows."

Skeeter felt a pang of grief for the people who planned to attend those shows. He could warn them. He could call the police. He could drink himself into oblivion to atone for his sins. Or he could stop pretending that he wouldn't go to hell and back to be with Edie again.

"Are you going to kill Rafael?" Skeeter asked.

Nell sighed.

"Yes."

"Then I'm taking you home to see your mama."

CHAPTER TWENTY-SEVEN

Chicago Joe's Italian restaurant was proudly old-fashioned. Housed in the same brick building for decades, the red and white checkered tablecloths and Christmas lights that lined the walls had probably been there for decades as well. Originally built to give a taste of home to the East Coast gangsters who had invaded Las Vegas, it was now a tourist attraction. Lt. General Buck Carter, Special Agent Easter, and Special Agent Zavala sat at a table close enough to the kitchen that they could hear the clatter of pots and pans.

"This is the best lasagna I've ever had," Carter said.

"How can you tell?" Zavala said. "You're scarfing it down like you're afraid it's going to run away."

Easter knew from his own experience as a Marine that speed eating was a common trait among members of the military. After Easter left the service, it took him months of conscious effort to unlearn the habit.

"As much as I appreciate you buying us dinner," Easter said, "I feel like we're celebrating when there's nothing to celebrate."

Carter pulled a slice of garlic bread from a basket on the table.

"We still have to eat, so why not eat well when we have the chance?"

"That works for me," Zavala said.

Carter drained the red wine from his glass and refilled it from the bottle on the table. He offered to refill Zavala's glass, but she declined.

"You must have some idea where Slagle is hiding," Carter said.

"We've narrowed it down to the United States and Mexico," Zavala said.

"Nell is on a mission," Easter said. "She wants those who profit from the sword to die by the sword."

"We're highly confident that she's going to attack a gun show. We've focused our search on shows between Arizona and east Tennessee."

Carter glared at the special agents.

"Why stop in Tennessee? Why not go all the way to the East Coast?"

"Since leaving Vegas, Nell has been traveling steadily east. We believe her destination is her home in Cleveland, Tennessee."

"Be that as it may, the area you mentioned is a sea of red states. That's a lot of fucking gun shows."

Zavala cut into her eggplant parmigiana.

"We talked to the Bureau chief this morning. He agrees with our theory and he's working with state law enforcement agencies to increase security at gun shows in their jurisdiction."

Carter finished his lasagna and sopped up leftover sauce with garlic bread.

"What are you doing other than waiting for her to kill more civilians?"

Easter dabbed his mouth with his napkin.

"We're investigating the possibility that Nell is getting assistance."

"We have a person of interest," Zavala said. "A truck driver named Terry Foote. He told someone that Nell robbed him before the convention shooting. His description matched Nell. But when Agent Driscoll spoke to Foote, he denied it was Nell and described a completely different person."

"Foote's on the road heading east. We believe Nell is also heading east and that the two are traveling together."

Carter nodded.

"Should I send my men to follow him?"

"No need. Agent Driscoll and Agent Teal left this morning."

"Send me Foote's GPS. If he does lead your agents to Slagle, then my men can quickly take over. Anything else?"

Easter shook his head.

"That's all we have for now. Like I said, nothing to celebrate."

CHAPTER TWENTY-EIGHT

Nell and Skeeter arrived in Longview, Texas after sunset. Streetlights cast a yellowish glow on the road as Skeeter drove until he found a trucker-friendly hotel.

Nell's room was old, but it was clean. She capped her recently colored hair before taking a shower. Afterwards, feeling fresh and clean, she dumped the contents of her shopping bags on the bed. The smell of new clothes filled the room. She'd been eager to try them on since they left the Austin Flea Market. And to finally put on new underwear.

Nell performed a fashion show for herself in front of the mirror and experimented with different combinations. The clothes made her look like a regular human girl, and she almost felt like one too.

The last thing she tried on was the Nell Slagle Halloween costume. She turned to the side to get a better view of how her butt looked in snug camo booty shorts. She wondered if her butt really was too small. There was a time when men preferred women with cute little behinds. Now, the bigger the better. If only Nell had thought to ask Honeydew to enlarge her posterior while they were making her bulletproof.

Nell stripped down to her underwear and got under the covers in bed. She considered reading her romance novel, but she was too full of nervous energy. Tomorrow was a big day. What she needed was a good long run to clear her head. She would need another shower after her run but so what? Rummaging through her new clothes, she laid out sweatpants, a hoodie, and running shoes.

The air had a pleasant crisp coolness as she jogged along the access road. She ran past gas stations and fast-food restaurants. The streetlights that lined the road created pools of light. She ran from one pool to another.

Nell increased her speed but still couldn't outrun her memories. They popped into her when she least expected, delivering fresh shock and pain. The most persistent had to do with eyes; one of Peggy's beautiful blue eyes staring at Nell, the other one replaced with a black hole, Carson's cold blue eyes, devoid of emotion, right before he shot her.

Nell stopped under an overpass to catch her breath. She held out her hands and gazed at her palms. Her brain decided now was the time to revisit excruciating memories from her time at HARD-SOW. Most of them had to do with less fortunate test subjects. They had been her friends. Grace, whose skin became as scaly as an alligator's, died in her sleep, one of the lucky ones. Lenny, whose skin fell off because it couldn't contain his invulnerable skeleton. The scientists wrapped him in something. He screamed until his voice became hoarse. Nell wasn't sure how he died. If Honeydew killed him, it was a mercy killing. And Robby. They had kissed and done other things late at night when she was supposed to be asleep in her own bed. Robby melted. Just melted into a blob of skin and oozing internal organs. He was sitting next to Nell during dinner when it happened. She cried for days, and couldn't eat for a week.

Then there were the memories of injections that shot fire through her veins and caused convulsions so severe she broke her arm. As she flopped around like a fish on dry land, a scientist calmly took notes but never offered comfort. When Honeydew scientists popped Champagne corks to celebrate the success of Project Bulletproof, Nell looked at her hands and realized the full meaning of what they had done to her, what she had agreed to let them do to her. She had given away her humanity for a warm place to sleep and three meals a day. As they drank Champagne and didn't offer her any, she thought what have I done? What have I done? What have I done?

The rumble of trucks rolling across the bridge above her brought Nell back to the present. She used to think of the rumble as a lonesome sound, the yearning of men a long way from home. Traveling with Skeeter, the road had begun to grow on her. If she wasn't on the run, she could easily see his truck as her home. Maybe she would become a truck driver in Canada.

Not that Nell had any delusions about life as a trucker. Skeeter groused constantly about how big carriers and government regulations were squeezing out owner-operators like himself. He was a dying breed as the trucking industry became consolidated, automated, and the truckers themselves became isolated from the rest of society. However, when Nell asked Skeeter why he kept driving if being a trucker sucked so badly, he'd said that there was no better job in the world.

When Skeeter decided to stick with Nell, she felt more relief than she thought she would. She could have found a way to continue her journey without him, but she liked having company. She liked *his* company, which was too bad because there was no way they could stay together. Sooner or later, someone would figure out who she was, or find his hidey hole.

Once they got to Cleveland, they would go their separate ways. There was no other choice.

CHAPTER TWENTY-NINE

No matter how much she tugged and pulled, Saffron Winer couldn't get the camo T-shirt over her bulletproof vest. As she struggled, Saffron debated whether to take the T-shirt back to the costume store for a larger size. After more determined yanking, she finally succeeded. Standing in her bedroom, she looked at her reflection in in the mirror. It was obvious that she was wearing armor. Either that or she had square boobs. At least the matching camo booty shorts were a perfect fit. Saffron was proud of her firm ass, not because it was sexy but because it showed her dedication to her yoga practice.

She pinned her purple hair to the sides of her head, slipped on the blonde wig, and wrenched it into place. Saffron couldn't resist flipping the yellow tresses back and forth before putting on a stiff new ballcap with a Bulard Arms logo. She wasn't happy about the cap's chemical smell, but she wouldn't be wearing it that long.

Lacing up her favorite cherry red Doc Martens gave her a sense of familiarity after donning the fresh-out-of-the-plastic-bag-clothes. She had considered shaving her legs, but decided there was no reason to start now. Looking at her reflection again, Saffron struck a superhero pose, legs apart and fists on her hips. Grinning, she thought she made a decent Nell Slagle.

Saffron hadn't told anyone about her plan. Not her parents, her sister, or her friends. Not one of her lovers, past or present. No one in her yoga class or at her food co-op.

She didn't tell her downstairs neighbor, Ms. Nina Williams, when she asked her to look after Saffron's cat, Emma Goldman. Ms. Williams was used to Saffron leaving for days at a time to attend a political march or a consciousness raising conference. Emma Goldman was always welcomed to join Ms. Williams's clowder of cats until Saffron returned. And if for some reason she didn't return this time, Saffron knew her cat would have a good home. Saffron hugged Emma Goldman and fed her some of her favorite organic cat treats before dropping her off downstairs.

She definitely didn't tell anyone at Feminists for Freedom, also known as Triple F.

Saffron had been one of the St. Louis chapter's most trusted employees until last week, when she spoke to a reporter at an anti-gun march in Washington, D.C. The reporter had asked Saffron what she thought about the Las Vegas Convention shooter. Saffron had never been afraid to speak her mind, even if it got her into trouble. As the American historian Laurel Thatcher Ulrich had said, "Well-behaved women seldom make history."

"The gun lobby is a terrorist organization," Saffron said. "Gun lovers give the gun lobby money, so that makes them terrorists too. Nell is fighting terrorism."

"But she's killing innocent people," the reporter said. "How do you justify that?"

Saffron shrugged.

"Nell said it perfectly. 'Those who profit from the sword should die the sword.' The people at that death merchant convention, the ones she killed, they weren't innocent. They got what they deserved."

When Saffron's comments appeared on national news that night, Triple F was furious. They put out a statement to the press immediately that stated that Triple F did not condone violence or the use of guns for any reason. They certainly didn't endorse the actions of a deranged mass killer. They further clarified that Saffron Winer's views did not reflect the views of Triple F, and that Ms. Winer was no longer employed as the organization's community engagement manager.

Saffron's frustration with the anti-gun movement had been growing for some time. The reporter's questions had prompted her to put those feelings into words. Marching had achieved nothing. Marches hadn't stopped mass shootings. They hadn't saved school children. Every common-sense gun restriction was shot down in Congress.

But then along came Nell. Her attack on the WAR Show had made a bold statement stronger than any march. Nell had demonstrated bravery, risking her life to tear down the military industrial complex, and she had done it using their tools of oppression. Saffron decided that if she truly believed in making a difference, then she must be willing to risk her life as well.

She went to her apartment's breakfast nook where the early morning sun shone through the window on a hard plastic rifle case sitting on a small dining room table. Flipping the latches, Saffron opened the case and gazed at her brand new Beastmaster. The cool black metal death machine was beautiful the same way scorpions and black widow spiders were beautiful. The smell of plastic and metal fought the smell of organic coffee and brown rice.

The salesman at the sporting goods store had looked like he was going to come in his pants when Saffron asked for a Beastmaster by name. Certainly, he didn't suspect that she chose the specific semi-automatic rifle because it was Nell Slagle's weapon of choice.

Saffron saw how the salesman looked at her tattoos, the one that said GRL PWR and the female symbol with a fist in the circle. He must have thought that she was another misguided liberal who had finally come to her senses and realized that guns were the answer to all of society's problems, because he had suggested she get a bump stock for her Beastmaster.

"If you got a bad guy coming for you," he said, "this will fill him full of holes in seconds."

"In seconds?" Saffron asked.

"Seconds can mean the difference between life and death."

"I'll take it."

The salesman had attached the bump stock on the Beastmaster for her and helped her load cartridges into the extra magazines she requested. It had given him time to ask her for a date. Saffron told him that she had a girlfriend, which was a lie. She used to have a girlfriend.

Saffron had a moment of panic when she got home with her new rifle. She had never fired a gun. There had to be more to it than just squeezing the trigger. The problem was easily solved by watching a few YouTube tutorials.

Saffron carried the Beastmaster back to the bedroom and posed once again in front of the mirror. Now she really looked like Nell. Her decision to dress this way was inspired by an ad for the Chaos Emporium that she happened to notice in the Riverfront Times. It was the store's quirky name that caught her attention. The fact that it was a costume shop didn't interest Saffron until she spotted the woman in the ad wearing a Nell Slagle costume.

The news said that Nell's slutty army girl outfit at the WAR Show was a disguise. She had posed as a booth model to gain entrance into the restricted convention. Saffron knew there was more to it than that. By dressing as a sexy soldier, Nell had taken possession of the gaze of male gun lovers. They were part of the patriarchy that enslaved women and forced them to be either madonnas or whores but never individuals with thoughts and dreams of their own. What could be more of a mindfuck for those pigs than to have the woman of their dreams shoot their tiny dicks off?

Saffron aimed the rifle at the mirror.

"Bang, bang, motherfuckers."

She put the rifle back in its case and placed the five extra magazines into her local NPR station tote bag. Peering out the kitchen window, Saffron was relieved that there were no signs of life in the apartment building's parking lot. Then again, it was a weekend morning, and most of the other tenants wouldn't be getting up for another couple of hours. Saffron carried the rifle case and the tote bag to her red Prius and stored them in the trunk. She then drove twenty miles from her home in Botanical Heights to the Machinist's Hall in Bridgeton.

The parking lot was crowded. Saffron drove around for five minutes before she found an open space between two pick-up trucks. Turning off the engine, she sat in the car and did a brief meditation to calm her nerves.

"If not now, when?" Saffron said.

She got out of the car. The bulletproof vest itched. The sun seemed too bright. Everything around her, from the cracked asphalt to her chipped nails, were in sharp focus and at the same time felt overexposed. Saffron popped open the trunk. She slung the tote bag over her shoulder and took the Beastmaster out of the rifle case. Cradling the rifle in her arms like a baby, Saffron walked toward the building. She felt like she was detached from her body and floating above herself. At the entrance was a banner that read Bridgeton Gun and Knife Show.

Inside the glass doors, a man and a woman sat behind a table. Four people stood in a line on the other side. Saffron joined the line. As she got closer, she learned that the woman was collecting a ten-dollar admission fee and the man was making sure no one carried a loaded gun into the show. Saffron was sorely tempted to run back to her car, drive home, and hide under the covers in her bed. But it was too late. She was at the head of the line.

"Ten dollars, please," the woman said.

"Is your rifle loaded?" the man said. "Can't take a loaded rifle inside."

Saffron stared at them, unable to move and her throat too dry to speak.

"Ten dollars, please."

"Is your rifle loaded?"

She felt very small and vulnerable. A shiver ran down her spine.

"Ten dollars, please."

"Is your rifle loaded?"

She couldn't give up. She had to demonstrate bravery.

"Those who profit from the sword should die by the sword," she said softly.

"What was that?" the man asked. "I didn't hear you."

"I think she said she had a sword," the woman said.

"I don't see no sword."

"Maybe it's in her tote bag."

Saffron pointed the rifle at the woman and squeezed the trigger. Many things happened at once. The Beastmaster shook and made a loud rapid stutter. Empty cartridges jumped out of the rifle. The gun's recoil that vibrated inside her wasn't as extreme as she worried it would be. The woman's blood splattered Saffron's face and arms. It felt like warm sprinkler water. The woman slumped in her chair. The salesman had told the truth. Saffron had filled her full of holes in seconds.

She had fired a gun. She had killed a fellow human being. Saffron felt a confusing mix of excitement and shame.

Time slowed down. People in the gun show ran from the sound of gunfire. The man sitting next to the dead woman took a gun from a holster on his belt. In a panic, Saffron swung the gun at him and squeezed the trigger again. The man jerked like a fish out of water before he fell to the ground.

Maybe it was a case of the first death being the hardest, or maybe Saffron accepted that there was no going back. The pain in her stomach disappeared. Adrenaline rushed through her in a tingling excitement. She was at the top of the roller coaster and ready to plunge into action.

She moved around the table and entered the main room filled with tables and people. Guns and rifles covered the tables, and people who had been looking at the guns were now looking at Saffron.

"Those who profit from the sword should die by the sword!" Saffron shouted.

At least, she thought she shouted. She was half-deaf from the gunfire so close to her ears. Everything sounded like it had fallen down a deep well.

Saffron opened fire on the crowd, moving the gun from side to side. People ran in all directions. A clicking noise let Saffron know that she had emptied the first magazine. She had fired thirty bullets in less than a minute. She removed the empty magazine, dropped it clattering to the floor, and replaced it with a loaded magazine from her tote bag.

There was too much recoil to think about accuracy. She just pointed it in the general direction of people and fired. The heavy bursts of bullets found plenty of bodies.

She emptied the second magazine and quickly replaced it with the third loaded magazine. As she searched the room for new victims, Saffron thought she heard a gunshot, and felt like someone had hit her chest with a baseball bat. She fell to the floor as pain blossomed through her body. Gritting her teeth, Saffron looked down at her chest. There was a hole in her camo T-shirt and a slug nestled in the vest. She was still on her back when a man ran over and pointed a handgun at her.

"Don't move!" he yelled.

Fear gripped Saffron. She screamed, swung the rifle toward him, and fired. Bullets ripped into his chest. He toppled to the ground. Ignoring the pain in her upper body, Saffron scrambled to her feet.

At first, she thought the silence was a result of her near deafness. Many of the attendees had fled the building. Saffron looked around the room. There were so many guns, so many rifles, and so many knives. So many ways to maim and kill. There were ugly anti-liberal bumper stickers and endless pro-gun mugs, T-shirts, and posters. They said things like, *Ban Idiots Not Guns, If You Are Too Stupid to Get an ID You're Too Stupid to Vote*, and *God Created Man Guns Made Them Equal.* So much rage, just so they could keep their damn toys.

And then there were dozens of dead people either on the floor or sprawled on tables. There were also a good number of wounded people begging for help. She almost choked on the taste of metal from blood and killing machines. The carnage she had created had happened quicker than she imagined it would.

Way far away, Saffron could hear sirens, and through the glass doors, she saw flashing lights. The police had arrived. She looked at the people she had murdered. They were white and people of color. Old and young. Men and women. Their red blood mingled together on the floor.

Saffron prayed that she had made the right choice and that something good would come from this.

Police officers entered the building with their guns drawn.

"Put the gun down!"

Saffron looked at the Beastmaster in her hands. The barrel was smoking from firing so rapidly. She didn't know how many bullets she had left in the last magazine she'd loaded. It didn't really matter. What was it they called what she was about to do? Suicide by cop?

"Put the gun down! Now!"

She had come here today to risk her life to make a difference. Just like Nell Slagle. Saffron straightened her spine and took a deep calming breath. She would have repeated the thing Nell had said about the Beastmaster, but she couldn't remember what it was.

Crouching behind a table, Saffron counted six officers. They were coming toward her, guns raised. She opened fire. One of them went down. They returned fire, the shots echoing. She felt burning pain in her left arm and leg. And then, a policeman's bullet ripped through the Bulard Arms logo on her ballcap and entered her brain.

CHAPTER THIRTY

SKEETER PULLED OFF a two-lane road into the empty parking lot of Oil Bowl Lanes, parked, and kept the motor idling. Everything in this part of Longview felt flat and empty, as if the life had been pressed out of it.

"How far is the truck stop from here?" Nell asked.

"About ten miles," Skeeter said.

"Is that far enough? Maybe you should go to Shreveport and wait for me there."

"Ten miles is far enough."

"I just don't want anything to happen to you."

Skeeter crossed his arms.

"Since when did you get so worried about me?"

"You're my ride. If something happened to you, I'd never find another truck with a hidey hole like this one."

Nell climbed out of the truck and slipped her canvas backpack onto her shoulders. In the backpack was a loaded Glock, four extra magazines, a taser, her money roll, and the blonde wig and Bulard Arms logo ballcap of her Nell Slagle Halloween costume. She wore the camo T-shirt and camo booty shorts under a gray long sleeved T-shirt and jeans.

Skeeter drove away. She waited until the truck was out of sight before walking in the opposite direction. Nell trudged past a roofing and gutter supply company, a self-storage building, and a drywall installation company. Each place had battered pick-up trucks parked in front that were either red, white, or blue.

The entrance to the Maude Cobb Convention Center stood out from the hardscrabble businesses. The sign included an LED display that announced the latest event. Today it read, Longview Gun Show. The grounds were professionally land-scaped with well-tended grass and clusters of trees. Rather than follow the winding driveway to the convention center, Nell took advantage of the cover provided by the trees.

Her plan was to find a place close to the building where she wouldn't be seen changing into her costume. Once she was in disguise, she would hide her backpack before rushing the entrance with her Glock and Taser. And then, all hell would break loose.

As far as plans went, it didn't seem too shabby.

Moving through the shade of the wooded area, Nell breathed in the earthy scent of oak and pine trees. At the end of the landscaped forest, she stood at the edge of the parking lot with a clear view of the building. Two cops stood at the entrance. They wore shades and rested their forearms on their duty belts. A police car was parked nearby.

When Nell was a teenager, Peggy had dragged her and Carson to dozens of gun shows. The most security Nell had ever seen at those shows was one off-duty police officer at the entrance. The police car today meant that the two officers guarding the entrance were not picking up freelance work. They were assigned here by the Longview police department. Nell wondered why there was extra security.

A tree line flowed around one side of the parking lot. Nell kept on the outside of the trees as she made her way to the back of the building. Along the way, she saw that the metal doors on the loading docks had been rolled up so that vendors could bring in their merchandise. The doors were guarded by scruffy men wearing body armor over Hawaiian shirts. They carried semi-automatic rifles and looked around like they expected an immigrant invasion of murderers and rapists to arrive at any moment.

Nell decided she would enter the gun show at one of these service entrances instead of the front door for two reasons: she disliked shooting cops, and the dipshits wearing the "Aloha" print shirts were prime examples of those who profit from the sword should die by the sword.

The tree line ended at the rear of the back parking lot. Nell was debating where to change into her costume when a man emerged from a cluster of shade trees and called out to her.

"Hey there, young lady," he said. "Hold up."

Nell groaned. So much for going unnoticed. She leaned against a pick-up truck. He waved as he snaked between cars. Once he got closer, Nell got a better look at him. He seemed to be in his forties. He wore a green army jacket, a green ballcap, and jeans. There was a patch on his jacket that read, THOSE WHO LIVE BY THE SWORD DIE BY THE GUN. On the cap was a silhouette of an assault rifle and the words, COME AND TAKE IT. The man didn't know it, but he had just volunteered to be Nell's first kill of the day.

"You going to the gun show?" the man asked.

"That's the plan," Nell said.

"You been inside?"

"Not yet."

He grinned.

"Today is your lucky day."

Nell knew his game. She had met guys like him before. Going to a gun show with Peggy always included a trip through the parking lot in search of independent dealers selling guns from the trunks of their cars. As much as Peggy had loved guns, she had loved a bargain more. These guys were not licensed dealers, their guns were cheaper and didn't require a background check.

"I'm Dan Stump, but everybody calls me Stumpy," the man said.

"And you let them?" Nell said.

Stumpy wagged his finger at Nell.

"You're funny. I like a woman with a good sense of humor. It means she knows a good bargain when she sees one."

The sun beat down on them. Last night's heavy rain had left the air thick with humidity. Sweat trickled down Nell's shirt.

"It's hot out here," Nell said. "Could we hurry this along?"

"Right to the point," Stumpy said. "I like that too. Look. I love gun shows, but the prices are too damn high. Don't get me wrong. I got nothing against the dealers in there. They're good people, but they have to recoup the cost of their table and pay local taxes. They do that by marking up their merchandise. I've got the same guns they got but a hell of a lot cheaper."

Nell scanned the parking lot as she wiped sweat off her forehead with her sleeve. There were no people around but them.

"Prove it," she said.

Stumpy grinned.

"Follow me."

He led Nell back to a brown sedan parked underneath a cluster of shade trees. The car had been backed into the space so that the trees and the remote section of the parking lot hid the trunk from anyone walking by. Stumpy opened the trunk to reveal a pile of firearms.

"See anything you like?" Stumpy asked.

Nell peered into the trunk and pointed.

"Is that a Beastmaster buried down there?"

"Why yes it is."

Stumpy moved weapons about so that he could get to the Beastmaster and handed it to Nell.

"It's a damn fine rifle," Stumpy said. "How much were you thinking of spending?"

Nell returned the Beastmaster to the trunk.

"It doesn't matter. I'd have to lug it into the gun show to buy ammo for it. I'd rather buy both at the same time."

"Ammo? No problemo."

He opened the back door and took out a duffel bag full of various ammo boxes. He sorted through them until he found two boxes of .223 Remington Ammunition.

Nell knew that it was customary to haggle over the price. She offered a number for the rifle and ammo. Stumpy countered with a higher number. They went back and forth until they agreed on a number in the middle.

"Let me get my wallet," Nell said.

She slipped off her backpack and dug around inside. Stumpy alternated between watching Nell and watching the parking lot. Instead of money, Nell pulled out her Taser.

"Hey!" Stumpy said. "Don't point that thing at me."

Nell pulled the trigger. The two electrodes flew out and stuck in his chest. Stumpy howled as electricity coursed through him. His eyes rolled back, and he collapsed. Nell knelt beside him and dug his car keys out of his pants pocket.

A crow cawing from a nearby tree was the only witness to Nell's attack. But their privacy couldn't last. There were too many cars. Someone was bound to return to their vehicle and any moment. Nell unbuckled Stumpy's belt and removed it.

"Heeeey," Stumpy said. "Are you are you are you trying to take take advantage of me?"

"You wish," Nell said.

She turned Stumpy over onto his stomach. He tried to stop her but was too weak. Nell used his belt to secure his wrists and the Taser's copper wires to tie his ankles.

"Help!" Stumpy shouted. "I'm getting robbed here."

Nell rummaged around the trunk for something to gag him and found an oily rag among the firearms. Tearing the rag in two, she rolled one half and stuffed it into his mouth. She tied the other half around his head to keep the gag in place. There was fear in Stumpy's eyes.

"You were going to be my first kill of the day," Nell said. "But I changed my mind. Don't worry. I promise I'll kill you later."

She loaded ammo into the Beastmaster. Since Stumpy had plenty of firearms and a duffel bag loaded with ammo, Nell helped herself to two shotguns and a semi-automatic handgun along with the Beastmaster. She loaded the weapons and placed them on the car's passenger seat. She found an ankle holster in the back seat and slipped her Glock into it.

Nell dropped Stumpy into the trunk and was about to

change into her costume when she heard talking in the distance. Two men had entered the parking lot. She slammed the trunk lid down and got behind the wheel. As she watched them in the rearview mirror, she hoped that they wouldn't come close enough to hear Stumpy bumping around in the trunk. If they did, Nell would have to waste time killing them and hiding their bodies. They walked to a pick-up truck on the other side of the lot.

She waited until they drove away before stripping off her long sleeve T-shirt and jeans and putting on the blonde wig and Bulard Arms ballcap. She strapped the ankle holster to her right boot, stuffed her clothes into the backpack, and opened the trunk. Stumpy made whimpering sounds as he wiggled about.

"Watch this for me," Nell said as she stashed her backpack next to him.

Nell closed the trunk, got in the car, checked her face in the rear-view mirror, started the engine, and rolled down the windows. She turned on the radio. Skeeter would never let her choose what they listened to in the truck, and he only listened to NPR because no matter where he was in the country, he could always find the local station. Nell twisted the dial until she found a top 40 station. *Wrecking Ball* by Miley Cyrus was playing.

She drove to the convention center and idled in front of the loading dock. The Hawaiian shirt men checked her out. She waved at them. They grinned and waved back. Nell turned the volume on the radio up all the way. The guys gave her a thumbs up. Nell laid on the horn as she floored it. She rumbled up the loading dock ramp. They dove out of the way as she entered the convention center's backstage.

Going so quickly from bright sun to dark interior left Nell

momentarily blinded. She bumped into something and rolled over something else. The back window exploded, and gun shots pinged the car's exterior. Glancing in the rearview mirror, Nell could see dark figures chasing after her. She thought about stopping to kill them, but she was anxious to get to the actual gun show. There was a light ahead and Nell drove toward it.

The doorway was wide enough to drive through, but Nell still managed to scrape the side of the car as she sped past. A row of folding tables covered in weapons was dead ahead. Nell slammed on the brakes, screeching as she crashed into the tables. Guns and rifles toppled to the floor. People screamed and ran in all directions.

Nell looked over the weapons on the passenger seat.

"Eeny, meeny, miney, moe," she said before grabbing one of the shotguns.

She got out of the car and climbed onto the hood. The convention center wasn't as vast as the one in Las Vegas, but it was much bigger than she would have guessed for a city the size of Longview, Texas.

"Those who profit from the sword should die by the sword!" Nell shouted.

They probably didn't hear her, what with people yelling their fool heads off and the car radio blasting, but it didn't matter because actions spoke louder than words. Nell flipped the safety off, pointed the shotgun at the crowd, and squeezed the trigger. Shotguns are noisy bastards with loud booms, and this one was no exception. People fell and blood splattered the guns on display. Nell pumped the shotgun ¾ *clack clack* ¾ and fired into the human herd again.

Multiple bullets slammed into Nell's back. The unexpected impact caused her to lose her balance. She fell off the hood and landed on the convention floor without losing her grip on the shotgun.

Sitting up, Nell panicked. She was blind. Then she realized that the wig had slipped so that the hair covered her face. She turned the wig back around.

Ducking behind the car, Nell surveyed the area where the gunshots had come from. Four Hawaiian shirt men were coming toward her. She waited until they reached the car before standing up.

"I'm so glad you came," Nell said. "I was afraid I'd have to hunt you down."

She aimed the shotgun below the closest man's bullet-proof vest and squeezed the trigger. The blast hit his left leg. He screamed and sank to the ground. The three other men opened fire, but she was ready for them. Nell held her ground as their bullets bounced off her. She took her time pumping the shotgun and aiming just below their vests. Soon, all four were on the ground clutching either their stomach, legs, or private parts.

Nell came around the car and stood over them. She put the shotgun against the head of one of the men and pulled the trigger. The next man managed to ignore his pain and fired his rifle at her. Nell kicked the rifle out of his hands and shot him. The third man tried to crawl away, but Nell turned him onto his back, placed her boot on his chest, and aimed the barrel at his head. She pulled the trigger, and nothing happened.

"Darn," Nell said. "I ran out of shells."

"Thank Jesus!" the man said.

His Hawaiian shirt was yellow with pineapples and flowers. His blood had turned the shirttail bright red.

"Don't worry," Nell said. "I have another gun."

She tossed the shotgun aside, removed the Glock from the ankle holster, and used it to kill him and the fourth man.

A bullet glanced off her shoulder. The two policemen that she'd seen at the entrance were firing at her. Certainly, they had called their dispatcher and reinforcements were on their way. Nell didn't want a shootout with the Longview Police Department if she could avoid it. They carried guns as part of their job, not because it fulfilled their patriotic fantasies.

Nell went back to the car and gathered the three firearms on the passenger seat. Running across the convention floor to where a crowd of people were bottlenecked at an exit, she laid her weapons on top of a display of handguns. A woman pushing in vain at the people in front of her turned around, her face white with fear, and screamed. Nell picked up the second shotgun and fired in the direction of the woman until it was empty, killing her and a dozen people around her. Dropping the shotgun, Nell grabbed the semi-automatic handgun and moved to the next exit crammed with people. She emptied the gun's magazine into the crowd.

Gunshots whizzing past her let Nell know that more officers had arrived. Despite her reluctance to shoot police officers, she grabbed the Beastmaster.

"You can't be the Beastmaster forever, but I'm the Beastmaster today!" she shouted before returning their fire. She aimed for their chests in the hope of hitting their bulletproof vests. It would hurt like hell, but they'd still be alive.

Nell wasn't sure how many times she hit her intended targets, but she managed to drive them back. Savoring a moment of calm before the next storm, Nell looked around. There were dead people everywhere lying in their own blood. The wounded were begging for help. Tables were overturned. Guns and rifles littered the floor. It was a tragic mess, but had she killed enough people who profited from the sword to make her point? Had she sufficiently scared the bejesus out of the remaining gun lovers?

The carnage she'd created in just a few minutes would have to be enough. Soon more policemen were going to arrive making it harder to get out of here.

Nell hurried back to Stumpy's brown car. She had kept the engine running. The radio was still playing the latest pop hits. Her intention was to drive out of the convention center the same way she'd come in, but there were a lot of guns and dead bodies on the floor that weren't there when she drove in.

The decision was made for her when a hail of gunfire ripped into the car. A group of gun show attendees had returned armed and most definitely dangerous. They were carrying all manner of firearms. Their bullets flattened the tires and killed the engine, which in turn killed the music. A trail of bullet holes went from hood to the trunk.

"Oh shit," Nell said. "My backpack. Stumpy!"

She opened the trunk. Stumpy was almost as full of holes as his car.

"Sorry," Nell said. "I know I promised to kill you, but somebody else got to you first."

She grabbed her backpack and braced herself for the next attack. Instead, Nell witnessed a shouting match between armed citizens and armed police over who had right of way to shoot her. Nell took this as her cue to make her retreat. She left the Beastmaster next to Stumpy and headed toward the loading dock.

Worried that she wouldn't have time to put her clothes on over her costume, she snatched a hoodie that read BLACK GUNS MATTER off a clothing table. Backstage, she found a dark corner to slip it on. She practically drowned in it. On the plus side, it completely hid the camo T-shirt and booty shorts. Pushing the sleeves to her elbows, she stuffed her Nell costume ballcap and wig in the backpack along with the ankle holster and the Glock. She almost made it to the loading dock door when a flashlight shone in her face.

"Hold it right there!"

Nell almost attacked but decided to try and bluff her way out instead. To do that, she did something she hadn't done in a very long time. She screamed like a girl.

"Oh my God, oh my God, oh my God," Nell said. "Please don't shoot."

The flashlight moved out of her eyes. Two policemen had come in through the landing dock. They lowered their rifles.

"Have you seen the shooter?" one of the policemen asked.

Nell shook her head.

"As soon as the shooting started, I came back here. I've been hiding the whole time."

"You did the right thing. Go down the ramp and join the others."

"Thank you. Thank you. Thank you."

Nell ran past the policemen as they continued their search for a blonde in sexy camouflage carrying a rifle. At the bottom of the ramp, she was greeted by another policeman who instructed her to hold her hands up and get in line with the other survivors. Outside, police cars with lights flashing, ambulances, and a fire engine stood ready. News trucks waited behind caution tape stretched across the entrance to the parking lot.

Policemen kept the survivors moving in single file to the open field beyond the parking lot. Nell kept her head down and listened to the conversations.

"I don't know what happened to Dean. He was right behind me."

"Has anybody seen Kelly Ann?"

"This is why it's bullshit that we can't take loaded guns into a goddamn gun show."

"If I had had bullets in my gun, she'd be the only dead person here today."

Policemen instructed them to stay calm and not to leave. Nell hovered at the outer edge of the group and looked for an opportunity to slip away without anyone noticing.

Divine intervention arrived in the form of a determined gun lover. Driving a massive pick-up truck with a vanity plate that read YESGAWD, he roared past the news trucks and ripped through the caution tape like he'd won a race. The crowd scattered to avoid getting run over. He screeched to a halt at the front entrance and hopped out with his semi-automatic rifle in his hands. The man looked to be in his early fifties, with a salt and pepper beard and an impressive beer belly.

"Stand aside!" he shouted. "I'm here to do what needs to be done!"

The police surrounded him. Being that he was a white man, and this was Texas, rather than demand he lay down his weapon before they shot him dead, they begged him to let them handle the situation. An argument ensued, with people in the crowd joining in with their opinions about Second Amendment rights and police jurisdiction.

With everyone's attention on the armed savior, Nell slipped away. She crossed a dirt field and entered the adjacent neighborhood. She passed by apartment buildings, single family homes, fast food restaurants, baseball fields, and churches. The wail of sirens grew more distant until she couldn't hear them at all.

Nell followed a back road to a railroad track and followed the tracks until they crossed the four-lane highway that would lead her to the truck stop where Skeeter waited for her. The grumble of traffic and the crunch of her boots on the gravel on the shoulder provided the soundtrack for her journey. The afternoon sun painted the sky in pinks and blues.

CHAPTER THIRTY-ONE

Agent Wayne Driscoll and Agent Jenni Teal caught an early morning flight from Washington DC to Austin, Texas, rented a car, and drove north, following the GPS signal of the Freightliner Semi-truck owned by Skeeter Foote. At 2:15 p.m., eleven miles outside Longview, they pulled off I-20 and slowly circled a TA Express truck stop until they had a visual on Skeeter's eighteen-wheeler. Once they were parked where they could observe him without being conspicuous, Driscoll called Special Agent Zavala.

"We've got eyes on Foote's vehicle."

"Is Nell with him?" Zavala asked.

Driscoll heard a call for a flight to St. Louis.

"Are you at the airport?" he asked.

"I take it you haven't been listening to the news."

"No. What did I miss?"

"Two active shooter incidents today. Same time. Different cities. Survivors at both locations claim the shooter was Nell Slagle."

"But…that's impossible."

"What's impossible?" Teal asked.

Driscoll held up his finger.

"Just a second."

"Either one of the shooters is a copycat," Zavala said, "or Honeydew cloned Nell and didn't tell us."

"Which cities were hit?"

"St. Louis and Longview."

"We're in Longview."

"Looks like you were right about Foote's involvement."

"Any arrests made?"

"Longview Nell got away. St. Louis Nell was killed. The fact that the St. Louis shooter is dead pretty much proves she's a copycat, but Easter and I are going there to confirm."

Teal grabbed Driscoll's arm and pointed at a young woman wearing an oversized hoodie walking across the parking lot.

"I can save you a trip," Driscoll said. "We have eyes on Nell."

"You can confirm it's her?"

Driscoll took out his binoculars and peered at the young woman.

"Affirmative."

"Don't approach her," Zavala said. "The military will take it from here. If anybody has a chance of containing her, it's them."

"She altered her appearance. Dyed her hair black and cut it short."

"I'll let them know. I want you and Agent Teal to return to headquarters. You did a good job, Archie."

"Thank you, Dora."

Nell climbed into Foote's truck. A minute later, the eighteen-wheeler drove away. The FBI agents headed in the opposite direction back to Austin. They weren't aware of Harry Pigott's mission to find Nell, otherwise they might have noticed Harry's Land Rover Defender on the other side of the parking lot.

Harry and Kat sat in his front seat. Grover and Dale sat behind them. Kat pointed at Nell as she walked toward Skeeter's truck.

"There she is," Kat said.

Grover leaned over the seat, giving Harry and Kat the full force of his bad breath.

"That's not her."

"Yes, it is," Kat said.

Grover sat back.

"Nell has long blonde hair."

Kat turned in her seat to face him.

"Spider, are you telling me that you are incapable of recognizing a woman if she changes her hair?"

Grover looked at Dale for help.

"No way she went into a beauty salon and had her hair done," Dale said.

Kat rolled her eyes.

"Boomslang, I adore you, but sometimes you're an idiot. She did it herself."

Grover and Dale stared at Nell as she climbed into Skeeter's truck.

"I still don't think it's her," Grover said. "That girl there is a lot lizard."

"She and I both have short black hair," Kat said. "If I stood next to her, would you be able to tell us apart?"

Dale put his hand on Grover's shoulder.

"Don't answer," Dale said. "It's a trap. If you admit they look alike, she'll kick your ass for calling her a lot lizard."

Grover turned to Harry for help.

"Commander. You saw Nell up close and personal. Is that her?"

While his men were arguing, Harry started the car and began following the truck from a safe distance.

"It's her. Everyone stay sharp. The mission is entering a crucial stage now."

Harry's phone rang.

"Yeah? What do you want?"

"Harry, it's Carol Fulcher."

Carole Fulcher was personal secretary to Chester Bulard Jr., CEO of Bulard Arms. She had a great figure despite having small breasts.

"What can I do for you, Carole?"

"Mr. Bulard wishes to speak to you. Stand by while I put your call through."

Harry did not wish to speak to Mr. Bulard, but he valued his job enough not to hang up. A moment later, Chester came on the line.

"Harry, how are you feeling?"

"I'm feeling fine, sir. Thank you for asking."

"That's good to hear considering the tragic experience you suffered recently."

"Yes, sir. What happened to those two brave police officers was a tragedy."

Harry could feel Kat staring at him. He shrugged.

"You chose an interesting form of therapy," Chester said.

"Sir?"

"I read about it in the Washington Post. You're apparently stalking the convention shooter with your personal militia?"

"Well, you know how the press likes to exaggerate the truth."

"Which parts did they exaggerate? And which parts are true?"

Harry stared at Skeeter's truck ahead. As much as he liked his job at Bulard Arms, there was no way in hell that he was going to give up his mission. Not when he was this close.

"My men and I are hunting the convention killer."

"Isn't that a job for law enforcement?" Chester asked. "I mean, isn't that why we pay taxes?"

"It's like you said, it's a form of therapy. The only way I can feel right about what happened is to terminate her with extreme prejudice."

"And law enforcement be damned?"

"No disrespect to the men in blue, but this one's mine."

Harry braced himself. Surely, Chester was going to fire him. It had been a good job while it lasted. The important thing was that Chester had no idea where Harry was, and even if he did, there was no way he could stop Harry from completing his mission.

To Harry's surprise, Chester laughed.

"Will you be speaking to the press again?"

"Sooner or later, I suppose."

"When you do, mention some of our fine products."

CHAPTER THIRTY-TWO

Nell and Skeeter arrived in Demopolis, Alabama at 1:00 a.m. and found a motel with truck and bus parking. Skeeter got connecting rooms number nine and ten. Once inside room ten, Nell dropped her backpack on the bed and went into the bathroom. She turned on the shower's hot water spigot and nothing happened. She tried twisting both the hot and cold taps all the way. Lukewarm water dribbled out of the showerhead for a moment before drying up.

She knocked on the connecting door. Skeeter let her into his room.

"What's up?"

"My shower doesn't work."

"Take a bath."

Nell wrinkled her nose.

"I've got sticky blood and who knows what else all over me."

Skeeter nodded towards the bathroom.

"See if this one works."

He leaned against the bathroom doorway as Nell tried the

shower. Hot water blasted out of the showerhead. Nell turned off the spigot.

"Mind if I use your shower?"

"Let's just switch rooms."

"You're not going to take a shower?"

"I don't have any blood on me."

Nell went back to her room, got her backpack, and went into Skeeter's room. He took his gear into her room and closed the door behind him. Nell stripped. She threw the hoodie she'd stolen from the gun show into the closet and washed her Nell Slagle Halloween costume, including the blonde wig, in the sink. She hung the camo outfit on a towel rack to dry and left the wig and ballcap on the bathroom counter. Turning the hot water on in the shower, Nell waited until it was hot enough to scald the skin of a normal person, and then got in. After the shower, she put on a clean T-shirt and panties and climbed into bed. Too tired to read or watch TV, she was asleep in minutes.

The people spying on them saw Skeeter enter room nine and Nell enter room ten. They couldn't see through walls, so they were not aware that Skeeter and Nell had switched rooms.

Harry followed Skeeter's truck until it pulled into the motel's parking lot, then he drove past the motel and parked at the barbeque restaurant next door.

"I'll do recon," Kat said.

"And I'll find a more secure base camp," Harry said.

"Right. It may be the middle of the night, but we don't want to take any chances."

Kat got out of the car, opened the trunk, and rummaged through their gear. She closed the trunk after locating a walkie talkie and binoculars.

Harry rolled down his window.

"I'll contact you for a report once we're in a secure location."

"Yes, sir, Commander," Kat said.

As Harry drove away, Kat melted into the shadows beside the barbeque restaurant. Harry drove empty streets exploring the surrounding area. He found a Walmart and a high school behind the motel. He chose the high school and stopped at the far edge of the parking lot near a clump of trees.

"This will do. Everybody out."

Harry, Dale, and Grover exited the car. They opened the trunk and removed the rifle cases.

"Commander," Dale said. "It's amazing how well you and Mama Kat work together. It's like you can read each other's minds."

"We are siblings," Harry said.

"Yeah, but I'm not like that with my sister."

Harry shrugged.

"Never gave it much thought. We've always been close. We've always shared the same values." Harry took out his walkie talkie. "Mama Kat. Report."

Her voice came through clearly on Harry's walkie talkie.

"Nell and Skeeter have side by side rooms near the ice machine."

"Room numbers?"

"Nine and ten."

"Which one is Nell's?"

"Ten."

Harry gave Kat their location and ordered her to rejoin the squad. When she arrived, she joined her fellow RAFF militiamen putting on their tactical gear and loading their weapons. Harry had Grover set up the camcorder for a pre-attack video.

Once it was recording, Harry spoke, with Kat, Dale, and Grover standing behind him.

"We have the mass killer's location and are preparing to make a citizen's arrest." Harry glanced at his watch. "It is now zero three hundred hours. At precisely zero four hundred hours, we will move in. If Nell Slagle doesn't surrender peacefully, we will have no choice but to use lethal force. That's all for now. God bless America." Harry paused for ten seconds then turned to Grover. "Get that online quick as you can."

Across the street from the motel, an AH-64 Apache helicopter landed in a field near two APCs, armored personnel carriers. A platoon of sixteen Navy SEALs wearing gas masks waited for Lt. General Buck Carter to exit the helicopter. Along with their normal combat gear, the SEALs had flash-bang grenades and tear gas launchers that fired canisters filled with sleeping gas. A line of oak trees hid the helicopter and the APCs from anyone driving by on the highway.

Carter climbed down. The men saluted and he returned their salute. Lieutenant Fernandez, the commander of the platoon, stepped forward.

"Status report," Carter said.

"Target is in the motel across the street," Fernandez said. "Room ten. We're ready to deploy at your command. However, there is an uninvited guest at the party."

"Explain."

"There's a high school behind the motel. In the school's parking lot are four civilians dressed in full tactical gear and armed to the teeth."

"You sure they're here for our target? They could just be out playing soldier."

Fernandez shook his head.

"They came in one car. Arizona license plate. Registered to a Harry Pigott."

"Why does that name sound familiar?"

"There was a *Washington Post* article about him recently. He said he was hunting Slagle and claimed to know how to find her. I thought it was bullshit, but now I see he really did have inside information."

Carter nodded.

"I read that article too. Do Pigott and his playmates have a clue that we're here?"

"No, sir. No one knows we're here."

That wasn't entirely true. The secretary of Homeland Security and the secretary of Defense knew they were here. Everyone at the Pentagon involved with Project Bulletproof knew they here. But Fernandez was right in that nobody in Alabama knew they were here, including the Demopolis police department.

"If Pigott attacks, then he's guilty of vigilantism, and if he gets in our way, it's criminal obstruction," Carter said.

"Even though we're a covert operation?" Fernandez asked.

"An operation that is in support of civil authorities."

Fernandez looked over at his platoon standing by.

"Just to be clear, sir, if Pigott gets in our way how should we respond?"

"Your mission is to get Slagle. Alive if possible. Remove any obstacles that get in your way in the most efficient manner possible."

Fernandez nodded.

"Understood, sir."

"Hopefully, it won't come to that. We never want to harm

civilians. However, I need you to have your full attention on Slagle. Let me worry about Pigott and his militia."

"Thank you, sir."

"I'll fly over to the school and put the fear of God and the United States military into them."

Fernandez saluted.

"We'll be ready to move in ten minutes, sir."

"I want your men breaking down Slagle's door eleven minutes from now."

Carter returned his salute and climbed back into his helicopter. Once he was strapped into his seat, he turned to his co-pilot, Chief Warrant Officer Sellers.

"Take her up," Carter said.

"Where to, sir?" Sellers asked.

"We have to go scare some grown men who never got over playing soldier."

Carter and Sellers arrived at the high school parking lot at 3:54 a.m. and hovered over an empty car. Harry Pigott and his companions were gone.

CHAPTER THIRTY-THREE

AT PRECISELY ZERO four hundred hours, Harry, Kat, Grover, and Dale sprinted across the motel parking lot, took positions outside room ten, and put on their night vision goggles.

"This is it," Harry said. "The moment we trained for."

"Can't tell you how thrilled I am to be here," Kat said.

"There's no one I'd rather share this moment with." Harry turned to Dale. "Boomslang. Breach the door."

Dale kicked the door open. Harry led the squad into the room. Though the bed was empty, the rumpled sheets showed that it had been occupied. Moving to the side, they saw the occupier's legs for a moment before they disappeared under the bed.

"Nell Slagle!" Harry bellowed. "You are under arrest."

"I think I saw a gun," Dale said.

"I feel threatened," Grover said.

"We must protect ourselves," Kat said.

The RAFF militiamen fired their Beastmasters at the mattress. Twenty seconds later, Harry held up his hand.

"Hold your fire!"

They stopped shooting. Bits of bedsheet and mattress pad floated in the air.

"We must confirm the kill. Spider. Boomslang. Move the bed."

Grover and Dale inched forward. Harry glanced at Kat. They both chuckled.

"Don't worry," Kat said. "Even if she's still alive, she's too full of holes to hurt you."

Grover and Dale put their rifles aside and grabbed the sides of the bed.

Harry heard the tinkling of glass breaking and felt something wet sprayed the side of his face. Kat slumped to the ground.

"Mama Kat?" Harry asked.

He knelt next to her. There was a hole in the back of head and a larger one between her blank staring eyes. And there was a bullet hole in the window. Harry realized the wetness on his face was Kat's blood.

"Everybody down!" Harry shouted.

They fell to their knees. Harry crawled to the window and peeked out. There was no sign of life. He didn't expect to see the sniper, but he thought he might at least see someone responding to the ruckus he and his men had created.

"What happened, Commander?" Grover asked.

"A sniper killed Mama Kat."

"A sniper?"

"It wasn't an amateur. My guess is either the Marines or Navy SEALs."

"Why?"

"They're pissed that we got Nell before they did."

"Shouldn't they be happy we killed her?"

"They should be pinning medals on us. But obviously, they don't agree."

Dale crawled to Harry and grabbed his arm. Tears streamed down Dale's face.

"How can you be so fucking calm?" Dale pointed at Kat's body. "Your sister's dead, and you act like it was no big deal."

Harry pulled his arm away from Dale.

"Of course it's a big deal. But I'd like to stay alive long enough to mourn her."

More bullets hit the window, shattering it to pieces. Humid air drifted in. Dale crawled over the broken glass, rested his rifle on the sill, and fired back.

"Boomslang! What the hell are you doing?" Harry asked.

"I'm not going down without a fight."

"The sniper is out of range of our guns. All you're doing is wasting ammo."

"They have to pay for what they did to my sweet, precious Mama Kat."

Dale fell back into the room and sobbed. Grover crawled to him and patted his back. Harry got as close to the window as possible without exposing himself.

"Nell's dead! If you want credit, that's fine with us. Just let us walk away."

Harry heard a helicopter overhead but couldn't tell how close it was. Sweat poured down his neck. The place had to be surrounded, cutting off any chance of escape. Either Harry negotiated a surrender, or he and his men were going to be as dead as his sister. Other than an occasional truck barreling down the highway and the whine of electrical lines, it was deathly quiet. When a voice finally called to them, Harry jumped at the sudden sound.

"You have one minute to get as far away from here as possible."

"You killed my sister," Harry said.

"You now have fifty-five seconds."

"I need time to get her in my car."

"We'll make sure her body gets to you."

"How does that work?"

"Harry Waylon Pigott. Divorced. No children. You own a two-bedroom house in Phoenix, Arizona. You've been employed by Bulard Arms for the last eight years. In the room with you are Grover Webb, Dale Klug, and your deceased sister, Katherine Pigott. You now have thirty seconds."

Harry groaned. If the three of them didn't want to join Kat, they needed to go. Now. That didn't make him feel any less shitty about leaving her behind. He stood by the door.

"Boomslang. Spider. Head back to the car. I'll cover you in case they change their minds about letting us go."

"What about Mama Kat?" Dale asked.

"The army will make sure she gets home," Grover said.

Dale's lower lip quivered. He bolted out of the room and ran in the direction of the high school. Grover waited a beat and then followed him. As Harry watched them sprint across the parking lot, he wondered if killing Nell was worth the sacrifice he'd made tonight. Maybe if he saw Nell with a bullet in *her* head it would ease the pain a little bit.

He looked at the bed and his eyes grew wide. The bed had been lifted and leaned against the wall. There was no body on the floor. Knowing the seconds were ticking away, Harry rushed to the bathroom. It was empty. The closet was empty. He glanced at his watch. His time had run out. He went to the door and took one last look back. That was when he noticed the other door. It must lead to the room next door. How did he miss it?

Swallowing his frustration, Harry bolted from the room. The air felt hot and sticky. He could feel the eyes of the hidden soldiers on him as he ran.

When Harry got to his car, his lungs burned, his legs ached, and he was covered in sweat. Grover and Dale didn't look at him. They sat on the ground and stared back at the motel. Crickets chirped their condolences.

Harry's hand shook as took his keys out of his pocket and unlocked the car. Silently, they stacked their rifles and night vision goggles in the trunk. They didn't bother taking the rest of their gear off. Grover and Dale climbed into the back seat. Neither rode shotgun. That was Kat's seat. Harry got behind the wheel and started the motor.

"I'm beginning to think a civilian militia like ours doesn't have a chance in hell against the real military," Grover said.

"Shut up, Spider," Harry said.

Harry got on the highway. They had the road mostly to themselves as they rode past trees and the occasional industrial business. Three miles outside the city, Harry pulled into the weed-choked parking lot of an abandoned diner. He climbed out, marched behind the crumbling building, and faced a pine forest. Normally, Harry enjoyed the scent of sticky pine sap, but at this moment, all he could smell was the stink of his grief.

Taking out his handgun, Harry screamed as he fired at the trees. He emptied his clip and reloaded. He fired again. When he finished the second clip, he could still hear gunfire. Dale had joined him in murdering timber.

After they ran out of ammo, they stood side by side and

listened to a hawk scolding them. Grover appeared at the side of the building.

"Commander."

"Not now, Spider," Harry said.

"Sir. The dot on the GPS tracker is moving."

Harry holstered his handgun. Now that he was calmer, he had questions. When RAFF squad broke into Nell's motel room, he'd only gotten the briefest glimpse of someone's legs as they squeezed under the bed. Were those legs hairy? Too hairy for a woman? Who picked up the bed and leaned it against the wall? And who was in the connecting room?

"Let me see that moving dot," Harry said.

They went back to the car and Harry studied the GPS tracker. Grover was right. The dot was moving.

"What does this mean?" Dale asked.

"Someone is driving Skeeter's truck," Grover said.

"They're heading east," Harry said.

Dale slapped the roof of the car.

"Skeeter got away. Big fucking deal."

Harry crossed his arms.

"It could be Skeeter. It's also possible we got the wrong room, and Nell's driving."

Dale stared at Harry.

"We got to catch that truck, Commander. I want to avenge Mama Kat's death."

"You and me both, Boomslang. What about you, Spider? If you want out, I won't think any less of you."

Grover saluted Harry.

"I'm with you, Commander. I loved Mama Kat too."

CHAPTER THIRTY-FOUR

Nell dreamed about shooting people who profit from the sword. They stood in a line, and she blasted them one by one. Her Beastmaster never ran out of ammo. She woke up, but the gunfire kept going. Someone was firing a weapon, and it wasn't her. Throwing the covers aside, she crossed the room and pressed her ear against the wall that separated her room from Skeeter's. A chill ran down her spine. The gunfire was coming from his room. Someone was shooting Skeeter.

The gunfire stopped.

Nell could hear talking but couldn't make out what they were saying. Cracking open the door that connected their rooms, she peeked in and could make out four figures in the dark room. She was about to go in when she heard glass break and one of the figures fell to the floor.

The others crouched down. As they discussed the death of their companion, the window shattered. One of them rushed to the window and fired his rifle outside. Nell saw her opportunity. She slipped into Skeeter's room. Enough light from the parking lot streamed through the shattered window for Nell to see that the four intruders were dressed in combat gear.

There was no sign of Skeeter. Nell heard a moan come from under the bed. She lifted it aside and found Skeeter on his back lying in a puddle. From the metallic smell, Nell knew that the liquid was blood.

Skeeter whimpered as Nell scooped him into her arms, carried him into her room, and lowered him carefully onto the bed. He pawed at her arm.

"Get my pants." His voice was weak.

"Now's not the time to worry about me seeing you in your boxers," Nell said.

Skeeter shook his head.

"My keys are in my pants. I don't want nobody to steal my truck."

Nell sighed.

"Okay. Where'd you leave them?"

"The chair next to the bed."

When Nell crept back into the Skeeter's room, a conversation was ongoing between one of the guys in combat gear and a man outside. As Nell grabbed Skeeter's pants, the man outside said a familiar name.

Harry Waylon Pigott.

Nell stared at the man hunkered down by the window. It was indeed Harry Pigott. He still had that stupid mustache. And as much as she wanted to kill him for shooting Skeeter, she couldn't right then because Skeeter needed her. She went to her room and locked the door.

"Skeeter. I got your pants. How do you feel?"

She tried to keep the quiver out of her voice but failed miserably. She put the pants next to him and then placed her hand on his chest. His lifeforce grew weaker by the second. She searched his body. Considering the amount of shooting Nell had heard, she was surprised to find only three entry wounds. That was more than enough. The Beastmaster was a high muzzle velocity weapon that released a huge amount of kinetic energy. When someone got shot by a Beastmaster, the bullet left a big hole and exploded inside the body.

Skeeter coughed. "I'm in a world of pain, so I must still be alive."

Nell fetched all the towels from the bathroom and ripped them into strips. The wound to Skeeter's left arm was nasty, the bone shattered beyond repair. Nell used a strip to tie a tourniquet above the entry point. She did the same for the wound to his right leg. The large hole in his side leaking dark blood worried her. She pressed folded strips into the wound before binding his torso.

"This is my fault," Nell said. "They were looking for me."

She put a pillow under Skeeter's head and brought his knees up. Holding his hand, she got more information from his body. The damage to his intestines was too severe. Even if an ambulance showed up right now, Skeeter was going to die.

"Remember the first time we met?" Skeeter said. "I thought you were a lot lizard."

"Easy mistake to make considering the circumstances."

"And then you tried to kill me."

Nell gasped.

"I never tried to kill you."

"Sure you did. You tied me up with cables and left me to die. I was in the cab for two days before the truck stop manager rescued me."

"Oh my God, I'm so sorry. I thought the knots were loose enough that you'd wiggle out of them in a couple of hours."

"No, ma'am. Those knots were so tight they ended up having to cut the cables."

Nell held up her right hand and flexed her fingers.

"When I first got enhanced strength, I crushed everything I touched. I turned forks and spoons into lumps of metal. Forget anything made of glass."

"I've seen you handle a fork," Skeeter said. "You didn't seem to have any problems."

Nell grinned.

"The scientists trained me to control my strength. It was a slow process, but I eventually learned. I have to be careful whenever I touch anything."

"I guess you weren't thinking when you tied me up," Skeeter said.

"It's not that. We never covered tying knots. I did my best guess."

Skeeter grimaced.

"I don't get it. I thought Harry was my friend."

"You know Harry Pigott?"

"Yeah. I did a lot of contract work for Bulard Arms. That's how we met."

Nell gently kneaded Skeeter's hand.

"I have a confession to make. I wasn't going to kill Raphael. I'm at war with gun crazy jerks. I have nothing against Raphael, and besides I thought if I did kill him, you'd end up regretting it later."

"Listen, Nell. About Raphael…"

His skin was pale and sweat shone on his forehead.

"Don't worry," Nell said. "I'll kill him. I promise. I'll go straight to Valdosta and kill Raphael."

"Listen," Skeeter said. "This is what I want you to do..."

His voice was weak. Nell had to lean in close to hear him. As Skeeter talked, he fumbled with his pants and took the keys to his truck from the pocket. He pressed the keys into Nell's hand. Nell held him close.

"Don't worry," she said. "I'll do it."

Skeeter closed his eyes and died.

Nell heard boots pounding the asphalt parking lot. She gently placed Skeeter's body on the bed then went to the front door and looked through the peephole. Soldiers stood outside her door. A guy wearing a T-shirt and boxer shorts, his hair sticking up, approached them.

"What's going on?" he asked.

"You were told to stay in your room," a soldier said.

"I've got a right to know."

"Get back to your room."

The guy mumbled something under his breath but walked away.

First Harry, now the soldiers. It seemed everybody knew where to find Nell and Skeeter. Soldiers filed into Skeeter's room. It wouldn't be long before they realized that neither Nell or Skeeter was in there and that there was a door connected to her room. As much as she wanted to stay with Skeeter, she knew she had to leave.

Stuffing jeans, combat boots, and Skeeter's keys into her backpack, Nell hurried into the bathroom and locked the door. There was a small bathroom window with a view to the dirt lot used for truck and bus parking.

The front door and the connecting door were busted open

one after the other. The boots she'd heard in the parking lot were now in her motel room. Nell's heart raced as she tossed her backpack out the window. She squeezed through and dropped to muddy ground. The stench of sewage was overwhelming. Grabbing the backpack, she started to run but slipped and fell.

She did a quick assessment of her situation. Her friend was murdered, she wore only a T-shirt and panties, was covered in blood and stinky mud, and soldiers were coming for her. And the sun wasn't even up yet.

Nell struggled to her feet and went to the dirt lot. To her surprise, no one was watching Skeeter's truck. The soldiers' overconfidence that they would catch her in the motel room was her first lucky break. Rather than hope that she got a few more lucky breaks, there was one thing she could do now to increase her chances of getting away.

It was painfully obvious that her partnership with Skeeter was no longer a secret. Every cop in America would be on the lookout for the truck's license plate number. Having another truck's plate might just buy Nell a little time. Maybe even enough to get her to Cleveland.

She switched the Georgia plate on Skeeter's truck with a Minnesota plate on the truck next to his. Thanks to her enhanced strength, Nell didn't need a screwdriver to turn the screws.

Climbing inside Skeeter's truck, Nell felt a rush of guilt sitting in the driver's seat. This was Skeeter's seat. After adjusting it to fit her shorter legs, Nell inserted the key in the ignition and started the engine. The engine's rumble was the first comforting thing she'd heard this early morning.

She didn't need to feel the truck to know how to operate it. She had been living in it for days and had already learned its secrets. Shifting gears, Nell checked the rearview mirror before turning right onto US 80 East. Nobody was chasing her. That was her second lucky break.

Four blocks later, she turned right onto US 43 South, a two-lane road that ran through a bucolic landscape of grassy fields, small lakes, and ranch houses with plenty of space between neighbors. In Grove Hill, Nell turned onto U.S. Highway 84 East. Her plan was to stay on it all the way to Georgia.

A mile outside of Grove Hill, Nell pulled onto a scar of dirt on the side of the road. She found a towel in one of the storage containers, stripped off her filthy clothes, and wiped mud and Skeeter's blood off her body before moving into the sleeper.

The bed smelled of Skeeter. The whole truck smelled like him. The truck was Skeeter. Nell's invulnerable body, enhanced strength, and the ability to learn a machine by touch were no match for grief and guilt. She curled up on the bed and cried.

CHAPTER THIRTY-FIVE

Easter stood in the bathroom of room ten and with gloved hands examined the blonde wig and ballcap on the bathroom counter. He did the same with the camo T-shirt and booty shorts hanging on the towel rack. This was the closest he'd physically been to Nell since he started searching for her.

He left the items for forensics to bag and tag. In the bedroom, he paused to look at Skeeter Foote's body on the blood-stained bed. The forensics team moved around Easter as they did their work. Zavala entered the motel room and stood next to him.

"Why did he help Nell?" Zavala asked. "Was it voluntary or did she force him to do it?"

"He had too many opportunities to escape," Easter said. "My guess is that they made a deal. She had something he wanted."

"Or he also wanted revenge on those who profit from the sword."

They left the motel room. Police cruisers, an ambulance, and an SBI (state bureau of investigation) mobile unit filled the parking lot. Katherine Pigott was already inside the ambulance. Once the forensics was done, Skeeter would join her.

"The chief of the Demopolis Police was not at all happy about the United States military being in his city without his knowledge," Zavala said.

"I don't blame him."

"Carter didn't help the situation. Told the chief to be a team player or get the hell out of the way."

Easter watched the traffic on the highway. A light rain had started to fall.

"I still can't believe she got away from Carter and his Navy SEALs."

"To his credit, he didn't try to put the blame on Harry Pigott's interference."

"We should have guessed that Harry and Skeeter knew each other."

Zavala scowled.

"Even if we had, there's no way we could have known that Harry found out Nell was riding in Skeeter's truck."

"Harry should have contacted the police and told them what he knew. If he had, then his sister would still be alive."

"Eventually, Carter is going to find her. Again. What if he can't bring her in? Again?"

"We have to come up with a plan. We know where she's going. If she gets by Carter, that's where we'll intercept her."

"Then what? What do we use to stop her?"

Easter shrugged.

"The power of persuasion?"

CHAPTER THIRTY-SIX

THE WAITRESS DELIVERED plates of fried catfish to Harry, Grover, and Dale. They had stopped for dinner at a ramshackle seafood restaurant on the outskirts of Dothan, Alabama. The tables were covered with checkered vinyl tablecloths and the walls were basic wood panels.

"Will there be anything else?" the waitress asked.

Harry held up his cup.

"Can I get some more coffee, ma'am?"

"You got it. What about you gentlemen?"

"I'm good," Dale said.

"Me too," Grover said.

"I'll get that coffee," the waiter said. "Enjoy."

Harry poked at his meal. He'd lost his appetite. He couldn't stop thinking about Kat's lifeless body on the motel floor. Watching Dale and Grover wolf down their catfish dinners was a reminder that people grieved differently. Especially Grover. Not only was he eating as if this were his last meal, but he was also deeply absorbed with a news story on his tablet.

"I'm sure that GPS signal will come back on," Dale said with his mouth full.

Harry shook his head.

"This isn't like before when we lost the signal in the hills. We're on flat land near decent sized cities."

"You think maybe it broke?"

"I think Nell figured out how to disable the truck's GPS."

Dale wrinkled his nose.

"Then how the hell we supposed to find her?"

The waitress swung by their table and filled Harry's cup. He sipped the steaming coffee and grimaced. It was burnt.

"Excellent question. I have no idea. But I'm open to suggestions."

Grover looked up from his phone and wiped his mouth with his napkin.

"I think I know where she's going, sir."

Harry puffed out his mustache.

"Really? I'm all ears."

Grover leaned forward as if he were sharing a secret.

"I read that article about us in the *Washington Post.*"

"I told the reporter that I knew where Nell was going, but that's no longer true."

Grover pointed at his tablet.

"After I read the article, I wondered if that reporter had written any other stories about us. So, I did a search on her."

"Did she?" Harry asked.

Grover mopped his forehead with his napkin.

"No. But it turns out this reporter, Dani Lewis, has written a lot about Nell Slagle, going all the way back to when Nell's brother shot all those kids in Cleveland, Tennessee."

Harry started to sip his coffee and remembered how terrible it tasted. He put the cup aside.

"I'm assuming this is leading up to something."

"In one of Lewis's articles, she talks about how Nell got a raw deal because everybody blamed her for what her brother did. The poor girl never even got a chance to say goodbye to her mother."

"Well, boo hoo," Dale said.

"Please, Boomslang," Harry said. "Let Spider talk."

Grover blushed.

"All this time Nell's been headed east. I think she's going home to see her mama's grave."

Dale and Harry stared at Grover.

"That's the dumbest thing I've ever heard," Dale said.

Harry grinned.

"No, Boomslang. It's brilliant. I wondered why Nell didn't go south to Mexico. And Spider figured it out."

"All we have to do is get to Cleveland before she does," Grover said.

"And wait for her to show up. Master Tzu couldn't have said it better himself."

Grover beamed and Dale looked confused. Harry began to eat his fried catfish.

CHAPTER THIRTY-SEVEN

NELL PULLED INTO a church parking lot in Quitman, Georgia, parked next to a sign that read, "We Love Our Military," and cried. This was the third time that day she had broken out in big heaving sobs. The first time was in the shower at a Flying J Travel Center in Dothan, Alabama. The second time was in the women's bathroom of Betty's Cafeteria in Bainbridge, Georgia.

How was she supposed to fulfill Skeeter's dying wish if she couldn't stop crying? Nell hadn't felt a hole this big in her heart since Peggy died.

She entered Valdosta's city limits around 9:00 a.m., passing building supply companies and open fields before encountering tree-lined streets, wide sidewalks, and large houses. Things changed as she got closer to Rafael and Edie's home. There were no more churches, fast food restaurants, or sidewalks. Along cracked asphalt streets were pawn shops, Family Dollar stores, and Mexican restaurants. Instead of grocery store chains like Publix and Winn-Dixie, there were *supermercados*.

Turning off the main road into the neighborhoods, houses were old but well-maintained. Lawns were mowed. There were lots of pick-up trucks, and Mexican flags hanging next to American flags. Kids on bicycles waved at her as she drove past them.

Vargas Painting and Home Improvement was in a two-bedroom red brick house that had been converted into a business office. It sat on a double lot; the other half was paved, with white lines painted to indicate parking spaces. As Nell pulled in, she broke a few tree branches that hung over the entrance. Skeeter's truck was too long, and three feet of the trailer's tail hung out on the street. No one seemed to mind. Cars drove around it and continued on their way.

Nell leaned back in the driver's seat. Coming to Valdosta, Georgia was the easy part. The next part wasn't going to be easy. Not even a little bit. She climbed out, walked around the cab, and found herself face to face with an angry woman.

"Where's Skeeter?"

"He's not here," Nell said.

"Why are you driving his truck?"

If Skeeter had possessed a photo of Edie, he had never showed it to Nell. But he had described her plenty of times, a fiery redhead in her forties with pale skin and lots of freckles.

"You must be Edie," Nell said. "I'm a friend of Skeeter's."

Edie gave Nell the stink eye.

"You'd better start explaining yourself, young lady, right quick. You hear me?"

"Is Rafael here?" Nell asked.

"That's none of your damn business."

"This is between me and him."

"You're driving a stolen truck."

"I didn't steal it."

"I'm calling the police."

"I wouldn't do that if I were you."

"Are you threatening me?"

Nell gazed up at the Spanish moss hanging from oak trees in the front yard.

"Skeeter was right. You're a pain in the ass."

Edie stepped back as if Nell had slapped her.

A Latinx man came out of the office. He cradled a girl in his arms who couldn't have been older than two or three.

"It's okay, Edie," the man said. "Let me talk to her."

He handed the girl to Edie. The girl had black hair and blue eyes. She was adorable. She wrapped her arms around Edie's neck.

"I'm Rafael," the man said.

He was handsome and younger than Edie.

"My name's Jolene," Nell said. She'd decided to use the name at the last moment, but really, she had been wanting to call herself Jolene since Las Vegas. "Is there someplace we can talk in private?"

"I'm going to tell my wife whatever you tell me."

"I promised Skeeter I would talk to you alone."

Rafael and Edie looked at each other. Edie gave a slight nod.

"We can talk in my office," Rafael said.

They passed through a living room had been converted into a waiting room. Rafael's office had been a bedroom. The thick carpet was so new it hadn't lost its chemical smell. A window air conditioner wasn't brand new and made a dripping sound. A child's drawing was taped to one of the wood-paneled walls. After closing the office door, Rafael sat behind a wooden desk that was too big for the room, and motioned for Nell to take one of the two visitor's chairs.

"You're lucky," Rafael said. "Normally, I would be out at a job site. But I happen to be catching up on paperwork today."

"Skeeter's dead," Nell said.

She hadn't meant to blurt it out like that or to start crying for the fourth time that day. Rafael stared at her but showed no emotion.

"How did he die?"

Nell wiped away tears.

"He was shot to death."

Rafael clenched his fists.

"Who shot him?"

"Does it matter?"

Rafael moved his hands off the desk to where Nell couldn't see them. He was trying to be quiet, but Nell could hear a drawer opening. Either Rafael was reaching for a gun or an antacid.

"It matters to me," he said. "How do I know you didn't kill Skeeter and steal his truck?"

"If I had, then why the hell would I come here?"

"If it wasn't you, then who? Skeeter never took anything that wasn't his."

"No. That's your specialty."

Rafael raised an eyebrow.

"Was he your boyfriend?"

"No. Just a friend."

Grief replaced her anger, and the tears returned. Rafael didn't speak. He waited for her to go on.

"Four people broke into his hotel room and opened fire on him. The room was dark. They thought it was me."

"You owed them money?"

Nell shook her head. "Their leader was angry at me for bruising his ego."

Rafael nodded. Nell could hear the drawer closing.

"I grew up in Mexico and I live in city full of rednecks," Rafael said. "I know all about what men do to women."

Nell looked down at her lap expecting to see Skeeter's blood on her clothes. But there was nothing there. After Nell had showered this morning, she had put on blue jeans, a pink T-shirt, and a gray hoodie. Her muddy blood-stained clothes were buried in a dumpster.

"Before he died, Skeeter asked me to come see you," Nell said. "He wanted me to tell you that he was sorry for the bad blood between you two. He said you were a good man and he's counting on you to take care of Edie."

Rafael shuffled some papers on his desk.

"Skeeter was very angry when Edie and I got together. He said he was going to shoot me. Edie said I was lucky he'd stopped drinking because if he hadn't, he probably would have done it."

Nell bit her lower lip. She had no intention of telling Rafael that Skeeter had wanted her to kill him. Or that Skeeter hadn't change his mind until he knew he was about to die.

"I only knew him for a short time, but he was like an uncle who isn't a blood relative but still family."

Rafael glanced at the drawing on the wall. It was of three stick figures: daddy, mommy, and daughter.

"I didn't plan to fall in love with Edie. These things just happen."

Nell laid the keys to the truck on the desk.

"Skeeter wanted you to have his truck. I don't know where

he kept the title. Maybe Edie knows. I just need to get my things out."

Rafael ignored the keys. He had gorgeous brown eyes. Nell could see why Edie had fallen for him.

"I have a good business," Rafael said. "I don't need a truck."

Nell nodded.

"Skeeter figured you could sell it and use the money for the baby."

The office door flung open, and Edie entered the room. Nell jerked back, but Rafael didn't move a muscle. Dramatic gestures were probably an everyday thing with Edie, and he had gotten used to them.

"Don't you dare touch those keys!" Edie said.

"You spied on us?" Nell asked.

Edie glared at Nell.

"It's my house. I can do what I want."

When Skeeter used to talk about Edie driving him crazy, Nell thought he was exaggerating. Not anymore.

"Don't worry," Rafael said. "I'm not going to take his truck."

Edie snatched the keys off the desk and thrust them toward Nell.

"Take it and get out of here."

"I'm sure it's worth a lot of money," Nell said.

Tears streamed down Edie's face.

"That truck took Skeeter away from me. It's cursed and I don't want anything to do with it."

Nell glanced at Rafael. He nodded. She took the keys from Edie. Rafael walked her out of the office. Nell felt sticky coming into the heat after sitting in the air-conditioned room. To her surprise, Rafael hugged her.

"Take care of yourself, Jolene."

"I'll try."

She climbed into Skeeter's truck. Edie came outside with the baby on her hip. Rafael joined her by the office door. Nell backed out of the parking lot, waved goodbye, and headed north toward home.

CHAPTER THIRTY-EIGHT

Nell took the entrance ramp onto I-75 North. Clouds had rolled in on what had been a bright day. But it didn't look like rain and there wasn't much traffic. A perfect day for driving an eighteen-wheeler on the highway. Nell turned on the radio. In honor of Skeeter, she searched the dial until she found the local NPR station.

"If you're just joining us," the announcer said, "we're discussing the so-called 'Nell Effect.' Gun shows have been cancelled all across the country for fear that they might be attacked by Nell Slagle or a Nell Slagle copycat."

"Whoo hoo!" Nell shouted.

Maybe, just maybe, she was starting to put the fear of Nell into those who profit from the sword. Maybe even enough to put some of them out of business.

Since Edie had basically given Skeeter's truck to Nell, she was tempted to stay on the road until the wheels fell off. But she knew she couldn't. There were only so many times she could change the license plate. Sooner or later, the police would find the truck. Nell would have to find new transportation soon.

A highway patrol car came up behind her with its lights flashing. Shit. Shit. Shit. This was her punishment for thinking ahead instead of keeping her attention on the here and now. But then the cruiser zoomed around her and pulled an SUV over. Nell was relieved, but confused. As far as she could tell, the SUV hadn't been speeding. Whatever. As long as she didn't get stopped.

Another patrol car whizzed past her and pulled over a sedan. Nell wondered if this stretch of I-75 was a speed trap. Though she was driving the speed limit, she downshifted to a slower speed. As she rolled along, gazing at billboards and the endless ribbon of road, it dawned on Nell that no vehicles were entering the highway from the on ramps. The back of her neck tingled. Something was wrong. Not only were no cars entering the highway, she had the road to herself. She looked to her left. There was no southbound traffic. This wasn't possible. It was the middle of the day.

Nell heard the chopping sound before she saw the helicopter fly over. It soared ahead and spun around to face her. This wasn't a police chopper. Dark green and looking like a giant insect, it was an advanced multi-role helicopter with laser-guided precision hellfire missiles, 70mm rockets, a 30mm cannon, and advanced target acquisition designation. Nell knew all this because she'd flown one just like it at HARD-SOW.

The helicopter hovered over the road. Nell moved toward it. Checking the rearview mirror, she saw armored vehicles pursuing her. The soldiers she'd narrowly escaped in Alabama were probably in those. But she had disconnected the GPS and changed the truck's plates. How the hell did they find her so soon?

She was in a rural area and the next exit was nowhere in

sight. There was a concrete barrier between the north and south lanes. They had her boxed in.

Nell had driven into a trap.

The helicopter fired a rocket at the truck. Nell swerved. It barely missed her, and hit the concrete barrier. The ground shook from the impact.

To her right was a farm with rows of green. Not a good place for a truck, but it was an open space and a possible escape route. Nell turned the wheel and drove off the highway. She struggled to maintain control as the truck rumbled across a ditch and tore through a chain link fence. The truck's heavy-duty tires trampled vegetables. The trailer was empty, which made it bouncy even on the best roads. It bounced so much Nell feared it would topple over.

Nell glanced at the rearview mirror and wished she hadn't. The armored vehicles were still after her. They were more suited to this terrain than a semi tractor-trailer. Ahead of her was a big red barn. Nell hoped there was a road on the other side of it.

There was a bang like a pistol shot to her left, followed by a thumping sound. One of her eighteen tires had blown out. Considering what she was dealing with, the flat wasn't worth a second of concern. But the sound caused her to look left in time to see the helicopter gliding over the field toward her.

The helicopter fired another missile. It was impossible to swerve in a vegetable field. Nell did the only thing she could do. She shifted gears and pressed the gas pedal to the floor. The truck lurched and gained enough speed so that the missile hit the trailer instead of the cab.

The explosion was deafening. Nell felt intense heat on her back. The cab's windows shattered. Nell was pushed into the driver's side airbag that had blossomed from the steering wheel.

The impact reduced the trailer to scrap metal and knocked the tractor onto its side. Nell felt a moment of weightlessness before it hit the ground. Smoke and the smell of diesel fuel filled the cab. The seatbelt held Nell suspended in a world that had gone sideways.

Every part of Nell hurt, a harsh reminder that being bulletproof wasn't painless. Nell didn't need to see the soldiers to know they were coming for her, but she was in too much pain to think clearly. She had to do something. Now.

CHAPTER THIRTY-NINE

Lt. General Buck Carter landed the AH-64 Apache helicopter in the vegetable field approximately twenty yards from the smoldering carcass of Terry "Skeeter" Foote's Freightliner truck.

"That was some good shooting, sir," Chief Warrant Officer Sellers said.

"The credit goes to the Apache's advanced technology," Carter said, "Makes it so even an old timer like me can't miss."

"Your first attempt only failed because Slagle got extremely lucky, sir."

"I didn't miss. My intention was to lead her to this field. It's a better location to engage the enemy than the road."

Sellers gazed at the field.

"I see what you mean, sir."

The truth was Carter had missed, though he shouldn't have. The Hellfire missiles are called Fire and Forget for a reason. Their guidance system guaranteed that they always hit their target. But Nell had maneuvered out of the first missile's path. And she had done it in a semi tractor-trailer, which would never be accused of being nimble. It was if she had sensed its trajectory. The ability to dodge missiles could be another unexpected benefit of Project Bulletproof and one more reason to get Nell back to Honeydew as soon as possible.

The second missile had struck exactly where Carter had intended it to hit. He had anticipated that Nell would speed up to avoid a direct strike to the cab. Carter had also wanted to avoid hitting the cab.

Even with her invulnerable body, a direct missile blast would have blown Nell to pieces. Rex Wilson had claimed that all his scientists needed to resurrect Project Bulletproof was a single body part. But Carter knew better. If he gave the Honeydew scientists a severed foot, they would say what they really needed was an eyeball or a tooth. Also, Carter wasn't in the mood to scrape bits of Nell into a bag. He intended to deliver her to Honeydew fully intact with no missing pieces.

Carter and Sellers departed the aircraft and stood in the field. Using his binoculars, Carter watched the two APCs halt within a yard from the truck. His platoon of sixteen Navy SEALs exited the vehicles wearing their gas masks. Two of the SEALs carried a clear plastic cocoon with oxygen tanks attached to portals along the side.

The cocoon was a portable negative pressure isolation bag. It was designed to let air in but not allow air out. They were used on small aircraft for transporting patients with infectious diseases. The tanks in the portals delivered anesthetic gas to keep patients calm while confined in the cocoon. Once the SEALs got Nell into the cocoon, they would use the gas to keep her unconscious for the duration of the journey to Honeydew's Atlanta facility.

The SEALs checked their weapons before surrounding the

toppled cab. Carter turned on his headset so that he could communicate with platoon commander Lieutenant Fernandez.

"Status report," Carter said.

"We're ready, sir," Fernandez said. "She won't slip by us this time."

"Proceed. With extreme caution."

Carter bent down and pulled a carrot from the ground. He stood and brushed the dirt off.

"My grandfather grew carrots."

He tossed the carrot aside. From his vantage point, Carter could see the tires and the belly of the cab. Half the platoon kept watch on the field while the rest took positions by the truck.

"Linton," Fernandez said. "Deliver the packages."

A SEAL climbed the side of the cab and tossed a flash-bang grenade into it. The bang echoed inside the cab and white smoke billowed out. Without waiting for the smoke to clear, the SEAL dropped a cannister of fentanyl into the cab. The hiss of gas lasted for a full minute while the metal container emptied its contents.

"Pruitt," Fernandez said, "Locate the target."

Pruitt climbed up the cab. He pointed his M4A1 assault rifle inside the shattered driver side window and looked around.

"No sign of the target, sir," Pruitt said.

"Come down," Fernandez said. "I'll take a look."

Pruitt climbed down and Fernandez went up. He mimicked Pruitt, pointing his rifle inside as he inspected the interior. Fernandez opened the cab door and went down inside. Carter couldn't see Fernandez, but he could still hear him. The metal scraping and banging sounded like Fernandez was inside a grain silo. Fernandez's head popped out of the door. He sat with his legs dangling inside the truck and shook his head.

"Pruitt is correct, sir. The cab is empty.

Carter put his binoculars down. "How does she keep doing this?"

The truck was in the middle of a field. There was no place for her to hide.

"Check the surrounding area," Carter said.

"Yes, sir," Fernandez said.

The lieutenant led the entire platoon across the field to search for Nell.

"The truck sustained a direct missile strike, sir," Sellers said. "How could she possibly still be moving?"

"Did you sleep through the briefing?" Carter asked.

"No, sir. Nell Slagle is latest development in advanced weaponry."

"Damn right she is."

"Sir. I believe I saw something move on the belly of the truck."

Sellers pointed at the truck. There was a flash of light that could have been a reflection of the sun on the metal belly of the cab, but then Carter saw that it was a panel swinging open. Nell crawled out. Her face and clothes were covered in dark smudges.

"Lieutenant Fernandez," Carter said into his headset. "Slagle's at the truck."

"We just checked the truck, and she wasn't there."

"I'm looking at her right now."

"But sir…"

"We can figure out how she did it later."

"Yes sir. On our way."

CHAPTER FORTY

NELL UNBUCKLED HER seat belt, fell out of the driver's seat, bounced off the passenger seat, and landed on the passenger side door. Outside the cracked windshield were rows of green leaves. Nell didn't know her vegetables well enough to know what was growing underneath them.

The back wall of the sleeper was charred black. Burnt cheese crackers were scattered everywhere. Her beloved fake Louis Vuitton handbag had melted into a misshapen lump. She pried it open. Her money roll had been reduced to ashes. The stench was thick and heavy.

The whirring of the helicopter and the rolling sound of the armored vehicles let Nell know that unwanted company would be arriving soon. She reached under the dashboard and flipped the hidden switch. The panel to the hidey hole slid open. Nell peered inside. The hidey hole was intact.

"Damn, Skeeter. You weren't screwing around when you built this thing."

Nell climbed inside and closed the panel. Since the cab

was on its side, she was able to stand up as she waited for the soldiers to come.

She didn't have to wait long. Five minutes later, Nell heard a man bark an order. His voice was slightly muffled.

"Linton. Deliver the packages."

The cab shifted and creaked from the weight of a soldier climbing to the top. A metal object clattered down inside followed by a deafening bang. Nell winced as her ears rang. Another metal object dropped into the cab. Despite her limited hearing, Nell could make out a hissing sound. Gas leaked into the hidey hole. Nell's head swam and her stomach lurched as she fought to remain conscious. She lost the battle. Her eyes grew too heavy to keep open and darkness enveloped her.

When Nell snapped awake, she had no idea how long she had been out. The voice she'd heard earlier spoke again.

"Pruitt is correct, sir. The cab is empty."

There was silence and then he spoke again.

"Platoon. Fall in!"

Nell heard footsteps receding. Gambling that the soldiers had left the cab to search for her, she pulled the lever and the hidey hole's bottom panel swung open. The stench of smoke and diesel fuel mixed with the scent of freshly turned earth. The clouds had retreated and the sun momentarily blinded Nell as she stepped into the field.

Peeking around the edge of the cab, Nell saw the soldiers moving toward a red barn. She scooted to the other side and was shocked by the mangled remains of the trailer. If the missile had hit the cab, she too would have been mangled remains. Beyond the trailer were two khaki armored vehicles. She only needed one to make her escape.

Nell scanned the field. A helicopter sat on the rim of the

field as if it was the opposing team waiting for the kickoff. Two pilots stood in front of the helicopter. Nell figured the pilot shouting and pointing at her must be an officer. She looked around the edge of the cab again. The soldiers were rushing toward her.

"Snitches get stiches!" she shouted.

Gunfire tore up the ground near her feet and pinged off the cab. Nell ran for the armored vehicles. She didn't even get close. There was too much open space. The soldiers fired on her. The hail of bullets hit her with so much force that she tumbled to the ground.

"My bruises have bruises," Nell moaned.

She got back on her feet and ran the rest of the way to the vehicle. The ramp had been left down, allowing Nell to enter from the back end. She hurried through the vehicle to the driver's seat, which looked like an office swivel chair bolted to the floor. Resting her hands on the steering wheel, she absorbed the vehicle's deepest secrets.

Nell started the engine. It grumbled like a grouchy beast. She pulled a lever and the ramp lifted. A metal canister smashed through the driver's side window and just missed Nell before it ping-ponged around the cockpit. It came to rest at her feet. She peered through the broken window and then down at the floor. The window was about the size of a loaf of bread, and the canister was only inches smaller.

"Damn," Nell said. "That was some impressive shooting."

The canister spewed gas into the cramped space. Nell grabbed it and tossed it out the window. Another canister flew in, followed by five more in rapid succession. There were too many to throw back. The interior filled with gas. Nell's head swam again as she stumbled out of the driver's seat. She felt like she'd fallen into a vat of molasses and had difficulty stringing two thoughts together. The row of padded seats looked like a nice place to take a nap.

"Don't do it, Nell," she said, slapping her cheek. "Don't go to sleep."

She opened her eyes.

Nell had no idea how long she'd been asleep. Getting back to her feet exhausted her, but she pushed on. The ramp lowered and soldiers poured in. Their gas masks made them look like aliens as they swarmed her. Nell's limbs felt like they were encased in cement, too heavy to move.

She fell asleep again.

When she jerked back awake, the soldiers were grabbing and tugging her. Their roaming hands triggered yet another of her many painful memories.

The terrible thing happened on a cold winter day while Nell was living in Emerald City's homeless camp. The shining sun seemed like an insult because it provided no warmth. Nell was in her wheelchair in front of her patchwork tent. Her body itched from the beginnings of withdrawal. Mother Hen had promised to fix Nell up with a speedball. She was late and Nell was getting anxious.

That was when a group of men rushed her. At first, Nell thought they were rolling her for her few possessions, but then one squeezed her breasts while another yanked her pants down. The cold air bit her bare skin. They didn't care that it was the middle of the day. Evil shit didn't wait for the cover of night in Emerald City.

"Why are you doing this?" Nell said."

The men answered with grunts and growls. Nell screamed and tried to fight but she was too weak. They pulled her out of her wheelchair, threw her on the ground, and rolled her onto her back. One of the men got on top of her, his weight pressing against her chest, his rank breath in her face. As he fumbled with his fly, the other men peered down at her with hungry eyes. Nell's pleas for them to stop only egged them on.

She heard a dull thud. The man fell off her. His head was bleeding. Mother Hen had come to her rescue. She'd used a cast iron skillet to beat the men off Nell. They scurried away like frightened rats.

Here Nell was again, too weak to fight back. Mother Hen wasn't going to rescue her this time.

The soldiers dragged Nell out of the vehicle.

"We have her, Lieutenant," a soldier said.

"Get her into the cocoon," the lieutenant said. "Don't give her time to regain her faculties."

The soldiers lifted her and carried her to a clear plastic thing that looked like a see-through coffin. Out in the open and away from the gas, Nell felt a fraction less sleepy but she was still too drugged to fight. In her head, she kept switching between the attempted rape in Emerald City and the soldiers carrying her in the vegetable field. Nell struggled to get away from both places. Her numb fingers knocked off helmets and slapped ears, earning curses partly muffled by their gas masks.

Nell could feel she was losing. She had inhaled too much gas and kept nodding off. Her fingers snagged something from one of the soldiers and pulled it loose. Maybe it was his gas mask or maybe it was his headset. Whatever it was, she tucked it inside her hoodie.

The soldiers lowered her into the cocoon and zipped it closed. Looking through the plastic made them appear wobbly. They twisted knobs on gas tanks attached to the sides of the cocoon. The hiss of gas and its now familiar sweet smell filled the tight space. Nell curled up on her side and pulled her hoodie over her head. The thing she had taken from a soldier felt both rubbery and solid. Though they sounded far away, she could hear the soldiers talking about her.

"We got her, sir!" the lieutenant said. "The tanks have been turned on. She'll sleep like a baby all the way to Atlanta."

The soldiers cheered.

"Should we load her in?" a soldier asked.

"Not yet," the lieutenant said. "Lt General Carter wants to have a look at her."

CHAPTER FORTY-ONE

Carter took out his phone and called Rex Wilson, CEO of Honeydew Industries.

"Rex. We got her."

"What's Number Forty-Eight's condition?" Wilson asked.

"Alive and in one piece."

"As usual, you have exceeded expectations."

Carter knew Rex Wilson didn't kiss his ass out of respect for the military. Wilson kissed his ass because Carter held the Pentagon's purse strings.

"What's going to happen to her?" Carter asked.

Wilson didn't answer.

"I asked you a question. What's Honeydew going to do to the girl after I deliver her to your lab in Atlanta?"

"We can't keep her asleep indefinitely," Wilson said. "And it's not safe to keep her alive. Our scientists will stop her heart, harvest her DNA, and then put her body in cold storage in case it's needed for further study."

"That's what I thought. See you in Atlanta."

Carter hung up his phone and turned on his headset.

"Fernandez," he said. "Don't load her in the APC yet. I'm on my way."

"Yes, sir," Fernandez said.

Carter turned to Chief Warrant Officer Sellers.

"Wait here," Carter said.

He jogged from the helicopter to the armored personal carriers. Carter was determined to see in the bulletproof flesh the little girl who had caused him so much trouble.

The platoon stood around the cocoon as if they were posing for a big hunt photo. They snapped to attention and saluted when Carter arrived. He returned the salute.

"At ease," Carter said.

He gazed inside the cocoon. In her dirty jeans and hoodie, she looked like a normal girl but looks were deceiving. Her back was to him. He'd have the SEALs turn her around so that he could see her face. But first, Carter would give credit where credit was due.

"Lieutenant Fernandez, your men did an outstanding job," he said.

"Thank you, sir," Fernandez said.

Carter smiled at the men, but then he frowned. They still wore their gas masks. Except for one man. Carter stormed over and stood inches away from him.

"Sailor," he said. "What's your name and rank?"

"Chief Petty Officer Travis Patterson, sir."

"Where's your gas mask, Patterson?"

Patterson looked like he had a sudden case of heartburn.

"Don't know, sir. Even drugged out of her mind, the girl had a lot of fight in her. She managed to pull my mask off, and I haven't been able to find it."

Carter put his fists on his hips.

"Patterson. Find your gas mask."

"Yes, sir."

Patterson searched the ground for his mask.

"Platoon," Fernandez said. "Assist Chief Petty Officer Patterson in locating his missing gear."

The SEALs spread out. Carter turned his attention back to the cocoon. Nell had turned over onto her back, but Carter still couldn't see her face.

"You can stop looking," Carter said. "I found it."

He pointed at Nell. Even though the gas mask obscured her face, Carter could swear that she was smiling. Carter backed away as Nell ripped open the cocoon as if it were a wet paper bag.

"Platoon!" Fernandez shouted. "Attack!"

The SEALs moved in on Nell. The first man to get within range of Nell was the first to die. She grabbed one of the cocoon's gas tanks and swung it against the side of his head. The tank clanged loudly as it cracked the SEAL's helmet and crushed his skull.

"Fire at will," Fernandez ordered. "Don't get caught in a crossfire."

The SEALs opened fire on Nell. She jerked about as if she'd been electrocuted. But the bullets didn't stop her. Nell leapt onto a SEAL, knocking him to the ground. She drove her fist through his body armor and into his chest cavity. She pulled her hand out. It was covered in the dead man's blood. Nell took his assault rifle and returned fire on the SEALs. When she ran out of ammo, she tossed the weapon aside, and replaced it with the nearest dead man's rifle.

Carter took cover behind an armored vehicle and contacted Sellers on his headset. The combined gunfire from Nell and the SEALs was deafening.

"Sellers!" Carter shouted. "I've taken shelter behind the APCs. Come get me."

"Yes, sir," Sellers said.

While he waited for the helicopter, Carter observed Nell in action. Honeydew had done a battery of tests on her body, but they never put her in a combat situation to see how she would perform. Her fighting style, if it could even be called a style, was primitive and intuitive. She knew exactly where to strike to cause maximum damage to her opponent.

The Navy's website said it best. Navy SEALs were expertly trained to deliver highly specialized, intensely challenging warfare capabilities that are beyond the means of standard military forces. They were the best of the best, the toughest fighters in the United States of America's armed forces. And yet, they were no match for Nell.

It wasn't for lack of trying. They threw flash bang grenades at her and tear gas canisters. They might as well have been tossing firecrackers and smoke bombs. Patterson's gas mask allowed Nell to level the playing field.

The SEALs brought out machine guns and grenade machine guns. The extra firepower knocked her down, but she kept getting back up. Carter was reminded of the catchphrase for a toy he had as a child. *Weebles wobble but they don't fall down.*

To make matters worse, the grenades that missed Nell blew deep holes in the carrot field and a couple of grenades flew past Nell and hit the barn. Carter hoped there were no civilians inside.

Within fifteen minutes, she had killed three SEALs and wounded six more. Among those bravely continuing the battle was Lt. Fernandez. Carter tuned into his headset.

"Fernandez. Abort the mission. I repeat abort the mission."

"She'll get away, sir," Fernandez said. His breathing was labored.

"We can't stop her."

"Even if I call a retreat, how do we know she won't keep killing my men?"

Carter cursed himself for trying to capture her instead of killing her with a direct missile strike. He felt a rush of wind behind him. Sellers had arrived and was landing the Apache helicopter. Carter could leave now and regroup. But that would mean abandoning the men who had put their lives on the line for him today.

"I'll make her stop," Carter said.

"That's like telling a tornado to stop spinning, sir," Fernandez said.

Carter stepped out from behind the APC. He marched toward the fighting and hoped he didn't get hit by a stray bullet.

"Cease fire!" he shouted. "Cease fire!"

Fernandez joined Carter in calling for a cease fire. The SEALs stopped firing and moved away from Nell. The gunfire still echoed in Carter's ears. Nell aimed her rifle at him.

"That goes for you too, young lady," Carter said. "Lower your weapon."

He knew it was a gamble. She wasn't a soldier. She hadn't been trained to obey a superior officer. Carter relied on his ability to give orders with such authority that Nell would do what he told her to do. Still. He would not have been surprised if she had shot him.

Nell lowered her rifle and removed Patterson's gas mask.

"I know you. The Honeydew scientists always made a big fuss when you came to visit. If the test subjects behaved around you, we got an extra dessert that night. Bet you didn't know that."

"Surrender while there's still time," Carter said.

Nell gazed at the carrot field. Wounded men were being attended to while the dead were carted back to the APCs.

"Why should I surrender?" she said. "I won."

"I fired the missile that hit your truck," Carter said. "I purposely aimed for the trailer. Next time I won't hold back."

Nell aimed the rifle at Carter's chest. He shook his head.

"That won't accomplish anything. I'm part of the largest military in the world. Kill me and another soldier will take my place. We won't rest until we reclaim our property."

"Is that all I am to you?" Nell asked. "Property?"

"That's right. The Pentagon paid for the technology that makes you invulnerable."

"You didn't pay me. You paid Honeydew. Ask them for a refund."

"You signed a contract giving Honeydew and the Pentagon the rights to your body."

Nell lowered the rifle.

"I never did read the fine print."

"I watched you in action," Carter said. "Very impressive for someone who doesn't have a clue what they're doing. Once we get that technology in the bodies of trained soldiers, America will never have to worry about our enemies harming us."

"I didn't mean to fight so hard. I was still woozy from the gas and wasn't thinking clearly."

"Really? You didn't mean to kill my men?"

Nell scratched her nose.

"Policemen and soldiers. They carry weapons as part of their job. I only kill them when I have no other choice."

A killer with a code of honor."

"Just like you."

Lt. Fernandez contacted Carter on his headset.

"The dead and wounded have been loaded onto the APCs, sir. The remainder of the platoon is standing by for your command."

Carter stepped closer to Nell.

"Come with me," he said.

"I have a better idea. You come with me."

"That's the same thing."

"Not exactly."

Nell quickly moved beside Carter and wrapped her arm around his waist. She positioned herself so that they were standing side by side like a couple watching a sunset. She pointed her rifle ahead of them.

"What the hell do you think you're doing?" Carter asked.

"You blew up my truck," Nell said. "So, I'm going to take one of your vehicles."

Nell nudged Carter and they headed toward the APCs. The SEALs aimed their weapons at her. She aimed her rifle back at the SEALs.

"Stand down," Carter said.

"But, sir," one of the SEALs said.

"Don't worry. She's not going to shoot me."

"Not unless I have to," Nell said.

"Why use me as a human shield? You're bulletproof."

"My clothes aren't."

"They're already full of holes."

"They don't need any more."

As they walked side by side, Carter looked down at Nell. Blonde roots were coming up in her black hair. Scrub away the soot, blood, and gore, and she would be an attractive young woman. The perfect disguise for an unstoppable killing machine. Carter would have to consider choosing a couple of good-looking females when he recruited soldiers for the next stage of Project Bulletproof.

They arrived at the first APC. It was filled with wounded men. They saw that she had taken Carter hostage and began to rise from their seats.

"Don't get up," Nell said. "I see a better ride."

The SEALs watched as Nell and Carter approached the Apache helicopter. Sellers stared at them from the cockpit.

"This is the one I want," Nell said.

"Get out Sellers," Carter said. "We're lending Ms. Slagle our aircraft."

"But, sir," Sellers said. "If we let her take the Apache, what's to stop her from using it to attack us?"

"Surrender the aircraft, Sellers."

"But sir!"

"I gave you an order."

Nell nudged Carter.

"That guy's a jerk."

Sellers was a jerk and a suck up, but he followed orders and climbed out of the helicopter. Carter had him join the other men. Nell released Carter and put her hand on the helicopter.

"This must be the deluxe model," Nell said. "It has all kinds of bells and whistles."

"I'm giving you one last chance to surrender," Carter said. Nell grinned.

"Sorry, but I can't accept your generous offer."

"I have found you twice now. I'll keep on finding you."

"And I'll keep getting away."

Nell climbed into the cockpit.

"I'll be waiting for you the second you land," Carter said.

Nell strapped into the pilot seat.

"Whatever."

Nell started the engine. The Apache's blades rotated and then the aircraft lifted into the air.

Hovering over the vegetable field, Nell looked down at the remains of Skeeter's truck. It was her fault that the truck had been destroyed, just like it was her fault that Skeeter was dead. Nell held in her tears.

"You can't cry now. Not while you're flying a helicopter."

Grief wasn't the only emotion twisting up her insides. A bubbling mix of guilt and self-pity was doing a pretty good job of messing with her head. And she couldn't forget the rage burning through her. She had plenty of it to go around. For Honeydew. For the military. For gun lovers. For whoever came up with spicy hot cheese crackers.

And for Harry Pigott.

He and his idiot friends had gunned down Skeeter just because he was with Nell. As much as she wanted them dead, there really wasn't time to kill them. The head start she had on Lt. General Carter wouldn't last forever.

Nell steered the helicopter away from the vegetable field. A mile away, she saw endless rows of cars and trucks on the highway. Police were directing them toward detours on side roads that could barely handle the volume of vehicles. News helicopters covering the traffic jam tried to hail her, but she flew away without responding.

The smart thing to do would be to use whatever fuel was left in the tank to fly the helicopter as close to the border as possible and then run like hell. Didn't matter which border. If she went south, she could hide anywhere between the Rio Grande River and Tierra Del Fuego. Her choices north were either cold Canada or freeze-your-butt-off Canada.

But Nell was too tangled up in her emotions to do the smart thing. What the hell. She was going to find Harry and kill his ass dead.

Normally, hunting Harry down would take weeks. But Nell had an Apache helicopter with all the extras. Some of those extras had the means to locate him quickly. Her fingers danced on the keyboard to her left. Information about Harry Pigott appeared on the central monitor, including the GPS signal for his Land Rover Defender.

"Holy fuckoley," Nell said. "Harry's in Georgia."

Harry was only a hundred and eighty miles away. The Apache's top speed was two hundred and twenty-seven miles per hour. She'd be there before she left.

CHAPTER FORTY-TWO

The Land Rover Defender was running on fumes when Harry exited Interstate 85 and rolled into a gas station in LaGrange, Georgia. While Grover and Dale hurried into the station to empty their bladders, Harry filled the car's tank.

The clouds that greeted them that morning as they crossed the Alabama Georgia border had wandered off, and though the sun was out in all its glory, the weather wasn't too hot. Once the tank was full, Harry parked on the edge of the parking lot to wait for Grover and Dale. Ten minutes later, they came out of the station eating chips and sipping sodas. Grover wiped his greasy hand on his pants before saluting Harry.

"Did you get me anything?" Harry said.

Grover choked on his chips.

"Sorry, sir. I forgot."

"I was kidding. I can get it myself."

Harry went into the station and got a bottle of iced tea and a bag of cashews. Back at the car, Grover and Dale had taken their Beastmasters out of the trunk and were loading them.

"Good thinking, men," Harry said. "We haven't reloaded since Demopolis."

Grover and Dale stared at the ground for a moment before continuing with their task. Mentioning Demopolis brought up bitter memories.

A few customers glared at Harry and his men openly loading their weapons while others gave them a thumbs up. Harry ignored the disapprovers. He had a legal right to carry his weapon.

But then he noticed people were staring at something at the sky. Shielding his eyes with his hands, Harry followed their gaze. A helicopter was approaching the station. As it got closer, the beating helicopter blades grew louder, drawing the attention of more people, including Dale and Grover.

"That's not a news chopper," Dale said. "That's a military helicopter."

"Spider," Harry said. "You're our resident expert on military gear. Identify that bird."

Grover took his binoculars out of the car and studied the helicopter.

"That's an AH-64 Apache advanced multi-role helicopter with laser-guided precision hellfire missiles, 70mm rockets, and advanced target acquisition designation."

"Is that right?"

"Yes, sir, Commander. She has a twin-turbo shaft engine. See there on the belly?" Grover pointed at the weapon attached to the bottom of the helicopter. "That's a 30mm single-barrel chain-driven autocannon."

Dale whistled.

"That's badass. I wonder what she's doing around here?"

The helicopter descended toward the parking lot creating

a whirlwind around Harry and his men. They were pelted with plastic soda bottles, candy wrappers, and cigarette butts. The aircraft got close enough for Harry to see the pilot. They locked eyes on each other. And then she waved at him.

"Well, men," Harry said, "we don't have to look for Nell anymore."

"We can't give up now, Commander," Dale said. "We've come too far."

"Boomslang. Open your eyes. She's flying the chopper."

The autocannon fired a single 30mm round. Made to penetrate armored vehicles and fortified bunkers, it hit Grover's belly and he exploded into a bloody mist. Bits of Grover splattered Harry and Dale.

"Take cover!" Harry shouted.

He ran towards the gas station. He didn't want to get caught out in the open, and if he could get past the gas pumps before she blew them up and burned him into a crispy critter, he would seek shelter inside the store. Looking over his shoulder, he saw that Dale had taken cover behind a minivan and was firing his Beastmaster at the Apache. His bullets pinged off the helicopter's metal exterior. Dale might as well have tried stopping a charging rhino by blowing spitballs from a straw.

The autocannon fired four rounds into the minivan causing a fiery explosion. Clouds of smoke which rose into the sky. A fire smoldered inside the vehicle's twisted metal frame. The rest of the vehicle and Dale were gone.

There was mayhem at the gas station. Cars tore out of the parking lot and zoomed onto the street. People screamed and ran in all directions. Harry made it to the store, but the glass doors were locked.

"Let me in!" he yelled as he banged on the door.

Frightened people stared at Harry and refused to let him in. A woman told him to go away. Harry aimed his rifle at the door.

"Open up, or I'll blast my way in."

The woman pulled a pistol out of her purse and pointed it at Harry. Three people took out their guns and joined her.

"Whoever is in that chopper is after you," the woman said. "Stay the hell away from us."

Harry looked back at the parking lot. The helicopter was spinning away from the demolished minivan. If he couldn't get inside the store, then he needed to get as far away as possible. In their panic, some people had abandoned their cars at the pumps. Harry dashed over to see if anybody had left their keys behind.

The door was open on a red Ford F-150 pick-up truck and a purse sat on the passenger seat. Harry climbed in, put his Beastmaster next to the purse, and pressed the ignition. Country music blared from of the truck's speakers.

"Shut the fuck up! She'll hear you," Harry said as he turned off the radio.

He couldn't see the helicopter, but he could tell that it was right above him from the deafening sound of the blades churning the air and the way the canopy over the pumps vibrated. The sound receded and the vibration ceased only to return a few moments later. The pattern repeated as Nell circled the station.

"You can't find me," Harry said, "if you can't put on eyes on me."

He couldn't leave yet. She'd see him and there was no way he could outrun an Apache. As the engine idled and the helicopter circled the station, Harry wondered about several things. How was he going to get away? How did Nell find him? Where the hell did she get an Apache?

The helicopter landed in the parking lot. Harry slid down in the seat. His heart pounded as he watched Nell exit the helicopter with an assault rifle in her hands. He put his foot on the brake and shifted the truck into drive. Nell's head swiveled back and forth as she approached the station.

"Harry. Come out, come out, wherever you are."

When she got closer, Harry's mouth went dry. There was dirt on her ripped jeans, dried blood on her hands, and bullet holes in her hoodie. Maybe she was a ghost.

"Don't lose your shit," Harry whispered. "Ghost don't fly Apaches."

Nell moved under the canopy. She bent down to peer under the cars left at the pumps.

"Come on, Harry. We can have a duel. Or do you only shoot unarmed people?"

Harry eased his handgun from his belt holster. Nell came closer and closer to the truck. Harry kept his foot on the brake and his finger next to the trigger of his gun. She got to a purple SUV with the pump nozzle still connected to its gas tank. One car sat between the SUV and the Ford F-150. Harry sank lower in the seat and watched Nell in the truck's side-view mirror.

She stood still and stared at the truck. Had she noticed the engine idling and the brake lights shining? Her gaze shifted and she caught Harry watching her in the side-view mirror. Nell winked.

Before either of them could react, a dog inside the purple SUV barked at Nell. Caught off-guard, Nell jumped back. Harry took advantage of the momentary distraction. He switched his foot from the brake to the gas and headed for the street. Glancing in his rearview mirror, he saw Nell running toward the helicopter. He cursed and drove faster.

Harry turned right onto the road and was almost hit by an oncoming car. The car honked and changed lanes. Harry was shocked that there was traffic, and that no police cars had shown up at the station with their sirens wailing. Apparently, the world at large hadn't yet discovered the hell that had taken place there or that two of RAFF's finest men had died in noble battle.

The road was in the open. Harry needed cover. Coming to a traffic light, he turned right onto a straight two-lane road that ran through a forest. As he zoomed around slow-poke cars, he searched for a side road into the woods where the trees would hide him.

Harry pulled onto the side of the road right before the forest gave way to open fields. If he kept going, he would be completely exposed. As he struggled to calm his jangled nerves, he considered his options.

He could get out of the truck and hike through the forest, using the trees as cover. If necessary, he could lie low until nighttime. But even if he made it out of town, it that would only be a temporary escape. If Nell could find him in the middle of nowhere, she could find him anywhere. He had to kill her before she killed him.

A car zipping past startled him. He rolled down the window, stuck his head out, and stared at the sky. He didn't see the Apache, but he could hear it in the distance. She was up there looking for him. Harry couldn't stay in the truck. If Nell caught him out in the open, one missile would turn the truck into his funeral pyre.

Harry went over Nell's attack at the gas station. She could

have fired a missile at the gas pumps, creating a massive explosion that would have obliterated both the store and the Waffle House next door. Instead, Nell had landed the Apache and hunted Harry with just her rifle.

"You made sure to only target me, Spider, and Boomslang," Harry said as he continued to watch the sky. "Since when did you start avoiding collateral damage?

This insight was the key to defeating Nell. As the *Art of War* states, securing ourselves against defeat lies in our own hands, but the opportunity to defeat the enemy is provided by the enemy himself. Quoting the *Art of War* calmed Harry and restored much of his confidence.

He got back onto the road and looked for a place that Nell wouldn't blow up. He passed an abandoned warehouse. That wouldn't do if he was in there alone, she'd happily blast it to smithereens. Then Harry saw the ideal shelter. A place filled with people. Nell would have to walk inside to find Harry, and when she did, he would be waiting for her.

Harry sped toward the middle school.

CHAPTER FORTY-THREE

The truck screeched to a halt in front of the school. Harry grabbed his Beastmaster and ran to the entrance. There was sign that read, "WARNING. Staff Members are ARMED and TRAINED. Any attempt to harm children will be met with Deadly Force."

"Good," Harry said. "I could use the extra guns."

He heard the helicopter before he saw it. The Apache descended onto the grassy field adjacent to the school's parking lot.

Shoving open the school's glass door, Harry had a moment of nostalgia for when he was in school. There was the scent of pimple cream and burnt pizza. The floors were waxed and shiny. A bulletin board was covered in cafeteria menus and announcements for special events. The hallway was lined with lockers.

He pushed the memories away and peered outside. The Apache had landed. Nell climbed out.

"Come on in," Harry said. "I'm waiting for you."

A voice on the intercom echoed off the walls.

"Invader in the school! Level Three Lockdown procedures now in effect. I repeat. Level Three Lockdown procedures now in effect."

The announcement was followed by a fire alarm ringing.

There was a gunshot and the glass panel next to Harry shattered. At first, he thought Nell had fired at him, but she was too far away. Harry looked behind him. A middle-aged woman trained a pistol at him. Her eyes were watery, and her hands shook.

"Hey! I'm here to protect the school," Harry said. "Put that down before you hurt somebody."

The woman fired again. Her second shot struck the wall. Her training apparently hadn't included steady nerves or common sense. If she kept firing at him, she might get lucky and shoot him, so he fired two rounds into her chest. She fell to the shiny floor and a pool of blood grew around her.

"Sorry, lady," Harry said. "You gave me no choice."

Along with the fire alarm's incessant ringing, there was shouting, doors slamming, and the sound of furniture dragged across floors.

Outside, Nell stood motionless at the edge of the parking lot. What was she waiting for?

The front entrance was too exposed. Harry needed a hiding place from which to ambush her. Before he went looking, he stopped by the dead woman. She reminded him of one of his mother's friends. He couldn't remember the friend's name.

He stomped down the hallway to the nearest classroom, but the door was locked. As he continued down the hallway, he found that all the doors were locked. Black shades covered the windows in the doors, preventing him from getting someone's attention to let him in.

Turning right at the end of the hallway, Harry entered another hallway with more lockers and more classroom doors with the window shades down. The third door on the left wasn't locked. Harry entered a dark room. Flipping on the overhead light revealed a group of kids huddled against the wall. They cowered and screamed.

"Shut up!" Harry shouted.

They stopped screaming but some of them blubbered.

"Please don't shoot us," a girl said.

"Where'd you get a crazy idea like that?" Harry asked.

"You're the shooter."

"No, I'm not."

"Then who are you?" a boy asked.

Harry straightened his spine.

"I'm the Commander."

The kids glanced at each other. A couple of them scowled.

"Where's Ms. Gardner?" the girl said.

"Who?" Harry said.

"Our teacher."

"She just left you here on your own?"

"Ms. Gardner took her gun to go kill the shooter."

Harry now had a name for the woman who forced him to kill her.

The girl poked the boy.

"Gavin was supposed to lock the door after Ms. Gardner left."

Gavin glowered at the girl.

"How can she get back in if the door's locked, Kayla?"

Harry closed the door and tugged the edge of the shade. The hallway was empty. He released the shade.

"Is that blood on your clothes?" Kayla asked.

Harry allowed himself a smidgeon of grief.

"Yes, it is."

"Did you cut yourself shaving?" Gavin asked.

"It's not my blood. It's Spider's blood."

"Ewwwww!" the children said.

Harry groaned.

"Hey, listen up kids. I'm going to teach you an important lesson about gun safety."

Kayla crossed her arms.

"What?"

"Never point your gun at anything you don't intend to shoot."

"I knew that," Gavin said.

"Good. What do you do if somebody points a gun at you?"

Gavin made a gun with his finger.

"Shoot to kill."

"Wrong."

"What are you supposed to do?" Kayla asked. "Let them shoot you?"

"No," Harry said. "You shoot to stop the threat. If the person dies because you had to defend yourself, that's on them."

"What's the difference?" Gavin said.

"If Ms. Gardner points her gun at somebody, they have no choice but to stop the threat. If she gets shot and dies, it's on her. Not me."

"You killed Ms. Gardner?"

"I didn't say that."

"Did you?"

Harry turned out the lights and tugged the shade so that he could watch the hallway. "No more lessons for today. And no more talking."

CHAPTER FORTY-FOUR

"Damn it, Harry," Nell said. "Of all the places to hide, why did it have to be a school?"

As she stood at the edge of the school parking lot, memories of the other middle school flooded her mind. Nell had been unconscious and bleeding when Carson had killed the children at Red Clay. Her only experience with the actual shooting was the TV news reports she'd seen from her hospital bed.

Police cars and ambulances had filled the carpool lane. Kids had run out of the school with their hands in the air as if they were surrendering their innocence. Worried parents had stood in clusters expecting the worst. Some of them had been able to hug their children as if they would never let them go again, while others had continued to wait in hellish limbo. Finally, a parade of gurneys carried shellshocked survivors and bloody sheet-covered children who would never be hugged again.

The school's fire alarm began to ring, bringing Nell back to the present.

Harry Pigott wasn't Carson Slagle. He wasn't a young man with an untreated mental illness and an indulgent mother who refused to face reality. Harry hadn't gone into the school to kill children, but the teachers and students didn't know that. And Harry was willing to kill to get what he wanted. Just ask Skeeter Foote's ghost.

Nell sank to her knees. She had been accused of not doing enough to stop her little brother. Her accusers had been right, and the guilt had almost crushed her.

She hadn't stopped Carson, but she would stop Harry. But not with a gun. Enough with the goddamn fucking guns! Whatever she had been trying to accomplish with them, she didn't want to do it anymore. They were only good for creating pain, and she already had enough of her own. Nell got to her feet and realized she was cradling the rifle like a baby.

"You can't be the Beastmaster forever," Nell said. "And I can't be the Beastmaster anymore."

She removed the magazine and cracked it open. Bullets rained down on the grass like seeds of death. She held the assault rifle with both hands and brought it down on her raised thigh, cracking the weapon in two. Tossing the pieces aside, Nell ran toward the school. She felt like her feet barely touched the ground.

Entering the school lobby, Nell found a woman on the floor. The woman's eyes were glassy, and she held a gun in her right hand. Nell didn't need to feel for a pulse to know there wouldn't be one.

"Quick! Come inside."

A man in a dress shirt and bowtie beckoned Nell from the office door. She went over to him.

"Do you know where he went?" Nell asked.

"The police are on their way," the man said. "Hide in here where it's safe."

Nell nodded at the dead woman.

"Who was she?"

The man choked back tears.

"That's Ms. Gardner. She taught seventh grade."

Nell started down the dark hallway. The man left the office and grabbed Nell's arm.

"Don't go down there. Come with me."

He tugged on her arm, but she didn't budge. He looked her over.

"Good Lord. What happened to you?"

"I had a rough morning." Nell gently pulled her arm free. "Don't worry. I was made for this."

She headed down the hallway. Other than the fire alarm's endless ringing, the school was hushed, as if everyone and everything was holding its breath.

Nell considered knocking on classroom doors and asking if an asshole in fatigues and a long rifle was in hiding inside, but worried that might cause them to panic. Better to let Harry find her. She walked in the middle of the hallway so that she could be seen easily.

Reaching the end of the hallway, Nell paused to drink from the water fountain before checking out the next hallway. It was just as dark and quiet as the first one. She wiped her mouth with the back of her hand.

"I'm not armed, Harry," she shouted. "Come out and talk to me."

Harry didn't respond.

Nell started down the second hallway. Her footsteps echoed off the walls. She came to the door to the cafeteria. Following the scent of overcooked vegetables, she was about to enter when she heard a door creak behind her followed by earsplitting gunfire. Bullets stung her back. Harry stood in a doorway about a yard from her.

"Now that you got that out of your system, can we talk?" Nell asked.

He answered with another burst of gunfire. After the bullets bounced off her, she walked toward him. His walrus mustache twitched in confusion.

"Why won't you die already?"

"How many times do I have to tell you?" Nell said. "I'm bulletproof."

More gunfire. The bullets ricocheting off Nell entered lockers and chipped the walls.

"You're lying," Harry said. "You're wearing some kind of high-tech body armor."

"I'm going to explain this so that even you can understand. A defense contractor made me invulnerable."

"That's impossible."

"Yet here we are."

Harry's eyes grew wide as the truth finally sunk in.

"Oh, shit."

As he retreated into a classroom, Nell heard children squealing inside. Her stomach clenched. They were in there with a man who was armed and desperate. And without an adult to protect them.

Nell tried the door. It was locked. She shouted to be heard inside.

"Harry. This is between you and me. Let the children out."

He called back to her.

"Can't do that. I'm protecting them."

"Harry. Please open the door and let them out. I promise I won't hurt you."

"That's a good one. Tell me another one."

Considering that she had just chased him with a military helicopter, she understood why he might not believe her intentions were peaceful.

"I don't want to hurt anyone anymore. Even you, Harry."

"Tell that to Spider and Boomslang."

"I'm sorry I killed your friends. I was angry because you guys killed Skeeter."

"He wasn't an innocent bystander."

Nell rested her cheek against the wood door. Her stomach still hurt.

"I'm sick of killing. I'm sick of guns. I just want to stop. Don't you want to stop, Harry?"

"Not until you're dead."

"I'm sure what happened in the lobby was a mistake. Don't make another one. Please, let the kids out."

"I didn't make a mistake. The lady shot at me first. It was self-defense."

A child shouted, "you did kill Ms. Gardner!"

There were screams and the sound of scuffling.

"Get off me!" Harry said.

There was a gunshot. Nell gasped.

"Stand away from the door," she said. "I'm coming in."

She slammed her palm against the door. It fell forward and landed with a loud thud. Nell walked over it and entered the room. The children huddled in one corner and Harry stood in the opposite corner. His rifle was pointed up. Nell glanced at the ceiling and saw a hole.

"Don't shoot," Nell said, holding her hands up. "The bullet might bounce off me and hit one of the kids."

The fire alarm stopped. The silence didn't last long. Nell could hear sirens approaching. She put her hands down.

"It's over, Harry. The police are coming."

Harry scowled and pulled the trigger. Nothing happened. He pulled out the empty magazine and dropped it on the floor. Frantically, he checked his vest for a fresh mag. When he couldn't find one, he reached for his handgun. But the holster was empty.

"Where the hell is it?"

His face paled. Nell followed his gaze to the opposite corner. A girl had Harry's gun. She needed both hands to hold it. Harry lowered his Beastmaster.

"Your name's Kayla, right?" he said. "Kayla, remember what I told you about pointing guns at people?"

"Never point your gun at anything you don't intend to shoot," Kayla said.

Nell inched toward Kayla. The other kids looked from Kayla to Harry.

"That's right," Harry said. "Now put the gun down before you hurt somebody."

"I have to stop the threat," Kayla said.

Harry swallowed.

"I'm not the threat." He pointed at Nell. "She's the threat."

Nell moved closer. She was just a few feet away from the little girl.

"Kayla," Nell said. "Don't shoot him."

Kayla glanced at Nell.

"Why are you helping him? He tried to hurt you."

"If you shoot him," Nell said, "it will change you and not in a good way."

Kayla's lower lip quivered.

"I think he killed Ms. Gardner,"

"Two wrongs don't make a right."

Even though Nell was close enough now to grab the gun, she didn't. A sudden move might cause Kayla to pull the trigger. Instead, she knelt before the child.

"I pointed the gun at him, so now I have to shoot him," Kayla said. "He said so."

"Don't listen to him," Nell nodded at Harry. "With a mustache like that, how could you take anything he says seriously?"

Kayla shivered. She handed the gun to Nell.

"Thank you," Nell said.

She removed the clip and broke it open, spilling bullets on the floor. Checking the chamber, Nell removed the round inside. Kayla's mouth dropped open as she watched Nell bend the gun into a lump of metal.

Nell went to the doorway, picked up the door, and propped it against the wall.

"Okay, kids. Y'all should go now. If you run into the police, tell them where to find me and Harry."

The kids ran out of the room. With his back against the wall, Harry sank to the floor. Nell sat next to him.

"So, you're really bulletproof?" Harry asked.

"Yeah," Nell said.

"What I wouldn't give to be bulletproof."

"Not going to happen. Not if I can help it."

Harry rubbed his mustache.

"It was self-defense," he said. "Besides, Georgia's a stand-your-ground state. I was defending my life."

"Are you referring to your use of force against me or Ms. Gardner?" Nell asked.

"Ms. Gardner. Duh."

Voices barking orders were getting closer and closer.

"The cops will be here soon," Nell said.

Harry groaned.

"They're going to think I'm the bad guy with a gun. But I'm the good guy with a gun."

"No, Harry. You're just a guy with a gun."

CHAPTER FORTY-FIVE

Three weeks later.

THE SKY WAS solid gray, as if God had spilled something and hadn't gotten around to mopping it up. Nell's butt was freezing from sitting on a concrete bench. She would have sat on the grass, but it was still soggy from last night's rainstorm.

"I'm sorry I didn't pick a nicer day to come see you, Peggy."

She didn't know exactly where at Sunset Memorial Garden her mother was buried. Her father had her buried in an unmarked grave, because he had been afraid someone would deface her headstone. He had told Nell that Peggy was buried in Devotion II at the top of the hill near a concrete bench. There were a couple of sunken areas in the grass. Peggy must be buried in one of them. Nell spoke to the indention closest to the bench.

"You used to bitch about Dad all the time," Nell said. "But you have to admit, it was mighty nice of him to pay for your funeral. He caught hell from Wendy for doing it."

An eighteen-wheeler rolled past on the two-lane highway

next to the cemetery, dragging a harsh wind behind it. Nell pulled her denim jacket tighter around her.

"I could understand how Dad's new wife wanted to keep him away from his old wife," Nell said. "But Wendy didn't have to be such a bitch to me and Carson."

Other than a couple visiting a grave in another section, Nell had the cemetery to herself.

"Dad had Carson cremated. He planned to toss Carson's ashes into the Tennessee River but was waiting for me to get better so we could do it together."

Nell stretched out her legs and tapped her combat boots together. They were the only things she had on that wasn't stolen.

"But then, Dad had to go and die in a car accident. Wendy found Carson's ashes and threw them away. They're in a landfill somewhere. I know this is true because Wendy told me she did it. Again, why did she have to be such a bitch?"

Nell twirled a strand of hair around her finger.

"Do you like my hair this color?" she said. "I think I look good as a redhead."

Another gust of wind rolled across the hillside. Nell hugged herself.

"How old was I when I started calling you Peggy instead of Mom? Fourteen? Fifteen? You didn't notice. You were too busy dealing with Carson."

Nell's old jealousy of Carson tried to come back like a flare-up of acne, but she couldn't muster the energy to maintain it. Whatever resentment she had felt toward her little brother for sucking up all of Peggy's attention had been replaced with pity.

"I'm tired, Mom. Tired of running, hurting, being angry."

Nell wiped away tears. "I wish you could have met Skeeter. You two wouldn't have liked each other, but it would have been a blast to watch you in the same room with him."

Nell sat for another ten minutes listening to the wind and remembering how beautiful Peggy had been. Nell had inherited her mother's blonde hair and blue eyes, but not her perfect cheekbones and knockout body. Peggy had been an all-American goddess.

Nell stood. The seat of her jeans was slightly damp from the bench. She walked to the white Toyota Camry she had stolen from the parking lot of a McDonald's in LaGrange.

While the cops were busy arresting Harry, Nell had slipped out the back of the school and had wandered the neighborhood until she came to the restaurant. The car had been idling while the driver talked on his cellphone. Nell had opened the door and yanked the guy out. He gawked at her as she drove away. Nell had been driving the stolen car for three weeks now and had not been pulled over.

As she got to the Toyota, a gray sedan drove up and parked in front of it, blocking her from leaving. The couple who had been visiting a grave got out. The man was tall and handsome with short brown hair. The woman was Hispanic and slim. They both wore sport coats and khakis.

"Nell Slagle," the man said.

Nell glared at them then smiled.

"I know you guys. You're Special Agent John Easter and Special Agent Mara Zavala."

Easter and Zavala gaped at her.

"You have a good memory," Easter said.

Nell shrugged.

"Not really. When Carson killed those kids, most people

treated me like dogshit on the bottom of their shoe. You were among the few who treated me with kindness."

"We didn't want to disturb you while you were paying your respects to your mother," Zavala said.

"We're not armed." Easter opened his jacket to show he wasn't wearing a holster.

"We know you're bulletproof and got a thing against people pointing guns at you."

"We can't stop you if you decide to run."

"But you can't run forever. Sooner or later, you're going to get caught. Or killed."

"It would be much easier if you surrendered to us."

Nell stared at the muddy road.

"I can't surrender. I just can't."

"Sure, you can," Zavala said. "You just say, 'I surrender' and we do the rest."

"How much do you know about what Honeydew did to me?"

"Everything," Easter said.

"Then you know. They'll send me back to Honeydew to make more like me. I can't let them do that."

The FBI special agents glanced at each other.

"It's not your decision," Easter said. "The technology in your body belongs to Honeydew."

Nell sat on the hood of the Toyota.

"It was dumb luck that I won the Project Bulletproof sweepstakes. I was sure I'd be one of the human lab rats who died while screaming in agony from the crap Honeydew injected into our bodies."

Nell sometimes wondered what Honeydew had done with the test subjects who died. Where were the bodies of Grace,

Lenny, and dear sweet Robby? They had been her friends. Were they in unmarked graves like Peggy?

"By the time Honeydew made my body bulletproof, I had built a hard shell around my mind. I could no longer deal with the crap I'd been through. It was sort of a relief. Just do whatever Honeydew told me to do. When they told me to stand on stage and get shot by bigger and bigger guns, I was like okay. Sure. Whatever."

"We saw the video," Easter said.

"There's a video?"

"It's one of the few things that survived your attack on HARD-SOW."

Nell grinned. She had truly enjoyed destroying that place.

"During the presentation, I started thinking about that old movie 'Frankenstein.' Remember that one?"

"Sure," Easter said. "Dr. Frankenstein puts a criminal brain in the body of a superhuman monster."

"Exactly. What if that had happened? Like, what if it was Jesse standing here now getting his ass shot?"

"Who's Jesse?"

"He was one of the homeless vets who died during testing. I knew him at Emerald City. When he wasn't heavily self-medicated, the littlest things would trigger his PTSD, and he'd become a rage monster. If Jesse had been in my place, he probably would have flipped out and killed everybody there. He would have been like Frankenstein's monster."

Easter glanced at Zavala. She rolled her eyes.

"But you did flip out," Zavala said. "You were the monster."

Nell shook her head.

"No. I did what had to be done."

Zavala crossed her arms.

"I'm sure the military will do extensive screening before selecting which trained soldiers receive invulnerability."

Nell sighed.

"It won't matter how carefully they chose the soldiers. I'm sure Jesse was a good soldier. His injuries during combat weren't physical. Being bulletproof won't protect a soldier from PTSD."

"Not all soldiers have PTSD," Easter said.

"Okay, but what's to stop a bulletproof soldier from deciding that the army doesn't pay him enough to be superhuman? He could easily become an unstoppable mercenary for whichever country offers him the most money."

"It sounds like you've given this a lot of thought."

Nell watched another eighteen-wheeler roll by the cemetery.

"I spent hours riding shotgun with a long-haul trucker. He was a great guy, but not the world's best conversationalist. I had to do something to pass the time."

Easter faced Zavala.

"She's right. There's no test that can guarantee a soldier will always follow orders when he has the power to do whatever he wants to do. Soldiers are people. Even with bulletproof bodies, they're still vulnerable to temptation."

Zavala walked away and stood with her back to them and her hands on her hips. She came back and scowled at Easter.

"Maybe Honeydew will create an army of Frankenstein's monsters and maybe they won't. Our job is to bring in killers. And Nell is a killer."

"We can't take her in," Easter said.

"Bunny. Don't forget. After this we'll never have to investigate another active shooter incident."

"Instead, our job will be to bring in bulletproof killers. We were assigned active shooter incident investigations because we excelled at them. If we take her in, Honeydew is going to make bulletproof soldiers. Eventually, one of the bulletproof soldiers is going to go rogue."

Zavala gazed at the gray sky.

"And when he does, the Bureau is going to assign us to the case because we brought in Nell. If we did it once, we can do it again."

"Except you won't be able to catch him," Nell said. "The only way to stop him would be if the army dropped a bomb on him."

Zavala turned and glared at Nell.

"Let's put aside this make-believe bulletproof soldier and talk about bulletproof Nell. If you're so determined to avoid going back to Honeydew to prevent them from making bulletproof soldiers, then why make a spectacle of yourself?"

"That's not what I was doing," Nell said.

"You sure about that? Instead of sneaking away to someplace we'd never find you, you went to a convention center and made a lot of noise. You got the whole world looking at you."

"I had to use my power to make a difference."

"You used your power to kill people. And don't give me that excuse about those who profit from the sword should die by the sword."

Nell looked at Easter.

"She's not afraid to go there, is she?"

"It's one of the things I admire most about her," Easter said.

Nell hung her head.

"I'm not the Beastmaster anymore."

"That's all you have to say for yourself?" Zavala asked.

Easter gestured at Zavala. She gave Nell the stink eye before following Easter to their car. They talked with their backs to her. Nell could have taken this opportunity to run, but she held onto a slim hope that they would help her. She waited to hear what they had to say. And then she would run if she had to.

The FBI special agents came back to Nell.

"This goes against everything we believe in," Easter said. "But you're not like anyone we've ever dealt with."

"We're not going to take you in," Zavala said.

Nell smiled.

"You're going to let me go?"

"No," Easter said. "If we did, someone else would eventually catch you."

Nell frowned.

"Then what are you going to do?"

Easter rubbed his forehead.

"We're working on it."

Nell slid off the hood of the stolen car. She decided to trust them. And if she was wrong, she'd steal their car.

"Can we talk about it over lunch?" Nell said. "I'm starving."

Zavala shrugged.

"I could eat."

CHAPTER FORTY-SIX

DANI LEWIS SAVORED her first cup of coffee of the day while looking out the window of her Dupont Circle apartment. The sun had just broken the horizon. Lewis liked this time of year when the sharpness of fall replaced the fuzziness of summer.

The doorbell rang. Lewis checked the peephole. A man with salt and pepper hair and thick rimmed glasses balanced on his beak nose stood at her doorstep. Lewis opened the door.

"Dr. Troutman. You're early."

Troutman's head bobbed around like a nervous bird's.

"Should I leave and return at the agreed time?"

"No. Come in."

Lewis moved aside and Troutman entered her living room.

"Would you like something to drink?" Lewis asked. "I have coffee, soda, orange juice, and water."

"A glass of water please."

"Have a seat and I'll be right back."

Lewis went to her office and got her voice recorder, notepad, and a pen. She carried her things into the kitchen and filled a glass from the tap. She poured herself a second cup of coffee. When she returned to the living room, Troutman was seated in the middle of her couch. She put his water on the coffee table in front of him and placed her coffee, recorder, and notepad on the table. She sat in a chair across from him.

"Unless you object," Lewis said, "I'm going to record our conversation."

"I do object," Troutman said.

Lewis reluctantly set the recorder aside.

"Dr. Troutman, you contacted me. You said you have information about Nell Slagle."

Troutman sipped his water and then cleared his throat.

"I've been following your coverage of Nell Slagle. Unlike other reporters, your stories exhibit empathy and attention to detail. You have been more dedicated to getting the truth without taking the easy path of painting her as simply a villain."

"I appreciate the compliment, but most of my fellow reporters have also done an excellent job of covering Nell's story."

"But you know her personally."

Lewis shrugged.

"It's been years since we've talked. However, I can tell you that I care about her, and I'm worried about what she's become."

Troutman adjusted his glasses.

"So am I, especially considering my part in her creation."

He took a thumb drive from his coat pocket and placed it on the coffee table. The Honeydew logo was embossed on its shiny surface.

"And what exactly will I find when I open this drive?" Lewis asked.

"Proof that Nell Slagle is bulletproof. That's why nobody has been able to catch her."

Lewis grinned.

"I knew it."

"Bullets can't penetrate her skin. Her body is invulnerable, and she has enhanced strength."

Lewis frowned.

"Wait a minute. I thought you meant she's wearing some kind of advanced ultra-thin body armor. What you're talking about is impossible."

"She can also operate any machine just by touching it. A fortuitous side effect."

Lewis studied Troutman's face. He didn't look like he was joking. In fact, he looked like he was incapable of joking. But how could he possibly be telling the truth? She pointed at the thumb drive.

"And there is evidence here to prove your claim?"

"I'm sure you've already done a background check on me."

"I know that you are head of the research department at Honeydew Industries."

"I was lead developer on Project Bulletproof. Nell Slagle was one of our test subjects. If she hadn't destroyed our research lab with our only files, Project Bulletproof would have revolutionized body armor."

Lewis picked up the thumb drive and marveled at how much mayhem these small devices could hold.

"Will you go on record about Project Bulletproof?"

Troutman shook his head.

"Absolutely not. I have a wife and a daughter. I must remain anonymous and I'm depending on you to protect my identity."

Lewis stared at Troutman.

"Are you in danger? Hell. Am I in danger just having this drive in my home?"

"The project was financed by the Pentagon. They have kept it secret from the public because they are determined to protect their investment. They will make your life difficult, but I suppose you're used to that."

Lewis's mother had a saying for people like Troutman. Slicker than owl shit.

"You said Nell destroyed your lab and your files. What's on the drive?"

"Everything. Well, almost everything. Honeydew doesn't know I made copies of the project files. Because of my position, they never suspected me. But even if I gave them this drive, they couldn't replicate Nell's abilities because I destroyed key research elements."

Lewis sipped her coffee. It had gone cold.

"If even half of what you claim is true, this is quite amazing."

"I suggest you have a science expert vet it."

"Standard operating procedure. Why did you collect this data? Did you know Nell would escape?"

Troutman shook his head.

"I never would have guessed. She was one of our most docile test subjects. Halfway through the project, I began collecting the data because I knew I would eventually share it with a reporter like yourself."

"Really?"

Troutman cleared his throat.

"When I started this project, I naively believed that invulnerability would benefit everybody, not just soldiers. I imagined a world in which mothers wouldn't worry about their children getting hurt. Motorists wouldn't need seatbelts. Mass shootings would be nothing more than a painful memory."

Lewis wondered if all researchers needed this kind of self-delusion to complete their experiments.

"I could lie and say I had an epiphany after watching test subjects die in agony during experiments," Troutman said. "Instead, I realized how stupid I had been when I floated the idea of universal invulnerability during a staff meeting. Honeydew's CEO berated me in front of everyone at the meeting for daring to suggest we waste the Pentagon's investment on common people. Many of our test subjects were homeless vets. I realized that what we were doing didn't justify torturing them to death. They'd already done enough for our country."

"What about test subjects like Nell, who were not veterans?"

The morning sun began to fill the apartment with a yellow glow. Troutman stared out the living room's picture window.

"We had no right to do what we did to anybody. Project Bulletproof should never have happened."

CHAPTER FORTY-SEVEN

Nine months later.

Mavis Gathercole was eight miles from work when the skies opened up. The windshield wipers on her ancient Volvo squeaked as they struggled to clear away the pounding rain. Mavis hated driving in the rain, especially at night, but she was fortunate to have the graveyard shift at the truck stop. The string of hard luck events in Mavis's life that led to her present circumstances might have made a lesser Christian question their faith, but only made Mavis cling to her love for Jesus even tighter.

The car vibrated, informing Mavis that she had drifted onto the rumble strip. She was about to veer back into the lane when she saw something in front of the car. A thud and a jerk happened simultaneously. Mavis slammed on the brakes, and the car slid to a halt. She gripped the wheel as she waited for her heart to slow down.

"Sweet Jesus! I hit something."

Putting the car in park, Mavis left the motor running and the headlights shining. She retrieved her bucket hat and raincoat from the backseat and got a flashlight out of the glove compartment. Everything had happened so quickly she couldn't tell what she had struck. Mavis prayed that if it was a deer or a dog that the poor animal was dead and not suffering. It wasn't until she was out of the car and feeling the rain batter her that she remembered she was wearing suede boots she'd found in perfect condition at the Goodwill. Another thing ruined in her life.

Mavis went to where she thought the body would be, but there was nothing there. Considering the force of the impact, whatever she'd hit couldn't have just walked away. She was on a rural two-lane road that ran through an open plain. Dread washed over her as she imagined an injured animal somewhere out there limping toward a pitiful death. She swung her flashlight around. The light cut through the rain and out into the distance.

"Where did you go?" Mavis asked.

Standing in the rain wasn't helping anybody, least of all her. She trudged back to the Volvo to assess the damage. She was shocked to find a woman squatting by her car. Mavis aimed the flashlight at her. The woman was feeling the bumper with her open palm. She wore a long-sleeved T-shirt, tights, a ball cap, and running shoes. Other than being soaking wet, she seemed okay. She straightened up and faced Mavis.

"It's not as bad as it looks." The woman shouted over the driving rain. "You lost a headlight, but the engine's not damaged."

"How can you tell without lifting the hood?" Mavis shouted back.

"I know cars."

Mavis looked at her Volvo. The headlight was smashed and

the area around it was dented. It looked like she'd run into a metal pole.

"Let's get in my car," Mavis said.

"Why?"

Though the woman didn't appear to have physical injuries, Mavis wondered if she was in shock.

"To get out of the rain," Mavis said.

The rain was coming down in buckets.

"Okay."

They got in the car, dripping water onto the floorboards. Mavis turned on the heater and it coughed out lukewarm air.

"Are you bleeding?" Mavis said. "Should I call an ambulance?"

"I'm a little sore. Other than that, I'm fine."

"But I hit you. With my car."

"You just grazed me."

With only the light from the control panel, Mavis had limited ability to study the woman. She couldn't make out her face clearly, but from the way the rain had plastered the woman's clothes on her body, Mavis could see that she was all muscle.

"It's a miracle that you're not seriously injured," Mavis said.

"Or dumb luck," the woman said.

"Should I give you my insurance information?"

"Why?"

"I hit you. With my car."

The woman shook her head.

"I don't want to file a claim. Too much of a hassle, you know what I mean?"

"Yes, I do," Mavis said.

"When you do talk to your insurance company, you might not want to tell them you hit a person."

Mavis trembled.

"My Lord. You're right. What should I tell them?"

"You hit a deer, but it ran away"

Though Mavis hated lying, she agreed that it was the best thing to do. She made a mental note to ask for Jesus's forgiveness after she did it.

"Can I give you a ride?" Mavis said.

"I should finish my run."

"Please. It's the least I can do."

The rain drummed the roof of the car.

"Sure," she said. "Thanks."

"Where are you going?" Mavis said.

She hoped it wasn't too far. Not that she minded going out of her way but, she didn't want to be late for work.

"Do you know the truck stop off I-94?" the woman asked.

"S&R Truck Plaza & Café?"

"That's it."

"I do indeed. I was on my way there to work the night shift."

Mavis pulled back onto the road. Having only one headlight slowed her down but giving the woman a ride settled her jangled nerves. Doing the Lord's work by helping others always made her feel more at peace.

"My name's Mavis. Mavis Gathercole."

The woman paused before mumbling her reply.

"I'm sorry," Mavis said. "I didn't catch that."

"Jolene Foote."

Mavis thought the last name Foote was funny but didn't dare tell her that. That would have been rude.

"What brings you out on such a rainy night?" Mavis said.

"I was jogging. I can't sleep if I don't do my nightly run."

"Even when it's raining this hard?"

"It wasn't raining when I started."

They came to a stop light.

"I don't know how it happens," Mavis said, "but I always catch this red light."

"Keep driving," Jolene said. "We're in the middle of nowhere. There are no other cars around."

"I know, but I'm too much of a goody two-shoes."

Thunder shook the car. Lightning flashed across the sky and lit up the interior of the car. In that moment, Mavis got a good look at Jolene's face. She gripped the steering wheel to keep her hands from shaking.

"Green," Jolene said.

"What?"

"The light turned green. We can go now."

"Sorry. Spaced out for a minute there."

They continued on their way.

"Is somebody waiting for you at the truck stop?" Mavis asked.

"Just my rig. I'm parked there for the night."

"You're a truck driver?"

"Does that surprise you?"

Mavis shook her head.

"No. Seems like every day I meet more and more women drivers at the truck stop."

"You been working there long?"

"Coming up on two years."

For the next mile, they didn't speak. The only sounds were the windshield wipers squeaking and the patter of the rain.

"Running at night," Mavis said. "By yourself. Are you ever afraid?"

"No," Jolene said.

"But someone might try to hurt you."

"I can take care of myself."

"What if you ran into *her*?"

"Her?"

"Nell Slagle."

Mavis looked at Jolene for her reaction, but it was too dark to see.

"I read somewhere that Nell only went after people with guns," Jolene said. "I don't carry a gun. In fact, I hate guns."

"Me too."

Mavis fiddled with the cross on her necklace.

"I met Nell Slagle. In fact, she rode in this car. She sat exactly where you're sitting now."

"Really?" Jolene said.

"This was years ago when I lived in Cleveland, Tennessee."

"Do tell."

Mavis wasn't sure if Jolene was really inviting her to say more or was just being polite. It didn't matter. The opportunity had presented itself, and she was determined to take advantage of it.

"I was a volunteer at the hospital they took Nell to after her brother shot her. I felt so sorry for her. Her mother and brother were dead, and the doctors told her that she'd never walk again."

"But she did walk again," Jolene said.

"She didn't know it then."

"No, I suppose she didn't."

"There was a candlelight vigil for the Red Clay victims. I took it upon myself to convince Nell that she should go. She was one of Carson's victims. She needed the emotional healing that vigil would provide."

Mavis grimaced as she remembered that day.

"Nell wasn't supposed to leave the hospital. But I put her in a wheelchair, took her to the parking garage, and got her into my car without anybody seeing us."

"You were determined," Jolene said.

"I thought I was doing God's work."

Mavis glanced at Jolene, who was staring out the window.

"We got turned away at the vigil. They wouldn't even let Nell get out of the car. The drive back to the hospital is my most painful memory in a lifetime of painful memories. Nell didn't say a word. Didn't need to. I could see the agony in her beautiful blue eyes."

Up ahead, the truck stop's sign glowed like a beacon in the stormy sky.

"I had wanted to give Nell healing, but instead I may have made her wounds deeper. I was a foolish woman acting out of pride instead of understanding."

They arrived at the truck stop. Mavis drove past the store and café to where the trucks were parked.

"Which one is yours?" Mavis asked.

"That red one there." Jolene pointed at a semi-trailer truck sitting near the end of the row. "I have a load of radiator coils I'm hauling to Chicago."

Mavis parked in front of the truck.

"Thanks for the ride," Jolene said.

She opened the door, but Mavis grabbed her hand. The overhead light was on. Mavis could clearly see Jolene's beautiful blue eyes.

"I try to be a good Christian," Mavis said, "but I make bad decisions. It's why I got a divorce, why I had to leave Cleveland, and why I have fallen to the point that I'm lucky to be working the graveyard shift at a truck stop in Jamestown, North Dakota."

Mavis let go of Jolene's hand.

"I like North Dakota," Jolene said.

"I didn't mean to cast aspersions. There are good people here."

Jolene gazed at her truck as if it was the only friend she had in the world.

"Don't feel bad about what you did. Your heart was in the right place."

"So was yours."

ACKNOWLEDGEMENTS

I could not have written this novel without the generous feedback and encouragement from Jef Blocker, Daniel Meyer, Robert Gwaltney, Peter McDade, Marissa McNamara, and Elaine Neil Orr. Thank you Joe Friou for not being the Beastmaster forever. Special thanks to Jessica Handler. She gets me.

In 2003, I saw the Gun Poetry signs I used in the book along Highway 57 outside Champaign, Illinois. They may still be there.

Mother Hen is based on a homeless addict named Jessica. I got her story from a photo caption in an Atlantic photo story online from August 8, 2017, titled "Closing down a notorious heroin camp in Philadelphia."

Three books that provided valuable research are *The Art of War* by Sun Tzu, *The Writer's Guide to Weapons* by Benjamin Sobieck, and *The Long Haul* by Finn Murphy.

A portion of all book sales will be donated to Everytown For Gun Safety.

ABOUT THE AUTHOR

For over thirty years, Mickey Dubrow wrote television promos, marketing presentations, and scripts for various clients including Cartoon Network, TNT Latin America, and HGTV. His short stories and essays have appeared in *Prime Number Magazine*, *The Good Men Project*, *The Signal Mountain Review*, *Full Grown People*, and *McSweeney's Internet Tendency*. He lives in Atlanta with his wife, author Jessica Handler.

He can be found online at:

Facebook: https://www.facebook.com/mickey.dubrow/

Instagram: https://www.instagram.com/mickeydubrow/

Website: https://mickeydubrow.com

www.ingramcontent.com/pod-product-compliance
Lightning Source LLC
Chambersburg PA
CBHW022008310726
48972CB00006B/1575